CHAOS HUNT

A JORDAN ABBEY NOVEL

SHERYL R. HAYES

Cover Design by Fiona Jayde Media

Contact Information:

Stitched Wolf Press

PO Box 9033

San Jose, CA 95157

Email: stitchedwolfpress@gmail.com

Learn more at http://www.stitchedwolfpress.com

Published in the United States

eBook ISBN: 978-1-948480-02-4

Paperback ISBN: 978-1-948480-03-1

SHERYL R. HAYES

Chaos

A Jordan Abbey Novel

HUNT

1

———

I can do this, Jordan thought as she crouched beneath the bush.

The werewolf shifted her weight between all four paws. The breeze wafted the rich scent of deer and the green scent of oak past her nose. Her focus should have been on the deer grazing in the meadow. What kept echoing through her mind was the conversation she and Montgomery had earlier.

"Let me get this straight, Montgomery," Jordan had said, arms crossed over her chest. She shifted her weight mostly to her right leg and tilted her head as she studied the vampire. "You want me to go out to the middle of the woods so I don't kill anything, but while I'm there, I need to kill."

"Not quite," Montgomery said. "It's a rite of passage, of sorts." His lips curled into a half-smile, eyes focused on a distant memory. "As a stranger joining a pack, you need to prove you can provide for it. It's better you have a few kills under your belt before you have to prove you can do it." His smile grew wider. "And no, buying twenty pounds of kibble at the pet store doesn't count."

Jordan snorted. "Why would I want to do that? I'm a chaos

wolf. I have no intention of joining the Black Oak Pack." Them accepting her after that mess three months ago was an impossibility anyway. Between dealing with being bitten by a werewolf and finding out vampires were also real, she hadn't been at her most polite. Relations hadn't improved since she'd declared she wanted nothing to do with the pack. She could have handled the situation in a more diplomatic way, but they were the ones who'd threatened to kill her.

He'd deflated some, his focus sharpening on her. "Because someday you may need their help, and I want you to have the skills to fit in."

Fit in. Jordan huffed her annoyance since her wolf throat was incapable of human speech. Like she'd ever fit into the Black Oak Pack.

She eyed the herd of deer grazing in the middle of the clearing. The eldest doe caught and held her attention. Every time the deer placed her right hind hoof on the ground, she let out a small exhale of pain that rang as clear as a dinner bell to Jordan's ears. This was her prey for the evening. Jordan adjusted her stance, claws digging into the crackling, dry leaves.

All five heads snapped up, turning in her direction. Then they were off in a flash of white tails and black hooves. Jordan darted out of the bushes, focusing on the limping doe. Her chosen prey started close to the center of the herd but dropped behind until she was clear of the other bodies.

Soon the herd had left her behind as Jordan surged closer, snapping at the flashing legs. The doe twisted, aiming a vicious kick at her head. Jordan ducked to the right, hooves clipping fur off her shoulder. She stumbled, allowing her prey to pull a yard ahead of her. Jordan jerked back toward the deer and leaped. Midair, she shifted, switching from the pure wolf form to the werewolf. The claws tipping her paw-hands sank into the doe's furred shoulders as Jordan landed on her back. The deer bleated as it tumbled. Jordan rode the animal to the ground. She slapped a paw over the nose and twisted the doe's head to face her. Her jaws closed around the top of the neck. Bones crunched between her jaws. The doe convulsed beneath her and then went still.

Jordan kept her jaws clamped for a minute, despite the deer not moving. Then she let go and stepped back, watching for any rise and fall of the animal's chest. The doe lay there, head twisted so it stared upwards at an unnatural angle. Pride swelled in Jordan's chest. She had killed a deer on her own. She'd had no help, no aid, no pack to assist her. It had been one thing to sneak up on a rabbit, but this was the first animal over twenty pounds she had managed to take down on her own. Breathing heavily, she looked over the animal and then tilted her head back. She drew in a deep breath and let out a long victory howl.

Something slammed into her chest. She tumbled head over heels, landing on her back and unable to catch her breath. Snarls echoed in her ears. Teeth sank into her shoulders and flanks. Claws raked across her muzzle. She chomped down on a paw, and something yelped. A clawed foot slammed into her stomach as more bites scored her shoulders. While her attackers drew blood, they didn't have the same ferocity as Rhys, her self-proclaimed mate she'd rejected. They meant to hurt—but not kill—her.

Then a pair of jaws clamped around her neck, much like hers had the doe's. Jordan went limp, offering no resistance. Her only movement was the rapid rise and fall of her chest. The scents of several werewolves mingled in the air, scents she couldn't separate and identify. Footfalls thudded on the ground behind her. The only things filling her vision were the grass the deer had been cropping earlier and wispy edges of white fur out of the corner of her eye. Then a pair of bare feet stepped into her field of view, stopping in front of her. "Let her up," said a deep male voice.

The wolf holding her growled but did not let go.

"Angela." The displeasure was clear in his voice. "Let her up."

For a second, the pressure of Angela's jaws increased as if she was about to pop off her head in defiance. Then the pressure released, and she was let go. Jordan coughed and rolled onto her belly. She shook her head. A pure white wolf snarled in her ear, ready to strike. Two other gray-coated wolves flanked her, wearing similar expressions, although none were growling. But what was in front of her held most of her attention.

A bare pair of feet had stopped about a yard from her. Her eyes trailed up his well-formed calves and heavily muscled thighs. She tried to dart her gaze around his groin—she did not need to know the details of his anatomy currently on display—but she caught a peek.

His voice snapped her attention to his face. Alpha Shane, leader of the Black Oak Pack, frowned down at her. "Shift, chaos wolf. We need to have a discussion."

Chaos wolf. Three months ago, Jordan had claimed the designation given to a werewolf without a pack as a badge of honor. The way Alpha Shane said it, it was the dirtiest of curses. And despite her not being a member of his pack, he'd commanded her to shapeshift as if he had asked her to blink. For him, it probably was as easy as that. But Shane had been born a werewolf. Jordan was still learning how to use her newly acquired shifting abilities. Tonight was a full moon, so shifting into a wolf had been easier to do. Fine-tuning to the hybrid form in the heat of the hunt had been a matter of instinct. Shifting into the purely human form was a different matter, especially as she kept catching glimpses of the full moon, could feel it like an itch on her skin. Being commanded to do so with three other hostile gazes pinned on her throat did nothing to help her find the focus necessary.

Jordan closed her eyes. She could do this. She had to do this. She had proven she could shift before, and she would do it again. She closed her eyes and reached into herself for the human parts of her.

Nothing. No teeth flattening from points to blunt rectangles. No fur melting into finer hair. The humanity she grasped for slipped through her mental fingers. Brow furrowing, she tried again, ignoring the amused barks of the werewolves surrounding her.

It took five minutes of trying and failing before her bones shifted and reformed. Goosebumps rose on her bare skin in response to the cold night air and the poking grass blades. She squirmed into a sitting position, legs pulled up to cover as much of her torso as she could. While Shane was comfortable with his nudity, she was nowhere near ready to shed that human taboo.

"What do you want, Alpha Shane?" she asked, staring at his ankles. Looking at his feet had two advantages. She looked like she was showing him the appropriate deference, and she also didn't have to look at his groin.

"You're trespassing on Black Oak Pack territory." He nodded back toward the deer. "We caught you red-fanged in the act of poaching."

His words sent a shiver of ice down her spine. "Do not violate the hunting grounds of another pack" was one of the laws a werewolf was supposed to live by. Poaching was a serious accusation that could be used as an excuse to kill her. "I was told this is neutral ground," Jordan said around the lump of fear in her throat. "Talespeaker Diana assured me I could hunt here without any issues."

"Talespeaker Diana was not updated about our new territories. I reclaimed this hunting ground for the exclusive use of the Black Oak Pack. Now as to your crime, I am willing to show you mercy this time, but your kill is forfeit. And if I catch you hunting here again, there will be no forgiveness. Now go!"

This was mercy? Jordan bit her lip. Now was not the time to make a smart-ass retort. She hugged her legs tighter, curling into a smaller ball. She wanted to slink away into the night. But she needed answers if she didn't want to end up in this position again. "If I'm not allowed to hunt here, where am I allowed to hunt?" she asked, hating the puppy-whine in her voice.

"There are still places," Alpha Shane said, glaring at her. "I haven't claimed the territory out by Arroyo Secco yet."

Jordan eyes widened as the ball of ice gathering her stomach turned to fire. "That's a three-hour drive!"

"Finding you a hunting territory is not my problem, chaos wolf." Alpha Shane sneered. "If you were part of the pack, this would not be an issue. Because you threw your lot in with those leeches, you don't have any say in the matter. Now leave!"

Maybe it was the growl in his voice, a trick of the tongue, or the power of will from being the Alpha werewolf, but before she was aware of what she was doing, Jordan had shifted into her wolf form. She crashed through the nearest bushes, all attempts at stealth or even staying on a trail gone, tail tucked between her legs. The other wolves followed on her heels, nipping at her butt as she ran. Fur ripped out of her skin as she tried to pull ahead.

She tripped over a tree root and crashed into the main trail. Panting, she lay there, waiting for the pain of sharp claws and fangs. She felt nothing. Jordan lifted her head. In the woods, as if the trail were protected by an invisible shield, stood Angela and the other wolves, glaring at her.

Alpha Shane's deep howl echoed through the night, recalling his pack. Angela stepped farther down the trail. The two males whined and glanced behind them, ears pinned back. Angela growled as the second, more commanding howl echoed. The males slunk out of Jordan's sight. Angela glared at her before turning, stalking back into the brush.

Jordan's panting slowed to deeper, normal breaths. Then she stood and trotted up the trail toward the parking lot. At the trailhead, she didn't go straight to her car. Instead, she walked deliberately in the open to the shack at the edge of the lot, toward the silhouette of a man watching out the window. She stopped at the front door and pawed at it.

The door opened, as if for a pet wanting inside. The human male, barely into his twenties, smiled down at her. "So, how did it go?"

Jordan snorted as she stalked over to the desk. She tugged a duffel bag out from underneath it. She looked at it, then at him, ears tilting back. One hind leg tapped her claws against the wooden floor in an impatient staccato.

"Oh, yeah. Sorry." He turned to study the window.

Jordan took a deep breath and closed her eyes. *Calm, peace.* She focused on her heartbeat as she mentally chanted, trying to tame her adrenaline. It was easier to grasp her humanity and draw it forward without the immediate threat of other werewolves circling her. The human in the cabin wasn't as much of a threat, even though she had the skin-prickling sensation of being watched.

"It didn't go well," she said as soon as her mouth was human enough to form the words. She pulled on her clothes almost before she was done shifting. "You can turn around now, David." She fastened her necklace behind her neck. The pendant of a curved white wedge with a ruby hanging from the tip was identical to the design the young man wore on a ring indicating they were servants of vampires.

David glanced out the window and then back to her. "What happened? Did you run into those bear poachers we spotted the other night?"

Jordan winced at the word "poachers." She picked up the duffel bag and fished around in it for her car keys. "No. Something far worse. You heard those howls? Two of them weren't me. That was Alpha Shane. We need to inform Elder Marcus the Black Oak Pack is claiming Mount Ponderosa as its hunting territory. It may not be safe for any vampires or Family to stay here any longer."

"That doesn't sound good. Where are you supposed to hunt?"

Jordan sighed. "I have no idea."

2

———

David watched Jordan pull out of the parking lot and into the waning hours of the night. Jordan's words echoed in his head. The Black Oak Pack was reclaiming this territory. This couldn't be good.

He sipped at his coffee, shaking his head. Twenty years a famulus and he still wasn't able to stay awake at night. But at least he got paid a nighttime differential for his public-facing job watching Mount Ponderosa Park. Officially, it was privately held land a local benefactor opened to public use. Its true reason was slightly different. Some vampires didn't like the taste of human blood. Montgomery, in his early days of being a vampire, had been up here often, hunting the deer roaming the hills. It was common knowledge Montgomery had been a werewolf and believed he still needed to express those instincts even if he couldn't shapeshift. David hadn't witnessed him hunt, and the stories didn't say how he managed to bring his four-legged prey down. As time passed, he came to the park less and less often. There were also feral hogs here, which were almost as dangerous as the predators stalking them. Those were the ones who wanted the challenge of stalking prey without endangering human life.

Then there were the ones who needed a good place to stash the evidence of a feeding gone wrong. Jordan announcing to Elder Marcus the pack wanted to reclaim the land would not sit well.

He'd leave it to Jordan to tell him. He could call ahead, but it was up to Jordan to deliver the bad news. After all, she was a werewolf as well as a famulus, and the message had been delivered to her directly. But she could be naive at times. He wondered if she'd ever realize the light caused the window he stared at to show the reflection of the room instead of the woods outside. She was a pretty girl. Too bad she was a werewolf. Most of the vampire servants, if their patrons turned a blind eye, had affairs with each other. Some patrons encouraged it to establish a bloodline of servants, keeping it in the family as it were. But her lycanthropy put her in the look-but-don't-touch category. Still, he liked looking at her.

Someone knocked on the door. David jumped. The night had been still and silent since Jordan had pulled out of the parking lot. There were no other vampires in the area. Protocol demanded they check in with him so he was aware of who was moving through the area and could suggest areas for them to hunt. That way, they didn't inadvertently interfere with each other. Or they could be warned away because Jordan was using the area. Humans weren't allowed in after dark, although occasionally he had to evict teenagers looking for a place to make out, drink, or play at summoning the devil.

He stood up and walked over to the door. He hoped it wasn't the werewolves Jordan had run into. There had also been rumors about bear poachers in the area. Any poacher worth his salt wouldn't be knocking on the door to the security cabin in the middle of the night unless they were in need of help without other options. Most likely, it was drunk teens reenacting a scene from a horror movie. Still, he tucked his gun into the waistband of his jeans behind his back before he opened the door.

Nobody was there. He stepped off the front step and walked

out into the parking lot to get a better look around. "Hello," he called out. His mind flitted to the old Halloween stories about ghosts knocking on walls. No, the noises had been made by a human.

A stick snapped behind him. He spun around. It had come from behind the cabin. "I know you're there," he yelled. "Come on out."

No response. He walked toward the corner of the cabin, avoiding making any noise. Even if it was one of the werewolves who had harassed Jordan earlier, well, she was a lone, unarmed girl, even if she was a wolf. He had a gun and could convince them he was armed with silver bullets. Standing up to the entire pack and sending them fleeing might earn him some gratitude she'd express physically. At least he'd ask for a naked selfie of her. He reached behind his back and pulled out his weapon.

Back to the building, he slunk to the corner and paused. He could make out the light panting breath just at the edge of his hearing. He made sure the safety was off his gun and drew in a deep breath. This would be fun, no matter who was on the other side. Scared teens or werewolves trespassing, he'd run them off. If it was a vampire, while it could be a problem in the short term, he could talk his way out of any trouble. He'd claim he was within his rights since they hadn't announced themselves before hunting. He'd prove to Sabrina he was worthy of being turned. With a gleam in his eye, he yelled and jumped around the corner, gun held in front of him. "Gotcha!"

Except there was nobody there. Only trees in the distance and the nearby grass waving gently in the moonlight.

Pain knifed across his lower legs, just above his ankles, then something slammed him in the middle of his back. He fell, gun slipping from his grip as he tried to catch himself. He hit the ground face first. He attempted to push himself up, but his feet didn't respond, flopping uselessly at the end of his legs. David pushed onto his hands and knees. His gun lay on the asphalt just out of reach. He scrambled toward it, reaching for his only protection.

Something grabbed him by the legs and jerked him down. He fell, his fingers centimeters from the gun. Then he was flipped onto his back, weight settling on his legs. David's eyes went wide as he stared into the face of his death. "No! Don't!"

His pleas went unanswered. Agony slashed across David's belly. He looked at his stomach. Blood and intestine spilled out of the parallel slits in his skin and shirt. He screamed. Pain slashed across his throat. His scream turned into a gurgle. He tasted blood, his own, as it bubbled in the cut across his neck and filled his mouth. His vision went black as he wondered how vampires enjoyed the taste of the stuff.

3

———

The hum of the tattoo machines was a noise Thorn heard but no longer consciously acknowledged. They were part of the background hum indicating The Wilted Rose was doing a steady business. Steady business meant paperwork to organize.

The vampire with his hair in a gravity-defying mohawk sat behind his desk, riffling through receipts for the purchase order for the autoclave. He was amazed how Marcus kept such a clean desk despite the amount of documentation involved in running Rancho Robles. He probably hired people to do his paperwork so there was no risk wasting his precious blood to heal a paper cut. Hell, he probably hired people to do the paperwork for the people he hired to do his paperwork.

While he studied an invoice, trying to decide what the scrawled date was, booted footsteps approached over the tiled floor. He looked up as a woman with hair the same shade of red as a fire engine poked her head into the room. "Boss? There's a Detective Pamela Henricksen here to see you. Something about identifying ink one of our artists did for a client. Should I tell her to come back with a warrant?"

Thorn made a face as he stared at the invoice, deciding how to respond. While that was her excuse, there was another reason the detective was here. "No." He sighed. "I'll deal with her myself, Charla. Send her in."

He resumed turning the paper at different angles. In the hall, Charla said, "This way," and someone stepped into his office. He held out the lined slip of paper to Pamela. "What's the first digit, four or nine?"

Pamela arched her eyebrows. "That's not the greeting I expected."

"Quarterly taxes are due. Paid invoices don't turn themselves in to the accountant. And whoever signed for this has horrible handwriting." Thorn put the paper down on the messy pile on his desk. "What do you want this time? Is this something to do with your day job? Or are you going to try to dissuade me from staying in town?"

"Always, but we need to have a discussion about chaos wolves."

"Wolf," Thorn corrected. "Or are you counting Montgomery as one of yours even though you've shunned him for so long?"

Pamela's head jerked higher. "Montgomery's trail as a wolf has come to an end. Jordan still has a long one before her if she makes the right decisions."

"The decisions you approve of."

"Montgomery wasn't thinking clearly. His thoughts are still clouded by grief and betrayal. We both know he's an influence on her opinions of werewolves."

"Alpha Shane is just as much of one." He raised his eyebrows. "So is Angela Shane."

"And so are you."

"Is this a jealousy thing because I slept with her? 'Cause if that's all it takes to get you to leave her be—"

"Please," she snorted. "The chaos wolf—"

Thorn stiffened, fists balling. "Her name is Jordan. You say you're her friend, so why don't you use her name? Or are you only pretending?"

Pamela sucked in a breath, features tightening. "I'm trying to help her. She belongs with her own kind. You and Montgomery are confusing her."

Thorn rose to his feet. "No, we're giving her an educated choice."

Pamela crossed her arms over her chest. "Like you and Christine did Montgomery?"

Thorn mirrored the movement as he came out from behind his desk. "He didn't want to become the Alpha. He didn't want to go through with the arranged marriage his father set up without consulting him."

"So you suggested to him to get out of it by turning him?"

"Hey! It was Montgomery's and Christine's idea to make him a vampire. For once, I had nothing to do with it. In fact, I told them not to, that it was a stupid move that would only cause more trouble. He was the one who begged Marcus to sire him after Christine was destroyed."

"You didn't try to stop him then."

"I didn't see why I should, especially since Shane didn't so much as lift a finger to find out who attacked him. It was clear he couldn't return to any pack and needed to remain among us." He shook his head. "But you didn't come here to argue with me about Montgomery. This is supposed to be about Jordan."

"The chao— Jordan needs to make her own choices without your interference. She's intelligent and resourceful. This incident with the hunter has more than proven it. But she belongs with her kind."

"Her kind has done nothing but bully her. They weren't so helpful when she was bitten by the chaos wolf three months ago, and they're siding with Angela for the most part. So how am I supposed to convince an intelligent woman like Jordan to accept with open arms the people who are currently making her life a living hell?"

"Alpha Shane—"

"Will always side with his daughter. The same way Marcus did with his." He shook his head. "Why are you doing this? Sticking your nose into her business despite repeatedly claiming non-interference?"

"She's an innocent who doesn't realize how deep she's gotten herself." Pamela leaned closer to him. "Do you believe that other packs won't find out about her? Rhys may have been a chaos wolf, but there are people who will want revenge for what was done to him."

"If she's so innocent, why aren't you protecting her now?"

"I can't do that if she's with you and Montgomery. She made a mistake, even if it was out of ignorance. I'm trying to keep her alive in the long term." She leaned closer to Thorn. "We've both seen brutal deaths happen when werewolves and vampires make stupid decisions. Do you want that for her?"

"She's smarter than you think," Thorn said. "We can keep arguing this for years, and we won't convince each other we're right."

"I don't need to convince you. Just her." Pamela frowned as Thorn chuckled. "What's so funny?"

"That sounds like something Jordan would say. She reminds me of you a lot."

"Oh?"

"Yup. Hungry to learn, stubborn as hell, and loyal to a fault."

Pamela shook her head. "I'm flattered. But we both know where loyalty got me."

Thorn tilted his head. "Do you really want to help her, or is this your latest scheme to poke at me?"

"No, I was hoping you'd show some sense and help convince her she should join the pack. The only reason they aren't accepting her is her stubborn insistence that she's better off with

Montgomery. If she switches sides, she'll be praised for having seen the light."

"You do realize if she does change sides, she's signing her own death warrant. She'll have broken her Oath of Family, and if she crosses paths with a vampire, she'll be killed on sight. Are you telling me the pack will protect her?"

"Of course."

"Even Angela?"

Pamela stared at him, lips pressed firmly together.

"Thought so," Thorn said. "I think we're at an impasse. I'm not going to convince you, and well, I've told you my feelings on the situation. Now, I've got paperwork to finish sorting. If you wouldn't mind?"

Pamela's eyes remained hard. "I'll see myself out." Without any further words, she spun on her heel and walked out of the office.

A few seconds later, Charla stepped into the room again. "Everything okay, boss?"

"Yeah. But do me a favor. Be sure all our licenses up front are the current ones. Oh, and have the log for the autoclave cleaning handy. Just in case we get a 'surprise' inspection."

"You think that cop will cause a problem?"

Thorn shook his head. "No, but with my luck, she'll draw some attention. I'd rather be ready just in case."

4

———————

The sun was barely breaking the horizon as Jordan unlocked the apartment door. She didn't slam it behind her but pulled it closed with more than her usual force. She didn't give into the urge to lean against it in defeat. "I'm home," she called, not worrying about waking the humans in the adjoining apartment. The walls were soundproofed so their neighbors couldn't hear any late-night activities. Montgomery didn't usually fall asleep until a half hour after sunrise. And Thorn, Montgomery had commented more than once with a sly grin, could sleep like the dead.

She sighed, trying to push away all her fear and worry in that one breath. It became a yawn as she scratched her fingers through her hair. She didn't want to repeat the time she woke up the next night and found enough twigs for a bird to build a nest tangled in her hair.

"Welcome back," said a familiar baritone. "How did it go?"

Jordan jumped. Montgomery stood in the kitchenette by the electric range. "It's almost dawn," she said. "I didn't think you'd still be awake."

"Thought you'd like something after your hunt," he said. The kettle on the electric stove whistled. Montgomery pulled it off and poured the hot water into a waiting cup and stirred it. "Always helped me settle after."

Jordan inhaled. The powdery scent of cocoa and sugar that hadn't yet dissolved into the water tickled her nose. "I've never said no to hot chocolate. Do we have any of those little marshmallows?"

Montgomery smirked. "You tell me."

Jordan rolled her eyes. That was the new game they played, continuing her training. Just because she was now a werewolf didn't mean she fully understood what she was capable of. She had proven she could shapeshift, but she still had a lot to learn about her abilities and how they might subconsciously affect her. To aid her, Montgomery moved something she needed on a daily basis to a different location and had her find it, focusing on the scent alone.

She closed her eyes and drew in a deep breath, paying attention to the conflicting smells. Dish soap, last night's beef stew, the piece of cheese she'd snacked on before leaving, blood in the refrigerator, Montgomery's musk, Thorn's scent wafting in from the living room, and the faint scent of gelatin drifting down from . . .

Her eyes snapped open. She walked past him, reached for the cabinet where she kept the pasta and canned soups. He had moved them from their normal spot on the lower shelves as part of the test. Standing on her tiptoes, she fumbled around among a few boxes and then grabbed the squishy bag. The bag caught the corner of a box as she pulled it out and knocked it over. Elbow pasta spewed forth, scattering across the floor, some of it dropping into the mug. Jordan slammed her fist onto the counter. "Damn it!" One more thing gone wrong tonight.

"Hey, it's okay," Montgomery said. "I'll get another cup and clean up. You go sit in the living room and tell us what's going on."

Jordan huffed. The last thing she wanted to do was talk about how she'd had her tail handed to her. But she had to inform them about the change of ownership of Mount Ponderosa.

She stepped into the living room. Thorn was spread out on the couch, nose buried in a book with a pirate holding a mermaid in a lustful embrace on the cover. "Hey," he said and sat up, setting his book in his lap. "Rough night, Jo?"

"You could say that." She plopped down on the couch in the spot previously occupied by his legs.

Montgomery came in, carrying her mug. He handed it to Jordan and took his spot in the recliner. "So, what happened?"

Jordan looked down at the mini marshmallows floating in the chocolate. "Well, I brought down a deer."

"A deer? On your own?" Montgomery's smile widened. "For a single wolf, that's almost impossible. How did you manage it?"

She shrugged. "Got lucky and found one with a bad limp. Plus I tried to mimic what I saw on a TV show about lionesses hunting and jumped on it from behind."

"Hmm. That would work."

"From your expression, I'd have guessed the deer jumped on you," Thorn said. "Why aren't you howling the news of your great deed to the heavens?"

"I was about to. Right up until the Black Oak Pack showed up and stole my kill."

Thorn and Montgomery froze. It still freaked Jordan out when they went statue still, not even bothering to breathe. It always meant something bad. Montgomery leaned forward. "Tell me everything, Jordan."

"There's not much to tell," Jordan said. "Alpha Shane showed up with Angela and a couple others. They accused me of poaching, saying they had reclaimed Mount Ponderosa as the Black Oak's. Then they ran me off."

Thorn's frown deepened. "You're certain he called you a poacher."

"Yes. Said he caught me red-fanged in the act. When I told him Talespeaker Diana had told me it was okay to hunt there, he said that was the only reason I was being shown mercy. I told David, Sabrina's famulus, when I was on the way out of the park to give him a head's up in case more of the pack showed up at the public entrance next."

Montgomery jumped up. He paced the narrow space between the couch and the television. "He has no right," he grumbled. "He has absolutely no right to do this. Mount Ponderosa has traditionally been neutral hunting grounds open to all werewolves. My father offered it to the Conclave as an olive branch. It was meant as a place vampires could use, as well as any chaos wolf passing through the area." He snorted. "He's only reclaiming the territory to hurt us."

"So why didn't he do it when you were turned?" Thorn asked.

"Because then he was a new Alpha and still consolidating power. He was afraid of Elder Marcus. Obviously, he's lost that fear. Plus, reclaiming the territory back then wouldn't really have hurt me."

"But now it does." Jordan bowed her head. "Because of me."

"Hey, it's not your fault." Thorn put a hand on her shoulder. "Shane's the jerk here, not you."

She didn't find Thorn's declaration very comforting, even if it was the truth. Jordan looked at Montgomery as he still paced. She reached up to scratch an itchy spot on her scalp behind her ear. "So, what do we do now? Find me a new place to hunt? He said something about Arroyo Secco still being neutral."

Montgomery paused, not the same statue-stillness, but close to it. "That leaves two options—you'll have to drive a few hours away or hunt in the city proper." He tapped his fingers against his thigh. "Marcus won't tolerate you hunting inside the city. Too much chance of you getting caught or causing problems. Inadvertently," he added at her sideways look at him.

"Driving for hours won't make it any easier," Jordan said.

"True," Montgomery agreed. "We're not solving this tonight. Did you get a chance to eat?"

"Other than the marshmallows we left on the counter?" Jordan shook her head. "I feel like I could eat a horse."

"Sorry, no horse in the fridge," Thorn said.

"Figured as much. I'll make do with the pizza from last night."

She started to stand, but Montgomery waved her down. "Sit. I'll heat it up for you."

Jordan tilted her head in Montgomery's direction, watching as he walked to the kitchenette. "Aren't I supposed to serve as your famulus? What will the other vampires think?"

"They already think I'm nuts. This will just be more evidence. Am I right, Thorn?"

"Yup. He's already got the reputation of being nuttier than a fruitcake. And that was before he got involved with you."

"Har, har, har," Montgomery said, returning with a couple of slices of the meaty pizza on a plate. He handed it to Jordan and took a seat in his recliner. "So, what's on the agenda for tonight? Visiting the blood bank?"

"Besides telling Marcus about Alpha Shane?" She picked up one of the slices. "Your rations are supposed to be ready later this week. If they won't let me take out any blood for you since they won't let me donate, I'll go bribe the butcher. Or stop by the Asian grocery store that sells pig blood for cooking." Jordan shifted. "Tonight, though, I have an appointment scheduled with Rosanna."

The smile faded from Montgomery's face. "The fangs?"

"Yeah. She's refused to meet with me until now."

"Only because I leaned on Marcus to allow it." He shook his head. "Let me worry about Alpha Shane. I'll get a meeting with Marcus tonight. It'd be better if I am the one to tell him." He stood up and stretched. "I'm heading to bed."

Thorn straightened his shoulders. "Want us to join you, Mac?"

"No." Montgomery softened the abrupt tone of his refusal. "Jordan and I have a lot to do tonight. It would be better for us if we were well rested."

"Okay." She hoped she kept the disappointment out of her voice as well as Thorn kept it off his face. "I'll see you before you go."

Montgomery nodded. "Sleep well."

Thorn waited for the bedroom door to close before he turned to Jordan. "You sure you're okay?"

"Yes . . . No . . . I don't know," Jordan said. "I didn't want to cause more problems but that's apparently all I do."

"Hey, none of this is your fault. It would've happened sooner or later. You're the excuse, not the problem."

Jordan sighed. "That doesn't make me feel any better."

"Well, you should be proud of yourself. I don't think I've heard of a lone werewolf who's learning to hunt taking down a deer alone. Oh. Mac forgot to mention. Your parents called a few minutes after you left. They want to talk to you."

"Of course they do." Jordan's shoulders slumped further. "They probably want to find out why I've quit my job and dropped out of school. Oh, and moved in with two men."

Thorn raised an eyebrow. "Are they aware of me and Mac?"

"I haven't told them, but they'll find out about it sooner or later."

He looked down at the book on his lap. "Sometimes I wonder if I shouldn't have asked you to join us that night."

"Yeah, but who knows where we would've ended up. I may never have faced down Rhys. Or been able to shapeshift before the deadline Alpha Shane set. Montgomery and I'd be dead or worse, and maybe another war between werewolves and vampires would have started."

"Don't think they won't find another excuse," Thorn said. "Like I said earlier. We won't solve this tonight."

"For any of it." She looked at the closed door. Montgomery

had slept alone since Jordan announced she had no intentions of joining the Black Oak Pack. At first he claimed it was because he didn't want to disturb them with his nightmares. Now she wasn't so sure.

"Give him time," Thorn said. "He's still recovering from what Rhys did. Not to mention dealing with the memories of Christine." He eyed her up and down. "Are you regretting any of your decisions?"

"No, I think we're handling this the right way. For now at least."

"Yeah, it's just hard waiting." Thorn's gaze narrowed and traveled up and down her again. "For both of you."

Jordan squirmed. She was familiar with his assessing look. "You really think he'd be okay if we were doing the wild thing and leaving him out?"

Thorn shook her head. "Probably not. In that case, you probably should get to bed. You have a big night ahead of you."

Sighing, Jordan nodded. "Sleep well, Thorn." She picked up the half-eaten piece of pizza and took it to the kitchen, turning the situation over in her mind. There was no possibility of finding a solution this morning. Or maybe at all.

5

____

The sun radiated warmth on Jordan's skin. She squinted in the sunshine, relishing the sensation of light and heat not created by an LED lightbulb or a heating lamp. Being a famulus to a vampire meant she was available at all times, but especially during daylight hours. Montgomery had been on his own as a vampire for so long he was ridiculously self-sufficient. Most of his bills and business were handled over the phone or internet. The building he owned had a supervisor he'd hired as a layer of protection between him and the tenants. All Jordan had to do was run the occasional errand he didn't want to do, attend Conclave meetings with him, and pick up his rations of blood. Even the blood drives, as Thorn called them with a snicker, were a formality to remind other vampires and Family she existed.

That left her with plenty of free time during the days. Her normal schedule involved sleeping until two in the afternoon. Then she'd get dressed and take care of her checklist of things she needed to do, or anything Montgomery couldn't delay until the evening. The one task she looked forward to the most was taking Rex out to the dog park for Mrs. Clarke.

Exiting the apartment building, Jordan held onto the leash strained tight between her hand and the rhinestone collar. "Rex! Heel!" The Rottweiler's head turned back to her, the stump of the tail swishing back and forth. He leaned his weight against the tension holding him back.

Jordan sighed. While the dog had accepted she was a werewolf and not a threat, he still tested boundaries, wanting to be the top dog. "Rex," she said softly. She didn't growl at him like she had in the past. She no longer had to. Deciding he wouldn't win this one, he padded over to her, tail still wagging. He settled next to her leg and whined.

She reached down and patted the massive head. "Good boy." Mentally, she made a note to get a harness lead. Mrs. Clarke would be heartbroken if Rex broke free and ran away. "Let's go."

The walk to the dog park took about ten minutes. She scanned the fenced-in area, alert for any signs of other animals present. To her relief, the park was empty. She let herself and Rex in through the gate and unclipped the leash. Rex quivered next to her but remained at her side. Jordan produced a hard rubber ball larger than her fist from her jacket. She waggled it back and forth in front of his face. "Want it?"

Rex barked. He leaned forward on his forelegs, his stumpy tail high in the air.

She flung it a good twenty feet away. "Fetch!"

Rex bounded off. He grabbed the ball and shook it back and forth. Instead of bringing it back, he trotted on with it, dropping it, then picking it up.

Jordan laughed. "You're supposed to bring it back." Rex ignored her and continued pushing the ball this way and that with his nose. "Okay. We'll work on it."

The fence rattled behind her. She stiffened her stance, readying herself for a confrontation. All dogs smelled she was a werewolf within a sniff of meeting her. Rex recognized her as dominant, even if he continued to test her bounds. So did the

Scottish terrier who lived on the ground floor. If she kept her posture non-threatening, no fast movements and no challenges, they satisfied themselves with warning barks and growls. Their owners apologized, made a comment about their baby never acting like this before, and Jordan laughed it off and moved far enough away to let things calm down. The few times she had been attacked, it had been by smaller dogs, chihuahuas, terriers, and the occasional mini poodle. A quiet growl had been enough to send them yipping back to their owners before she was bitten.

She turned to face the newcomer, surprised there wasn't any barking. To her surprise, the man leaning against the fence didn't have a dog with him. He looked familiar. She guessed he was in his early forties from the traces of gray creeping into his short beard. His cinnamon brown hair was combed over from one ear on the other side in an attempt to hide a receding hairline. She studied his dark brown eyes set deep in tan skin and his aquiline nose. "Mr. Campbell? I'm Jordan Abbey. I was in your English Literature class last semester."

He frowned and then smiled as he put the name and the face to a memory. He had been one of her teachers at Rancho Robles Community College. "Jordan, of course. It's good to see you." Her former teacher leaned back against the fence and gestured at her. "I almost didn't recognize you, you're so pale. I didn't mean to interrupt you playing with your dog.

She looked at Rex, who was shaking the ball back and forth. "Rex isn't my dog. I walk him for a neighbor of mine."

"I wouldn't think you'd want anything to do with dogs, not after what happened to your roommate's boyfriend." He laid a hand on her shoulder. "I didn't get a chance to say how sorry I was. And I admit I was disappointed when you didn't return to class. I hoped it meant you had gotten into another college."

"Life has been a little crazy since then," Jordan admitted. She kept one eye on Rex, who was happily herding the ball about fifty feet away from them. "I've thought about going back to school, but right now I'm not sure how I could do it." She was still getting a handle on her abilities. Montgomery would back any decision she made. Or at least she hoped so. Technically she was supposed to follow his orders. They had discussed her going back to school after she was more grounded as a werewolf, but neither of them had broached the subject recently. If she wanted to and he said no, she wasn't sure how she'd react.

"I know it can be tough, especially after a break, no matter how short." Mr. Campbell picked at a piece of lint on his sweater. "What's holding you back?"

Jordan sighed. "Pretty much every decision I've made since I left," she said. Her phone buzzed, not the pattern of an incoming call, but an alarm. "I'm sorry, I have to get going." There were things she had to do tonight that she wasn't looking forward to but couldn't be late to. She let out a sharp whistle. "Rex! Here!"

"It can be daunting," Mr. Campbell agreed. He reached into his pocket for a small notebook and pencil. He scribbled something on a page and tore it off. "My contact information. I doubt you still have it. In case you want to talk or need a little encouragement about going back to school."

Jordan dredged up a smile as she tucked the paper into her jacket pocket. "Thanks." She called out again. "Rex! Here, boy."

Rex grabbed the ball and trotted toward her. But ten feet away from them, his attitude changed. He dropped the ball, planted his feet, and growled.

"Rex!" She stepped forward and snapped the leash to his collar. "I really am sorry, Mr. Campbell." She wrapped the leash around her hand to keep a better grip. "I don't know what's gotten into him." Gee, who did she sound like now?

"It's okay, Jordan." He took a step back as Rex lunged forward. Jordan planted her feet, gripping the leash tighter but unable to make the big dog budge. Mr. Campbell edged further away. "You've got your hands full, so I'll head on. But I do hope to hear from you sometime soon."

"Goodbye, Mr. Campbell." She watched as he waved goodbye and let himself out of the dog park.

Jordan held tight on the leash. Rex didn't relax until her former teacher had rounded the corner. "Rex." Jordan knelt down by him. "What's going on, boy?"

Rex turned to stare at her with deep brown eyes. Then he licked her cheek, stump of a tail wagging furiously.

"Eww! Dog drool!" She wiped her cheek with the back of her hand and stood and patted his head. "Well, I won't need a shower tonight. Come on. Let's go home."

She walked Rex home, her mind turning over the brief conversation. Seeing her former teacher reminded her of how much her life had changed in such a short time. Not all those changes were for the better. In fact, a lot of people from her old life would argue that none of it was for the better. Her parents were at the head of the list. If they hadn't found out about her withdrawal from college already, they'd find out at the end of the semester.

Rex's attitude was subdued as well, as if picking up on her pensiveness. He padded along at her side, leash limp between them as they walked into the apartment building, no longer the eager goofball pulling her along. When they reached the elevator, he nudged her hand, giving it a quick swipe with his tongue.

Jordan smiled down at Rex and tousled his ears. "Good boy," she said as the doors slid open. She continued to scratch his ears as they rode the elevator to the third floor. She walked to 302 and let herself in. "Hi, Mrs. Clarke," she said as she unclipped Rex's leash.

"Hello, Jordan dear." The elderly woman shuffled out of one of the back rooms. The dog's stump of a tail wiggled back and forth as he ambled over to his owner. "How was the walk?"

"Fine, Mrs. Clarke." Jordan smiled. "Rex had a fun time today."

"I'm glad to hear that. Thank you again for walking him."

"You're welcome. I'll be back tomorrow afternoon to take him out again."

When she stepped into the hall, the smile dropped from her face. Now she had to get ready for the rest of the night. And given who she'd have to visit, she'd rather face a full dog park.

6

———

Jordan pulled Montgomery's car into his underground assigned parking spot in the Rancho Robles shopping complex. She slipped out of the driver's side while Montgomery got out of the passenger seat. "My meeting will probably take longer than yours," he said. "Wait for me in the hotel's lobby."

"See you there." As she watched her patron walk away, she slipped her hand into her jacket pocket to make sure the jewelry box was still there. If she lost it, there'd be multiple hells to pay. Reassured by the brush of velvet against her fingers for the fifteenth time, she walked out of the parking structure.

The faux-gas lamps glowed softly, adding light to what shone out of the store displays. The restaurant had turned on their outdoor heaters, and most of the tables clustered around them were filled with people drinking and eating. None of them probably had a clue that the most powerful vampire in Rancho Robles owned the complex.

She stopped in front of one of the stores showing three headless mannequins wearing tight, stylish dresses. Jordan checked her reflection in the glass of the window and made sure the pendant of her necklace was visible in the "v" formed by her jacket. She pulled her phone out of her purse, set it to vibrate, and returned it. Then she squared her shoulders and stepped into Eleganza Discreta.

She walked up to the counter, past displays and racks of cocktail and formal dresses. Despite her best efforts, she still felt underdressed even though she was wearing a black pinstripe pencil skirt, cream blouse, and matching jacket. She was here to make an impression, and she hoped it would work in her favor. Part of her still considered herself a little girl playing dress up, much as she had been when Montgomery had first brought her here. This time, she planned to play the part without any hesitation.

The clerk behind the counter eyed her with the usual disdain. "May I help you?" she asked in a voice like frost on glass. The tension in her posture was only matched by the tightness of her bun.

Jordan looked her in the eyes. "I have a meeting with Ms. Lombardi."

The clerk's eyebrow arched. She looked Jordan up and down and paused roughly at her neckline. Her pose stiffened, and some of the hostile attitude drained away. "Whom should I say is here to see her?"

"Ms. Jordan Abbey. She's expecting me."

The woman paled at the mention of her name. "Ms. Abbey. Of course." Obviously, her reputation preceded her. Jordan wasn't sure exactly what that reputation was, but she'd use it to her advantage. The clerk stepped out from behind the counter and gestured for Jordan to follow her. She led Jordan past the racks of sample dresses and displays of high-end costume jewelry to a plain door marked "Employees Only" in fancy script. "She will see you in her office, the first door on the left."

"Thank you," Jordan said. Without showing any hesitation, she passed through the door. The plainness of the back area was a shock after the opulence of the store itself. The walls here were painted a flat beige, almost the same color of the cement floor. In the room to the right, she glimpsed a few vinyl-back chairs and a table that would have been at home in her grandmother's house. To the left there was a door marked "Management." The font was blocky, unlike the elegant lettering of the customer-facing sign. She straightened her shoulders and knocked.

"Come in," responded the French-accented female voice.

Jordan stepped inside. The spartan look of the outer area continued into the office. Calendars and schedules covered the walls. Invoices and receipts were stacked on the desk. And Rosanna Lombardi sat behind the desk. The red-haired vampire still managed to look imposing despite the pencil tucked behind her ear. "You wished to see me, Jordan Abbey."

"Yes, ma'am." She had practiced the speech in her mind many times. Montgomery had coached her over and over on both the proper etiquette and the phrasing. Now it was up to her to deliver it. She stood up straight and reached her hand into the pocket for the velvet box. "I thank you, Rosanna Lombardi, child in the blood of Elder Marcus, for this audience. Your brother in the blood Montgomery Cooper wishes to know the status of your famulus Bridgette."

Rosanna's expression never flickered "She passed."

"Oh." That wasn't good. There were rumors Brigette had survived the attack of the werewolf stalking Jordan, and like Jordan was now a werewolf. There were also rumors Rosanna had put her down rather than suffer the presence of a werewolf among her servants. Even more quietly whispered were the rumors Bridgette hadn't been changed, but that Rosanna had killed her due to her scarred appearance. She wasn't here to probe any of those rumors, despite her morbid curiosity. "I'm sorry for your loss."

"I'm certain you are." Rosanna removed the pencil from behind her ear and put it on the table. "Now tell me. Looking into the status of my famulus cannot be the reason your patron requested this audience. Why are you really here, Jordan Abbey?"

Thrown by the question, she spoke less formally. "Montgomery sent me." She pulled the blue velvet box out of her pocket and offered her the box with both hands and a slight bow, using the time to regain her footing. "I have come on his behalf to present you with a gift, ma'am."

"A gift?"

"Yes, ma'am." Jordan said.

Rosanna accepted it with a dubious expression. She raised the lid. Nestled inside on the silk lining as if they were precious jewels were four large incisors. From tip to root they were at least three inches long, marking them as werewolf teeth. "You told my patron you would only forgive him if the fangs of the werewolf who wronged you were in your hand," Jordan said softly. "Here they are. He wishes to learn the answer to one question. Does this repay the debt?"

Rosanna hesitated, and then one finger stroked the length of one fang, lightly caressing the tip. A shudder ran through her. Jordan wasn't sure if it was fear or pleasure Then she snapped the box shut, placed it on the table, and shoved it toward Jordan. "No. I refuse"

Jordan's skin felt cold as her spine stiffened. Montgomery had said that if Jordan showed Rosanna the proper respect, she'd accept the fangs and things would be right between the two vampires. She had recited her speech flawlessly. Or had she blown it? "I'm sorry. Was it something I said? I meant no offense—"

"You have given none, little wolf. Your patron, however, should be not sending his famulus to perform an act of contrition he should be doing himself." Rosanna clasped her hands, interlacing her fingers. She looked Jordan up and down and gestured for her to sit in the chair opposite her desk. "Now, allow me to give you a word of advice, little wolf, even though I am not your patron."

Jordan sat, perching on the edge. "Advice, ma'am?"

Rosanna leaned on her forearms. "You do realize one day you will be forced to make a decision." Her tone was conversational, but the words held the weight of doom. "You will not be allowed to remain with a foot in both worlds. You will have to choose between the ones who saved you and the ones who are your own kind."

Hadn't she already done this by deciding not to live with the Black Oak Pack? Jordan shook her head. "I'm not sure I understand, ma'am."

Rosanna waved a hand, encompassing the room. "I'm certain you've been told bedtime stories about the big bad Bat and the innocent little Wolf, the gods most werewolves worship. You must have realized it is the excuse that werewolves use to hunt down vampires with fire and fang and claw and stake. They will do everything to encourage you to join in on their hunts, especially since you are Family and are privy to our secrets. They will take you back to where they lair and use you to give birth to the next generation, whether you wish it or not." She held up one slim finger. "But there is a way for you to avoid that fate."

The cold in her spine crept over her skin. Of course she had realized the things Rosanna had just mentioned. But she was only in thinking in terms of the werewolf who had bitten her, not the entire Black Oak Pack. While they had not accepted Rhys, it didn't mean the pack didn't share the same beliefs and opinions about vampires. She swallowed, finding her voice. "How do you propose I avoid that, ma'am?"

"Become a vampire." Rosanna made a little shushing motion before Jordan managed to protest. "No. Think about it before you speak. It solves so many of your problems. Even if you joined them, do you think Alpha Shane's followers would ever accept you now that you've been tainted by vampires? The pack will cease to harass you as they must be doing now. You will be accepted as a full member of the Conclave."

"But I'll be dead."

"*Un*dead, darling. There is a difference." Rosanna leaned over the table to her. "Think about it, little wolf. Not only would your problems with the werewolf pack disappear, but so would a lot of pesky mortal issues. You'd be forever young. And with careful planning and a century or so, you could be rich and free to indulge your love, your lust, your hunger with whomever you want. You have a chance to have what so many want, but so few obtain."

"And Alpha Shane?"

"He would not be happy, but you would have the protection of the Conclave since you would no longer be a mere servant, but a full-fledged member."

"Are you offering to do it?"

"If you asked. Or I could help arrange for another. Has Montgomery offered to sire you?"

There had been a little discussion but nothing serious. Jordan blinked at her in confusion, unable puzzle together Rosanna's angle. "Why? I didn't even think you liked me. What's your gain?"

Rosanna's face shifted to something reptilian. "Bridgette was my famulus. Mine!" she hissed. "And she was taken because of him. The werewolf may be dead, but that does not pay for what I have lost. If you become a vampire, it will not be full recompense, but it will be enough." Her face froze into its normal icy facade. "Please consider my offer, Ms. Abbey. And please relay my message to your patron about the gift, and emphasize it was not your lack of manners that led to my refusal."

Jordan picked up the box, her hands turning it this way and that as she gathered her composure. This had not gone how Montgomery said it would. She bowed to Rosanna. "I will convey your message and consider your offer, ma'am. I bid you good evening." She turned and walked out of the office and out of the store. Jordan took a deep, cleansing breath the moment she stepped over the threshold. It could have gone worse, but not by much. Montgomery wasn't going to be happy.

She pulled her phone out of her purse. It vibrated in her hand. Jordan glanced at the screen and froze when she read Montgomery's text.

Marcus's office! ASAP!

Jordan stared at the message on her phone. Her stomach clenched. She double-checked the timestamp then scrolled to the clock. Montgomery had texted her just after her meeting with Rosanna had started. Hopefully Elder Marcus wouldn't consider it a grave insult she hadn't responded immediately.

She hurried past the parking structure toward the street-level entrance of the Hotel Cataluna. While the restaurants and bars were still full, the sidewalks were empty. She didn't run, but walked with more speed than the casual shopper. She entered the lobby of the hotel and headed to the elevator flanked by an older man in a modified bellhop's uniform. Richard nodded a silent greeting as he removed the velvet rope blocking the elevator.

On the ride up to the 7th floor, she double checked her appearance in the blurry reflection of the metal doors. At least she had dressed up for the meeting with Rosanna instead of wearing her usual jeans, not that it would make much of a posi-tive impression. Elder Marcus wouldn't have forgotten about her leaving his presence without permission at their last private meeting. Then there was the fact she had chewed him and Alpha Shane out about their bickering instead of helping her find Montgomery. The only reason she hadn't been punished was because she had pulled off the rescue on her own. Was he planning on punishing her now? Had she broken an unknown rule when dealing with the Black Oak Pack last night? There was only one logical reason she could think of. He wanted specific details about what had happened last night. She wasn't looking forward to reliving her humiliation again.

The doors opened directly into the lobby for the quarters of the Elder Vampire of Rancho Robles. It could have passed for the waiting area at a tech company with the leather couches, glass tables, and chrome accents. Helen, tucking a strand of red hair behind her ear, rose from her desk. "You're expected," she said as she walked to the security door behind it. She gestured Jordan over. "Do you remember the procedure from last time?"

Jordan nodded to the vampire. "Walk to the end of the hall, knock on the door, and enter when he says I may."

"Good." She punched a number into the key panel. The light on it flashed from red to green. Helen opened the door. "Now don't dawdle. This is a grave situation."

When wasn't it? She walked into the hall. The heavy steel door closed behind her with an ominous boom. Then there was the silence of the hallway. But her ears picked up the faintest whir of a security camera turning to focus on her. Head up and spine straight, she walked down the hall, trying to display complete confidence. Her hands balled into fists and the way she bit the inside of her lower lip gave her away.

The second doors loomed in front of her. Unlike the security doors, these were carved with an ornate scene of a bat flying before the full moon and a small wolf on the hill, howling. It comforted her that while the focal point was on the Bat, the Wolf was also present. Her fingers brushed over the carving, then curled into a fist again. She knocked on the doors three times.

"Come in," a voice boomed. She drew in another deep breath and pushed them open.

The office was mostly the same as the last time she had attended a meeting. The paintings and statuary had been swapped out for more modern pieces, but the same sense of power, dignity and restrained menace permeated the walls. Three vampires sat around the desk. Montgomery's expression was a neutral mask, but she could read the small twitches of tension in his jaw. The blond woman opposite him in the other guest chair eyed her with ill-concealed anger and disgust. She was vaguely familiar. Melissa? No. Sabrina. She had been one of the witnesses to her induction into the Family. David was her famulus. Now she was certain why she was being called here.

But most of her attention was on the man sitting behind the desk who watched her approach. He was tall and thin. Light reflected off the dark skin of his bald head. Any human who met him, if any who weren't Family ever did, would consider him African American. Jordan guessed he didn't consider himself one or possibly even the slurs once used to describe his race. Montgomery had said that Marcus never told him how old he was, and Jordan couldn't begin to hazard a guess. The source of the menace and the power resided in his gaze. She stopped short of the two vampires in the guest chairs and bowed low, as Montgomery had taught her. "Elder Marcus," she acknowledged him.

"Famulus Jordan Abbey," Marcus said, his voice resonant and stern. "We need to know where you were and what you did last night. We especially need to be told of anyone you may have seen or anyone who may have seen you."

Jordan glanced at Montgomery. He sat motionless, shoulders pulled back and hands balled into fists. Was she being asked to provide an alibi? Was she being accused of something? She squared her shoulders, meeting Marcus's gaze. "I spent the full moon last night hunting at Mount Ponderosa Park. While there, I was attacked by members of the Black Oak Pack, who informed me they were reclaiming the park as part of their exclusive hunting territory. They accused me of poaching."

Marcus leaned forward a few millimeters. "Who, specifically?"

"Alpha Shane, his daughter Angela Shane, and the twins Ryan and Brian. I don't know their last names."

The female vampire sitting to her left stirred, her glare crashing like a pallet of bricks on Jordan's shoulders. But Jordan's attention remained focused on Marcus. "Did you speak to anyone else?" he asked.

"Famulus David Crossley. He was there when I arrived and shifted. He was also there when I returned and got dressed. I told him what the Black Oak Pack had said and suggested he leave the area."

"When was this?"

Jordan bit her lip. "I got home around sunrise. So five o'clock a.m.-ish? I can't say for certain."

"Had the Black Oak Pack been in the area before you arrived?"

Jordan shook her head. "I don't know. I wasn't aware they were there until they blindsided me."

"And they only threatened you?"

"Yes." The knot in her stomach was growing tighter. Something was very wrong. "May I ask what happened?"

Out of the corner of her eye, she watched the vampiress stiffen. "This morning, Sabrina's famulus was found dead inside the gates of Mount Ponderosa. The coroner's report will reflect that he was mauled by a bear. They most likely will make notes of the large tracks in the area."

Jordan swallowed, willing her stomach to keep its contents in their place. She hadn't come across any signs of a bear in the area. "A werewolf killed him?"

He didn't confirm or deny. "You were the last person to have contact with him. Do you have anything you wish to add to your statement?"

'No," she whispered, more in denial of the death than a response to his question. "No," she repeated with more force. "I had nothing to do with it. If I had been aware of any threat, I would have stayed behind and protected him."

"It's a pity you didn't," Sabrina hissed.

Montgomery's head turned toward Sabrina, but Marcus didn't acknowledge her. "Ms. Abbey, please wait for your patron in the main office."

"Yes, sir." She bowed again and turned. Straight backed, she walked to the doors and let herself out. But when the door closed behind her, she dropped into a ball, the heels of her hands pressed to her eyes. Maybe if she had stayed there, if she hadn't let the pack drive her away . . .

She couldn't do anything about it now. Jordan wiped her tears from her eyes as she straightened up. All she could do now was wait for Montgomery and work through her guilt when she got home.

8

Once the door closed, Marcus turned to the female vampire. "Your thoughts, Sabrina?"

She sighed, her eyes still narrowed. "She still could have done it. She has no alibi."

"What is her motive?" Montgomery asked.

Sabrina made a broad wave with her hand. "David was known to show an interest in the female famuluses. He could have made a pass at her. Or perhaps she caught him looking at her as she dressed. She might have lost her temper and attacked him."

Montgomery shook his head. "No. She'd admit to me if she did."

Sabrina glared at Montgomery, fangs descending. "And you believe her?"

Montgomery stared back, his own fangs descending as well. "Are you questioning her truthfulness, or mine?"

"Enough," Marcus snapped. He glared at Sabrina and then at Montgomery. Both vampires sank back in their chairs. While their fangs didn't retract immediately, both covered them with their lips. "Sabrina, I have dealt directly with this girl before. She wouldn't use a humiliating defeat at the hands of the other were-wolves as an alibi unless it was the truth."

Sabrina took a deep breath and sat back into the chair. "I will accept your word, Elder Marcus."

Montgomery's shoulders relaxed. A fight had been averted, even if Sabrina was only paying lip service to Elder Marcus. He tensed again at the next words his sire said. "Now what do we do about Alpha Shane hunting Family members?"

"I'm not sure he is," Montgomery said.

"Really?" Sabrina arched an eyebrow.

"It doesn't feel like a move Alpha Shane would make."

Marcus arched an eyebrow. "You're certain, Montgomery?"

"No. But . . ." He shrugged, searching for the words to explain the nebulous feeling. "It's too aggressive. If he did things like this, I'd have died a long time ago."

Sabrina frowned, turning to face him. "If it's not your pet werewolf, and not the Black Oak Pack, then who?"

Montgomery sat back in the chair. "There could be another chaos wolf in the area. We've seen how well Alpha Shane patrols his territory. Jordan's proof of his failures since she was created by a rogue in his territory he was not aware of. Or . . ."

"Or what, Montgomery?" Marcus asked.

"Or Alpha Shane's daughter lost her temper and attacked David and is hoping we distrust Jordan enough we'll jump to the conclusion that she killed him."

Sabrina fingers clenched the arms of the chair tighter. "Do you think that's possible?"

"She and Jordan don't get along. It sounds like she was more than willing to help Alpha Shane bully Jordan off the territory, which makes sense if she sees Jordan as a rival. And if the rumors are true, she has her eye on being Alpha after her father. If she's grown impatient, this might be her opening move in an attempt at a coup. Or she did it and Alpha Shane isn't aware yet. But another chaos wolf is more likely."

"I thought strays were uncommon." Marcus tapped his fingertips together. "I haven't heard of any before the chaos wolf who turned up here a few months ago."

Montgomery shrugged again. "They are. But if Alpha Shane is getting a reputation of being a lax guardian, packs and wolves searching for territory may be testing his strength. Send in a few lone wolves they can claim were kicked out of their packs if caught."

"This is all very interesting," Sabrina said in a tone that sounded anything but. "But what will be done about the death of my famulus?"

"We will investigate it thoroughly before we decide our next steps." Marcus turned to his child in the blood. "Montgomery, I want you to go to Alpha Shane on my behalf and find out what he knows about this."

Montgomery swallowed. The timing of this request could not be worse. "Sir, not that I'm questioning your orders, but is it wise, given recent events?"

He fixed Montgomery with an even gaze. "Is there anyone else who would be better suited to approach him?"

Montgomery looked down at the floor. "No, sir."

Marcus turned to Sabrina. "Do not worry. You will be avenged for this insult, no matter who the guilty party is."

Sabrina smiled coolly at Marcus. "Thank you, Elder. I trust your word." She stood up. "I thank you for looking promptly into this, sir." She looked at Montgomery. "Mr. Cooper." With no further words, she swept from the chamber.

Once the doors were shut, all of Marcus's attention focused on Montgomery. "How likely do you believe any of the Black Oak Pack are responsible?"

Montgomery relaxed into the chair. He could speak freer now. "I'd say fifty-fifty. I'm not sure about a lot of the younger pack members. But when they want to make a name for themselves, they will do very stupid things. If Jordan was aware of another chaos wolf in the area, she'd say something. But she might not have picked up on their presence."

"You are the only one in the Conclave with firsthand expertise of internal werewolf pack politics, Montgomery. Can I trust that you won't do something stupid and antagonize Alpha Shane?"

"My mere existence antagonizes him," Montgomery grumbled.

"You do nothing to help the situation. And he is in the right, since you took it upon yourself to train Jordan instead of handing her over to him."

"I know, and it was a mistake. But I couldn't let him—"

"Yes, you could." Marcus's voice was cold. "She is your responsibility now, but you are not to be her advocate among werewolves. Have I made myself clear?"

"Yes, sir."

"I will contact Alpha Shane. You will speak with him tomorrow night at his home, and take your famulus with you."

Montgomery tapped his chin. "He won't be happy to see Jordan again, especially with me. If he agrees to meet with me at all."

"Exactly." A menacing smile spread across Marcus's face.

Montgomery's eyes lit up. Now the move in the chess game his sire was playing was revealed. This was one of the few times he wouldn't mind being used as a pawn. "I understand." Montgomery put his hands on the chair arms but didn't rise. "Is there anything else you wish to discuss?"

"Not until we find out what Alpha Shane's take on the situation is. That will direct our next moves."

Montgomery rose and bowed. "Until tomorrow evening then." With no further words, he walked to the exit, debating how much to tell Jordan.

9

———

Jordan pulled herself together enough to get outside to the waiting area. She took a seat in the corner, hoping her eyeliner wasn't too smeared from her earlier tears. Helen focused her attention on the computer, typing something and punching one key at a time.

The door opened and Jordan looked up. To her disappointment, it was Sabrina. The vampiress glared at her as she swept out of the room.

Helen looked up, one finger resting on a key, asking without words what Jordan had done this time. Jordan dropped her gaze. No matter what she said or did, it would be twisted into her being guilty. The slow-paced clicking resumed, counting out the seconds.

The door opened and Montgomery stepped out. Helen relaxed. "It took you long enough. I was worried I'd have to come and rescue you."

"You still might have to." Montgomery sighed. "I'll be reporting back tomorrow night. See you then."

Jordan stood up without saying a word and followed him

through the door into the elevator. "What do you mean you'll be back tomorrow?"

"Not here," Montgomery said. "Once we're in the car."

They didn't say anything as they rode down to the first floor. Nor did they speak as they crossed the lobby, her a respectful length of a yard behind him, the proper distance for a famulus following her patron. She could tell from how he held himself coiled and about to spring that Montgomery wasn't happy about something. Was he being asked to hand her over for punishment for a crime she hadn't committed? No, it didn't make sense. She wouldn't be allowed to leave now if it were so.

Once in the parking area, she trotted to catch up with him. Neither said anything until they were inside Montgomery's SUV. Jordan settled behind the wheel and slipped the keys into the ignition. "Sabrina thinks I killed him."

Montgomery nodded. "Yes, she did at first. I think I changed her mind. Marcus believed you, or at least I believe he does."

"Thank God for small favors," Jordan grumbled as she started the engine.

"Hey, now. You should be grateful. If Marcus thought you had any part of it, you wouldn't be coming home with me."

She blew out a ragged breath through her nose. "Sorry." She backed the car out of the parking lot and waited until they were on the main street before speaking again. "He'd be alive if I had stayed."

"You can't be sure of that." Montgomery sighed and reached over, resting a hand on her shoulder. "You'd just had your ass handed to you. Shane probably would have killed you if you'd tried to fight back. And you did warn David there were other werewolves in the area."

"But—"

"But nothing, Jordan. You aren't responsible for his death."

"That wasn't what I was about to say." Even though her guilt insisted otherwise. "Alpha Shane doesn't seem like the kind who kills without warning. For all he knew, I didn't warn David Black Oak was out there. And if there was a confrontation that ended in David's death, it would tip us into the conflict he supposedly doesn't want."

"In other words, what's changed?" Montgomery said. "It's a game of good cop, bad cop. Given the interactions I've seen between the two of you before, I wouldn't be surprised if Angela wasn't trying to get you in trouble. Make your life so miserable with us that you feel you have no choice but to come crawling to him for protection.

"Kicking me out of the hunting grounds I get. But killing a famulus? That's way more than making my life miserable."

"Marcus said it would be publicly declared as a bear mauling as far as the mundane world goes. That doesn't mean other vampires will believe it, especially when word gets around that you were there before it happened. Alpha Shane is assuming any suspicion will automatically be cast on you. He may have seen an opening and taken it without thinking he or his pack would also be suspects."

"Acting without thinking it through? Sounds like something I'd do," Jordan said with a faint smile. "Besides, I thought an Alpha was supposed to be in control."

"Of his or her pack, yes. Some maintain control through violence and unpredictability. Some packs think it's the sign of a good Alpha werewolf." He shrugged. "Or at least that's what my father told me."

Jordan's ears perked up. The fact that Montgomery had been a werewolf before becoming a vampire was something they didn't discuss much. It was even rarer for him to mention his father. "What else did he tell you about being an Alpha wolf?" she asked, wanting to keep the conversation going.

Montgomery stared straight out the windshield. "I had a lot to learn about being one. I was too soft. I let too many people take advantage. I was too kindhearted." He glanced at Jordan. "He wouldn't have been too happy with my choice not to turn you into the pack when I found you. I'm sure he thought making me liaison to the Conclave would toughen me up. If he couldn't teach me, the vampires would." A small, bitter smile crossed his face. "You can see how well that worked."

Jordan smiled. "Personally, I think it worked very well."

Montgomery chuckled. "I forgot to ask. How did the meeting with Rosanna go?"

Her smile faded. She reached into her pocket and put the blue velvet box down on the dash.

Montgomery stiffened as he looked from it to her. "She refused?"

Jordan nodded. "She said I was perfectly polite, but I shouldn't be handing them over. You should."

Montgomery blew a breath out of his nose. He picked up the box containing the fangs and put them in his pocket.

"You don't want to face Rosanna without knowing you'll be forgiven. I get that," Jordan said. "But she's made it clear that you're the only person she'll accept them from."

"I know, but I can't . . ." He shuddered. "I still see him, them, in my dreams."

Them. Not Rhys. But the other werewolf attack had left scars on his soul. "You're still having nightmares." She and Thorn had been tracking the number of times they heard him wake up screaming. "But at least it's been two weeks since your last one, and it wasn't as bad as those first few nights." She paused, not sure how to bring up what had been on her mind since she'd learned who Montgomery had been. "That's the other thing we need to talk about. Christine. And what happened to you."

"What is there to say?" It was a little too quick of an answer for Jordan's comfort. "I loved her. I always will. But it doesn't mean I shouldn't move on."

But have you? Jordan swallowed. "Take me to her grave sometime? I saw it when I was searching for you, but I'd like to visit it properly. Maybe hear a bit more about her."

"I'd like that." Montgomery looked away, fine lines wrinkling around his eyes. "But not tonight."

"Yeah. Yeah, not tonight."

"Tomorrow we'll go and talk to the werewolves. Afterwards, you can pick up my rations while I debrief Marcus. He'll want to hear what Shane has to say."

"And you want me to go with you?" Jordan arched an eyebrow. "Are you deliberately trying to piss him off?"

A smug smile spread across Montgomery's face. "It was Marcus's idea, but I can't say I argued against it as hard as I should have."

"Okay," Jordan said. After cowering and fleeing from Alpha Shane, she'd be facing him again beside the one vampire who always managed to get under his skin. Her mouth stretched into a grin. *This was going to be fun.*

10

____

Jordan drew in a deep breath as she pulled up to the front gate to the Black Oak compound. *Why did Marcus insist I come along?* Montgomery approaching Alpha Shane made sense because he was the vampire with the most experience with werewolves, for obvious reasons. Given her history with the pack and her recent run-in with Alpha Shane, it was only going to cause more tension and hostility. But Montgomery said Marcus had been firm in his decision. They were the best to deal with the situation.

Montgomery looked over at her. She managed a half-smile as the gate rolled back far enough for them to pass though. *This is another test of loyalty,* she told herself. Marcus wanted to make sure she was loyal to Montgomery. Somehow, somewhere, Marcus was watching her. Once, Thorn had joked he had the entire city wired with spy cams and microphones. The more she learned of how he kept his hold on Rancho Robles, the less she believed it was a joke.

The trees cast shadows over the road, even in the moonlight, making it look like a movie scene set in a haunted wood. "I never realized how spooky oaks look at night," she said.

Montgomery grunted but didn't say anything. She focused on driving along the curves ahead of them, watching out for any animal darting into the road. She wasn't looking forward to this at all. The knot that had formed in her stomach the moment Montgomery had informed her they were to question Alpha Shane drew tighter the closer they came to the house where Alpha Shane kept his office and his quarters. Every so often, she spotted the greenish reflection of wolf eyes in the woods. Marcus wasn't the only one with spies.

She pulled up to the main house. The English manor style house looked out of place given the prevalence of faux Spanish and Mediterranean architecture. She had hoped there would be only one or two cars in the paved area reserved for parking. Instead, she counted seven. The entire pack was gathered. *Of course they would.* It was a good way to intimidate her and Montgomery.

Montgomery must have been thinking the same thing. "Ready to do this?"

"No," Jordan said. She put the car into park, shut off the engine, undid her seat belt, and opened the car door. "But we have to, so let's get this over with."

The night was full of eyes as they walked to the front door. "The bushes to our left," Montgomery said quietly.

"I can smell them," Jordan confirmed, deliberately staring at the bushes. She could just make out their outlines among the shrubs. Two werewolves crouched there, waiting for them to make one threatening move. She looked away, head held high, and walked to the front door side by side with Montgomery. He knocked on the door.

Jordan hoped that Bobby would be the one who opened the door. At least the two of them were on friendly terms, despite her not being part of the pack. Unfortunately, Angela was the one who stood on the other side of the threshold. "You are expected," she growled. Her glare was fixed on Jordan, the same stare as the night Angela had chased her off. Jordan tensed.

Montgomery stepped forward, the motion drawing both the werewolves' attention. "We are here as guests under the auspices of Elder Marcus," he said sternly. "Not to settle petty issues of rank with a half-grown pup who should have better manners."

Angela looked up at him, a clear challenge. Montgomery's expression never wavered as he stared back at her. Jordan began counting heartbeats. On her fourth, Angela's eyes cut to one side. "Follow me, sir," she said with considerably more respect.

She led the pair to the main living room. Most of the werewolves had gathered, but not all were in human form. Three lounged in relaxed menace against the wall in the bipedal wolfman form, while two were four-legged, hackles raised. It was an intimidation game, and Jordan had to admit, it was working.

Alexander Shane stood by the mantle, clad only in a pair of jeans. His eyes raked over her and then Montgomery as he folded his arms over his chest. "You wanted to talk to me?"

"Yes," Montgomery said. "We've come on Elder Marcus's behalf to inquire about what happened at Mount Ponderosa."

Shane snorted. "I'm surprised he'd take such interest in another vampire's slave being kicked out of territory she was trespassing on."

Jordan's fist balled, a growl bubbling up in her throat. She felt the weight of Montgomery's hand on her shoulder and halted, reminding herself he was deliberately baiting her.

Montgomery spoke, no hint of recognizing the insult in his voice. "While Elder Marcus found your treatment of my famulus interesting, that's not why he sent us here."

She glared up at Alpha Shane. The werewolf locked eyes on her. She stared for several seconds before dropping her eyes to the floor. Shane snorted. "Then tell me why you're here?"

"Last night, close to dawn, a famulus was killed by something with claws and fangs. We have no reason to believe it was a wild animal."

Soft growls surrounded them. Alpha Shane's response was less question and more statement. "You think one of us had something to do with it."

Montgomery held his hands out to his sides as if it was self-evident. "Jordan saw you accompanied by three others in the area shortly before the murder took place."

"The one in the cabin?" Shane's eyes narrowed. "We had nothing to do with his death."

"Then there is a stranger violating your territory?" Montgomery shook his head. "You'd think after the incident with Rhys, you'd be more diligent with your patrols."

Jordan's head jerked in Montgomery's direction. Was he trying to get Alpha Shane to rip his head off?

Several werewolves rose to their feet. Alpha Shane's fingers flexed like he was unsheathing his claws. He gestured the others back. "There are no strange werewolves in the area," he snapped. "We have increased our patrols to prevent any future incursions." He paused, narrowing his eyes at Montgomery. "And we had nothing to do with the death you're talking about."

Montgomery bowed his head. "I will relay your response to Elder Marcus." He bowed, something respectful and mocking at the same time. "We thank you for your hospitality. Now if you will excuse us, we will depart your territory."

Alpha Shane snorted. "Go crawl back to your master." He turned his back on the pair.

Montgomery turned and walked out of the room, apparently unconcerned with all the angry werewolves glaring at them. Jordan lengthened her stride to keep up. Outside, the two wolves were still in the bushes, watching as they passed. Jordan snorted, her nose picking up the stink of urine as they neared the car. A dark spatter marked the area of the rear quarter panel where the road dust had been washed off. *At least I locked the car so they couldn't mess with the interior.* "I'll take the car through the carwash as soon as they open."

Montgomery wrinkled his nose and shook his head. "Manners have gone downhill since I was part of this pack."

They climbed into the car. Fortunately, the smell was mostly cut out due to the cabin air filters. Jordan started the engine and drove back to the main road. Her heart hadn't stopped pounding at what Alpha Shane had said. Or what Montgomery had done. He was always correcting her if she showed the slightest hint of disrespect to the Alpha werewolf, and then he would turn around and do or say worse. She wasn't sure if it was a case of hypocrisy or a personal blind spot.

Once they were on the street, she couldn't keep her silence any longer. "What the hell was that about?"

Montgomery, looking pleased with himself, glanced in her direction. "What was what about?"

"Provoking Alpha Shane. I thought he was going to bite off your head when you reminded him of what happened to Rhys." Her eyes went wide.

His smug smile grew wider. "And?"

She frowned, thinking over what Alpha Shane had said. "And you got him to say there are no strange werewolves in the area." One werewolf sneaking under his nose could be excused. A second one indicated gross incompetence. Jordan smiled. She hadn't noticed the trap Alpha Shane had waltzed into. "He all but admitted it has to be one of the Black Oak Pack responsible for killing David, or he's not aware of what's going on in his territory."

"Exactly." Satisfaction suffused Montgomery's voice. "If he admitted he's not patrolling his territory properly, another werewolf could challenge him for his position. But if he claimed there are no chaos wolves in the area, he's implying that one of the pack killed David."

She pulled onto the freeway. "Could he have done it and is now trying to throw someone else under the bus?"

"No, I wouldn't go that far. He might have been involved in it distantly or was informed after the fact. Even if someone went rogue and killed without permission, he will still publicly protect whoever it is. He may punish them internally, but he won't want his appearance of control challenged."

"So, he may not be guilty himself, but he knows who did it." Jordan shook her head. "Even if we figured out who did it, what can we do?"

Montgomery's sigh was troubled. "Nothing, at least not at first," he admitted. "The Conclave isn't strong enough to take on the Black Oak Pack. It's part of the reason for the Treaty. It was put in place when we both had a chance at wiping each other out but weren't willing to risk it. We could demand the individual be turned over to face justice. It would be questionable if they did it or not. If the Conclave wanted to punish them, we'd have to call in reinforcements from other conclaves before moving against the pack."

"So, what's the next move?"

"That's the sixty-four-thousand-dollar question."

"The what?"

"Never mind. From before you were born." Montgomery stared out the windshield. "If he does nothing, Marcus will lose face. He'll have to watch out for a coup attempt, even more so than normal. If other conclaves found out, they'd respect his leadership even less and be less inclined to aid if he requested it."

"It's a no-win situation." Jordan's stomach clenched. "No matter what happens, someone has to call the other person's bluff. And it'll end in a fight." She shivered. It was almost the perfect storm. A little too perfect, the more she considered it. "Montgomery, are we sure it was a werewolf that killed David?"

"What do you mean?"

"David mentioned some people were spotted in the woods

after the park closed for the night. He thought it might be a poacher after bears. Maybe David caught him in the act and he killed him."

Montgomery chewed the inside of his lip. "I guess it could be possible. It's odd the poacher made the effort to make it look like an animal attack instead of just leaving him for dead."

"Let's assume that's the truth. How do we prove it?"

"I don't know. Just as I'm not sure how we'll keep everyone from each other's throats."

"This is what you were trying to avoid when I got bitten." It had been three months since the night Rhys attacked her, and tensions were still ramping up with no signs of easing.

"Yeah," he said. "We managed to keep things calm then. I'm not sure about now." He glanced into the rearview mirror. "Until this situation is resolved, I'd like you to stay closer to home."

"Exactly what do you mean?"

"You'll need to find new territory to run around in during the full moon. And as much as you don't want to, I think staying in the city would be better than driving several hours away. Also, I'd feel better if I went along. Or Thorn if we can talk him into it."

Her voice hardened. "Why?"

"I don't want some werewolf, or worse, a vampire, deciding you're part of the problem."

"Wait a minute." Jordan's head snapped over to look at him. "Sabrina thinks I did it?"

"Jordan! The road!"

She jerked the wheel, straightening the car out. "Sorry."

Montgomery shook his head. "You were there alone with him."

"So, she thinks I did it?" Jordan repeated. "I thought I was cleared. You told me you convinced her I was innocent!"

"No, but that doesn't matter. There are those who don't trust you and will believe you're involved, that you're a sleeper agent here to sabotage and destroy the Conclave from within." Montgomery shrugged. "They said the same thing about me when I became Christine's famulus." He paused. "Actually, they probably never changed their minds about me."

Jordan shook her head. "Gotta be a horrible way to spend eternity, being that paranoid."

"On the other hand, paranoia is probably why some older vampires like Marcus are still alive."

"So, obvious question. How do we convince them I had nothing to do with it?"

"Obvious answer. We find out who did it."

11

———————

When she and Montgomery stepped into the lobby of the Hotel Cataluna, several heads turned in their direction. Jordan was accustomed to sidelong glances and whispers by the other Family who worked in the lobby. They mirrored their patrons' attitude of distrust and in some cases disgust. It was part and parcel of being a werewolf famulus to a vampire who had also been a werewolf.

This time was different. In addition to the conversations fading to nothing, they looked away when Jordan attempted to meet their eyes. Tension filled the air, threatening to break and lash anyone who dared get in the way. Even Joe, who stood guard at the elevator and always had a smile or a sympathetic nod for her, kept his attention on Montgomery. An icy shiver ran down her spine. Rumors about David's death and her possible involvement were making the rounds. Montgomery didn't appear to notice. Or if he did, he didn't comment on it. Or maybe he was used to it from his days as a famulus. He merely nodded his greeting to Joe without acknowledging the silence surrounding them.

They stepped into the elevator. Montgomery swiped his

keycard through the access reader to gain access to the secure floors. The light flashed red. He repeated it twice more, failing both times. With a sigh, he looked at Jordan. Juggling the hard-sided cooler she was carrying to her other hand, she produced her own keycard and ran it through the reader. The light flashed green. Montgomery shook his head, a bemused smile on his face. "Another card demagnitized," he said as hit the buttons for the fifth floors Now that they were alone, the mask on his expression slipped, lips twitching in nervous anticipation. "I wish I could brief Marcus over the phone."

Jordan bit her lip to keep in the comment about old vampires being set in their ways. Better not to make a joke where she could be overheard, even if it was at Montgomery's expense and not Marcus'. They might be alone in the elevator, but she doubted they were unobserved. She adjusted the soft-sided cooler hanging off her shoulder as the elevator jerked to a halt, standing straight and proper before the doors slid open. "Wish me luck."

Montgomery patted her on the shoulder. He hit the button for the seventh floor. "You'll do fine," he said as the doors slid shut. "I'll meet you back at the car."

She walked down the empty hall, dredging up as much self-confidence as possible before she reached room 521. Like when she had entered the lobby, the chatter died away as she stepped into the office-cum-blood-bank. Apparently, this was her new normal. She strode to the desk, feeling each and every pair of eyes on her. Her head jerked a little higher as she reached the desk. "I'm here for Montgomery Cooper's weekly rations," she said to the secretary as she placed the empty cooler on the counter.

Emma's face and voice contained the forced politeness of professionalism. "May I see your ID, please?"

Jordan handed over her driver's license, resisting the urge to roll her eyes. It was a formality. All the Conclave had heard of the infamous chaos wolf famulus who belonged to the werewolf-turned-vampire.

"Thank you, Miss Abbey." Emma rose and handed her ID back. She picked up the cooler of the counter. "Wait here, please." She sashayed through a door into a connected room.

Unlike the first time she had picked up Montgomery's blood, they remembered to keep their voices down. Even with a werewolf's sharp senses, Jordan couldn't make out the words spoken in low, hushed tones. The one word she was able to pick up was David. Her lips twisted. Had the conversation about her being the killer had started before or after she entered the room? And were they debating who she would target next?

Emma returned with the cooler and placed it on the counter. There was a tremor in her hands only visible to a predator. Jordan took the cooler with a grim smile. Normally she would thank her and leave. A bubbling, acidic anger insisted she speak. She looked Emma in the eye. "If I were planning on killing anyone in this room, I wouldn't be doing it here. I couldn't sneak out without being noticed. And as far as I'm concerned, it's too much work to hunt you down during the day."

Emma took a small step back, a nervous fake smiling flashing across her lips. "Who said you killed David?"

Jordan leaned over the desk, pleased when Emma flinched further back. "I'm the most logical choice. I'm the big, bad werewolf. David was mauled to death. So, it had to be me." As fast as her anger flared, it snuffed out. She drew back to her normal posture. "Or at least that's what everybody thinks. It may have been a werewolf, but it definitely wasn't me." Her shoulders slumped. "And nothing I say will convince people otherwise."

Emma swallowed. "Do you really think a . . . nother werewolf did this?"

Jordan nodded. "I didn't see any pictures, but from how they were described, there were claw marks that didn't match a bear or a mountain lion."

"Do you think they'll start coming into the city?"

Jordan almost laughed. Did she think the Black Oak Pack stayed in their walled home up in the mountains? Wasn't she aware they came down into the city for groceries, for entertainment, for their jobs? "I don't think they will to kill," she said with a shake of her head. "Montgomery has told me the same thing."

"You and Mr. Cooper are the closest things to experts we have on werewolves."

Jordan rolled her eyes "Great. 'Cause I'm still learning." She grabbed the handle of the cooler. "I doubt the werewolves will invade *en masse*," she said loud enough for the people eavesdropping in the next room. "Alpha Shane was as interested in finding out who did this as we are." It wasn't the full truth, but it wasn't a complete lie either. It was, she hoped, comforting. She lifted the cooler. "I'll be back next week for Montgomery's next order. Are there any messages I should pass on?"

Emma shook her head. "Just remind him he needs to arrange for replenishment."

Jordan bit back a sigh. As a famulus, she should have been donating to replenish what Montgomery took out. However, no vampire was willing to drink a werewolf's blood, even willingly given. With all the other issues they had been dealing with, Jordan wasn't sure he had a solution. "I'll remind him." She turned around and walked out of the door.

She wasn't surprised when the chatter started before she shut the door. She sighed and walked to the elevator. That went so well. She needed a pick-me-up. Maybe she'd have time to get coffee for her and Montgomery before he was done. She ignored the looks as she went down to the lobby and outside and toward the coffee shop several stores down.

Ten minutes later, she was walking back to the parking lot under the hotel. The manager had been about to lock up the coffee shop when she came through the door. From the snippy attitude, she got the idea the employees were trying to leave early and her order of two lattes had interfered with their plan. At least this time the barista hadn't called her "Jerry Dan" like the one at the college coffee shop had. Cardboard carrier balancing the two medium cups, cooler and purse clenched in the other, she headed down the sidewalk toward the parking area.

The crowds had thinned out from earlier in the evening. Most of the shoppers had gone home, leaving couples and groups of friends heading toward the restaurants and bars and the movie theater. With a small smile on her face, she waved a greeting to the woman who was locking up Eleganza Discreta as she passed by. The woman, wearing a ring with a famulus symbol, nodded, but her mouth remained in a neutral line. Jordan sighed as she continued on. It was better than being glared at.

Jordan turned into the stairwell. She stepped around the corner . The coffee cup holder balanced on one hand jumped as someone slapped it. She squawked as coffee splashed on her and she backpedaled, dropping her cooler and her purse.

A hand grabbed her wrist and jerked. Jordan was swung in an arc, slamming against a concrete wall. Another hand shoved her cheek against her shoulder, baring her throat. Her vision doubled before a blond man, only a few inches taller than her, came into focus. He opened his mouth, revealing longer-than-human canine teeth.

She didn't have time to yell out who she was. Didn't have time to punch him. She raised her knee fast. Something crunched and the vampire squeaked. He backed away, clutching his groin.

Jordan slipped to one side, giving herself a free direction to run if needed. She grabbed her necklace, thrusting the pendant to him. "What the hell!"

The vampire, hunched over, squinted at the symbol. "You belong to . . . ?" he rasped.

She fought the urge to growl as she let go of the necklace. The pendant thumped against her chest. "My name is Jordan Abbey, Famulus to Montgomery Cooper."

He stepped back, his lip twisting in disgust. "The werewolf."

Jordan rolled her eyes. "Yes, the werewolf." She was probably going to regret being so mouthy to a vampire she didn't recognize, but at the moment she didn't care. "Either you're new to this or you're one of the worst vampires I've ever seen."

She'd hit another sensitive spot, if the way he drew himself up to his full height of five-foot-seven was any indication. "And why do you say that?"

"Several reasons." She ticked them off on her fingers. "One, I was holding coffees, plural. Someone nearby will be looking for me if I don't show up in five minutes. Do you really want to risk him or her seeing you with your fangs in my neck? Two, I'm wearing a Family symbol. You're supposed to ask and respect my choice if I say no, since I clearly am associated with another vampire." She arched her eyebrows. "And three, you attacked from the front, leaving yourself open to the oldest counterattack in the book."

He took a step closer, glaring at her. "And what is keeping me from attacking you right now and *accidentally* drinking too much, even if you taste like a dog, not seeing your necklace until it was too late?"

She locked her eyes on the vampire. "Because Montgomery is in a meeting with Elder Marcus right now. And if I'm not here when he gets back, well, how do you think the Elder will take to hearing someone is sloppily hunting literally in his back yard, and you've fed from and killed the famulus of his bloodchild without his permission?"

The vampire stared at her. She held herself relaxed, although every instinct screamed at her to make her move. The wolf howled to fight, but the human wanted to run. She wasn't certain who the winner would be if the vampire made a move toward her. He shifted his weight and she tensed.

He stepped away. "You're not worth the trouble," he spat and then walked toward the stairwell.

When his footsteps faded to silence, she leaned against the wall, gasping for breath as her heart pounded. She clenched the pendant and focused on slowing her breathing. "I'm safe," she chanted in a whisper. "Rhys is dead. I'm safe."

Her breathing returned to normal, and her heartbeat slowed. Jordan pushed away from the wall. At least she hadn't had to fight the urge to shift. Trying to focus on anything but the panic attack, Jordan looked for the cooler and her purse. They were on the floor, both still closed and their contents safe. She then looked down at her shirt. She pulled away the fabric where the brown stains were making it stick to her skin. Montgomery was going to be furious when she told him about her run-in with . . .

She smacked her forehead. She hadn't even thought to get her attacker's name.

12

Montgomery sat before Marcus's desk as he had the prior night. He had completed telling Marcus the events of the meeting with Alpha Shane. It was nothing that couldn't have been handled by an email or a phone call. Jordan had commented on it once, echoing a comment Thorn made about Marcus being set in his ways. Montgomery had reprimanded her, warning her never to make what could be construed as a negative comment about Marcus in public and to think twice about doing it in private. However, he had not disagreed with her.

Marcus's expression remained neutral. He interlaced his fingers and tapped them against the desk. "So, Alpha Shane claims there are no other chaos wolves present other than Jordan. Is he trying to cast blame on Jordan?"

"Perhaps," Montgomery said. "He could be trying to hide his incompetence in front of the pack. Or he believes she's responsible. There is another option though. His daughter and Jordan have had a few run-ins. Neither likes the other. Angela is showing ambitions of being the next Alpha, if I'm interpreting what Jordan is telling me correctly. If Angela did kill David in some rash bid for power inside the pack, even if she didn't try to make it look like Jordan was the guilty party, Alpha Shane would protect his daughter from us by misdirection."

"And what better way than to blame the chaos wolf." Marcus shook his head. "Sometimes I wonder what I was thinking when I let you make her Family." He sat back in his chair. "Are you sure it was one of the Black Oak Pack? Couldn't it be an unknown chaos wolf?"

For a moment, Montgomery considered what Jordan had asked. Had he dismissed the idea that it was another chaos wolf too quickly? Jordan would tell him if there was a stranger in the area, but that assumed that she was familiar with the entire pack. "I'm certain if he didn't condone it, Alpha Shane knows who did it."

"But we have no way to prove it." Marcus sank back into the chair, frowning as his fingers unlaced and drummed on the desk. "Can we trick this Alpha pup into admitting what she did?"

Montgomery shook his head. "Not without getting her alone. Shane won't allow that. And I don't think Jordan would be able to bait her into making such an admission."

"That's a pity. If you are given an opportunity, take it. I want the killer's head mounted on my wall."

Montgomery blinked. There had been stories about how Marcus had carved out a territory for vampires in San Francisco at the height of the Gold Rush. There had also been werewolf pelts rumored to decorate this office until the early nineteen eighties, when Montgomery's father, the prior Alpha of the Black Oak Pack, had offered an olive branch. "I will keep an eye on the situation."

"Good. Now onto other business. Would you care to update me on your situation with Rosanna?"

"She refused my gift of the werewolf fangs."

"Your gift? Or your famulus's presentation?"

"Jordan performed—"

"Yes, yes. She was perfectly polite and respectful. Her speech and actions were flawless. The problem is she shouldn't have been the one presenting the fangs. You should have."

Montgomery stiffened. "I was under the impression that it was considered acceptable for a famulus to present a gift in a patron's place."

"It is. Which is why she didn't kill Jordan for your slight." He leaned forward, lips compressed into a grim line. "I want you to set things square with her. I don't care if you have to sleep with her or order your famulus to sleep with her. I want the two of you presenting a united front, especially with this new threat from the werewolves."

It was an order couched as a suggestion, something Montgomery was familiar with. The last time he had heard that tone of voice, a vampire newly turned had persisted in questioning Marcus, despite increasingly blatant suggestions he not. But the vampire, oblivious or brazen, had continued. Or he had until Marcus had his tongue ripped out at the roots. It took a month for him to grow it back, and three months of speech therapy before he could speak properly again. He swallowed his defense and bowed his head. "Yes, sir. Is there anything else you wished to speak about?"

"There is one more thing." Marcus sat back, shoulders relaxing. "This is a bit of good news. I have a new famulus. I need you to administer the oath of loyalty, since I will not be able to, for obvious reasons."

"I see." All Family were indoctrinated in a ceremony involving a blood exchange, and a promise to serve the vampire. Marcus oversaw the ceremony, giving tacit approval to each one brought into the fold. Jordan had gone through it. He had gone through it as well, all those years ago. "But I'm the youngest. Why not have Rosanna officiate?"

"Because I want you to," Marcus said. He stood up and walked around the desk. "I want the Conclave to remember who you are." He laid a hand on Montgomery's shoulder. "It is a great honor, and one you are overdue."

Rosanna wouldn't perceive it that way. She was the elder, and the ceremonies Marcus was unable to perform should fall to her. For her not to would be considered by her, and by others, as an insult. But to refuse outright would be an insult to his sire. "Is this necessary?" Montgomery asked.

"Yes, it is." Marcus's voice maintained a steady tone, but not the taut control of when he was angered. "Your loyalty has come into question lately, and this should cement any doubts."

Montgomery's jaw tightened. "My loyalty?"

Marcus shrugged. "There are those who believe you are first and foremost a werewolf. This has been a long game you and Alpha Shane are playing, and Jordan is proof of that."

"That's ridiculous," Montgomery snorted. "Alpha Shane hates Jordan only slightly less than he hates me."

"He didn't always, or so you've told me. Not until you chose to turn your back on your pack. Most of the Conclave, however, haven't seen you or your famulus interact with him. We need to raise your profile to remind them you are not only a werewolf-turned-vampire, but my son-in-the-blood." His voice hardened. "Especially now that you have a werewolf for your companion. She may not have been born one, but you were. Isolating yourself and only showing your face here for the mandatory meetings does not help your cause."

In other words, because I don't live here with you. It was an ongoing sore spot between them. While technically not required to live with his sire, Marcus reminded him he had the option at every possible chance. He bowed his head, acquiescing. "Of course I will perform the ceremony, sir. When will it be?"

"The next meeting of the Conclave." Marcus withdrew, returning to his seat behind the desk. "Thank you, Montgomery. Now, if you don't mind, I have some things I need to attend to."

"Of course, sir." Montgomery rose and bowed. "I will see you at the next Conclave meeting."

Marcus nodded. "Until then."

Montgomery left Marcus's lair. He waved to Helen but didn't say anything. There were too many things going through his mind as he took the elevator to the lobby. The comment about ordering Jordan to sleep with Rosanna made his stomach twist. There had been a few incidents and breeches of protocol Marcus had helped smooth over. Had he made similar comments to Christine? And if Marcus ordered him to do so, what would he do?

He reached the car and wasn't surprised to find Jordan waiting there. She leaned against the driver's door, arms crossed across her chest. Her eyes were downcast, but her eyebrows lifted as she looked up at him. "You look about how I feel," she said. "Everything okay with Marcus?"

"He gave me something to think about," Montgomery said. No need to worry her. He looked her up and down. "Why is there coffee on your shirt?"

Jordan brushed at the stain. "It's a long story. Do you want to go first or should I?"

Montgomery sighed. "At least tell me you picked up the blood?"

She gestured at the cooler peeking over the edge of the back seat's window. "They reminded me we need to come up with a way to pay them back. She asked me if I knew who killed David, kinda accusing me. I lost my temper and sort of growled at her."

Montgomery bit back a sigh. Another thing he needed to smooth over. Maybe he should take on a human famulus in addition to Jordan to make things easier. Or he could try to work out his own deal with a butcher or an Asian market that sold pig's blood for cooking so he wasn't dependent on communal donations. It was a way for vampires who did not join a conclave to feed if they didn't want to bring too much attention to themselves. He'd talk it over with Thorn to find out if he had any ideas.

They got into the car and drove off. Montgomery settled into the passenger seat and stared ahead as Jordan wove though the narrow streets of the Row until they reached Main Street. "Okay," he said. "Why is there coffee on your shirt?"

Jordan sighed. "A vampire decided I looked like an easy snack. I fought him off. He didn't know or care who I was until I identified myself as a famulus. He eventually backed down but didn't want to. Fortunately, the lattes were the only casualties of the evening."

"What?" Montgomery turned toward her. "Who attacked you?"

Her cheeks turned red. "I didn't recognize him, and I forgot to ask his name."

"You're kidding."

"I wish I were."

"Wonderful." Montgomery stared straight ahead. He should report this to Marcus. But if Jordan couldn't identify who it was, blind accusations wouldn't go over well.

"Did I do something wrong?"

"Huh?"

"You're not talking," Jordan said. "You're brooding."

"I am not brooding." Montgomery sniffed.

"Yes, you are. You get a wrinkle in your brow when you're brooding."

He reached up and she was right. There was a wrinkle in his forehead. "No, you did nothing wrong. If whoever it was comes forward, your defense is he wasn't being cautious. I'm more concerned about Marcus asking me to do something I don't think will have good implications going forward."

"Let me guess." Jordan's lips curled into a smile. "He told you to give the fangs to Rosanna?"

"That and he wants me to swear in his new famulus."

"So, what's the problem?"

"It's normally an honor reserved for the eldest child."

"Oh." Jordan turned the wheel as she chewed on her lower lip. "How do you think Rosanna will react?"

"Not very well." He sighed. "Even under ideal circumstances, it would be considered an insult. Given the additional issues between us . . ." He raised his hands in an empty gesture.

"Yeah. Anything I can do?"

"Right now, nothing," Montgomery said. "She's made it clear she wants me to be the one to deal with her."

"So why are we leaving instead of heading over to talk to her?"

"Protocol," Montgomery said. "There's a way these things are done. For a formal apology, I have to request an audience. It's considered an insult to show up unexpectedly."

Jordan shook her head. "I get it, I really do. I just hope all of this formality isn't the death of us."

"You and me both."

13

Jordan ran under the full moon. The trees were familiar, but they didn't belong to Mount Ponderosa or to the Black Oak Pack's private territory. She didn't have the time to stop and study them. She was being hunted.

The panting of the predator behind her had a familiar rhythm. Jordan wove and ducked among the trees, giving up speed for obstacles that allowed her to gain some distance. She should have been running on all fours. She'd be faster and nimbler as a wolf.

She broke past the tree line. A fast-flowing stream with no sign of a bridge blocked her path forward. Jordan didn't hesitate. She charged to the bank and jumped. The stream was too wide for her to jump as a wolf, let alone as a human. And yet, she landed on her feet on the far bank.

She skidded to a stop, breathing hard. She had pulled off that jump many times before, but only in one situation. "I'm dreaming." This was her recurring nightmare about being a werewolf before she had learned to shift. She'd already faced this fear and had come through the other side. There was no reason to continue running. Panting to catch her breath, she backed up several steps and waited.

The ground shook as her hunter grew closer. Jordan shifted her weight to the balls of her feet before she caught herself. "She didn't hurt me then," she tried to reassure herself. "She won't hurt me now."

Her pursuer stepped out from between the screening trees. The giant wolf approached with the sure stride of a predator. It didn't jump the stream so much as lazily stride over it. Jordan was rethinking her decision to stand her ground when the wolf stopped in front of her. The top of Jordan's head was a good inch below the creature's lower jaw. Amber canine eyes locked on her brown human ones. Jordan took a deep breath, closed her eyes, and lowered her head, tilting her chin to her shoulder. Nape of her neck exposed, she waited for what came next.

Hot breath blew over her skin. Jordan twitched but held her place. A cold, wet nose nudged her neck, followed by the lightest pressure from a tip of a canine. Jordan, fighting to hold still, tried to remember if you died in a dream whether you died in real life or woke up.

The fang pulled away. Another wet thing nudged her throat, much rougher and warmer. Had she just been licked? Jordan opened her eyes and let out the deep breath she had been holding. She swayed and almost tumbled off her feet as the wolf sat on her hindquarters, making the ground shake. The werewolf's jaws parted in a proud smile. "You didn't run as much this time."

She opened her hands and loosened her stance, although now she felt more trapped. *It's only the wolf instinct trying to meld with my human mind.* There was no reason to be afraid. "I'm told that I learn, eventually," she said.

The wolf snorted again, amusement lighting up her eyes. She rose to her feet. "Walk with me."

She followed the werewolf deeper into the woods, away from where the dream-city was. She stumbled over a root and put her hand on the wolf's shoulder. "So, what is my subconscious trying to tell me this time?"

The wolf twisted her head to look at Jordan. "What makes you think I'll tell you outright?"

"The whole 'let me help you' thing." Jordan's fingers scratched the shaggy shoulder, like she petted Rex. "The last time I saw you was just before I figured out how to shapeshift."

The werewolf snorted. "That's part of your problem."

"Problem?"

"You keep referring to yourself as 'I' and me 'the werewolf' like you are two separate entities. Maybe if you started accepting what you are, you'd listen to me."

Jordan froze, her stomach clenching into a knot. Color drained from her face as she looked at her companion. "You mean you're—"

The muscles tensed beneath her hand and then disappeared. The Wolf swept around to stare her face to face. Hot breath blew Jordan's hair back from her shoulders. "I'm not some animal crammed inside of you." The werewolf touched her nose to Jordan's forehead and then shoved her. Jordan's stumbled, falling onto her back, cracking her head against a tree root. The sky spun around her as she opened her eyes. The Wolf stood above her, paws framing her body. The benevolent tone shifted to an iron snarl. "The sooner you learn to listen to your instincts, the better."

The Wolf's jaws spread wide and grew until the bottom one touched the ground and the upper one towered over the trees. Jordan screamed, crawling backwards on her elbows as they closed around her. She screamed as the fangs sliced into her arms and legs.

Jordan bolted up right, the scream coming out of her throat as a strangled gasp. She ran her hands along her arms and legs, searching for wounds and finding none. She sat on the edge of her bed, staring up at the ceiling, stretching her neck. She glanced at the clock and sighed again. 2:09 p.m. She should lay down. But whenever she woke up in the early afternoon, she had a hard time going back to sleep. She climbed out of her bed and pulled on her robe. Some hot chocolate usually helped.

She padded out of her bedroom and into the kitchen. Montgomery's door was closed. Thorn was stretched out on the couch, eyes closed and blanket spilling onto the floor. She turned on the kitchen light, blinking at the brightness. The creak of the sofa frame and feet hitting the ground were followed by footsteps coming toward the kitchen. "Something wrong, Jordan?"

She turned to face the voice. Thorn, wrapped in a blanket, stood at one end of the kitchenette. His bright blue hair draped over the side of his face. She dredged up half a smile for him as she poured milk into a glass. "Nightmare," she said as she put the glass in microwave. "Or at least I think it was."

"I thought that was supposed to be Mac's problem." He slipped an arm around her shoulders as she poked the buttons. "Wanna talk about it?"

Jordan cuddled in as the microwave's timer counted down. "There's not much to talk about. It's just a weird dream."

"What happened in it?"

"Oh, it's a new version of the stupid nightmare I had before I managed to shift. Running in the woods, a werewolf on my heels." She huffed a humored breath. "I guess my subconscious thinks I'm ignoring her."

"What did she say to you?"

"That I need to start listening to my instincts. I don't have a wolf stuffed inside of me, she's part of my psyche I'm ignoring. And if I don't start listening to her, I'll be in trouble." She frowned as the microwave beeped. "Huh. Maybe she thinks she's my mother."

Thorn grinned. "You know, Mac and I never talked about it. I wonder if he had nightmares about the Wolf after he became Family."

"I didn't." Jordan and Thorn turned their heads. Montgomery stood at the other entrance of the kitchenette.

"Sorry, didn't mean to wake you," Jordan said.

Montgomery waved away her concern as she opened the microwave and stirred the milk. "You didn't. I was already awake when I heard you talking. You said you had a dream about the Wolf? I never did either when I became Family. Or vampire. But then, I figure I haven't really done anything worthy of her notice. Or she considered me a lost cause."

"You have never been a lost cause." Thorn said. "Does the Wolf reveal herself to all werewolves who are being naughty?"

"No. Traditionally, the Wolf only appears to those who are supposed to be Alphas and talespeakers."

Jordan reset the microwave. "Somehow I doubt either will happen to me. Besides, she didn't say she was the Wolf. She said she was my wolf."

"You never know," Montgomery said. "You might get tired of this glamorous life and decide to take up Shane's offer."

"Or you might found a pack of your own," Thorn said.

Jordan laughed as she dumped the cocoa into the warm milk. "With what other werewolves?"

Thorn shrugged. "There might be other werewolves who pass through and decide they want to settle."

"Or some may decide they don't want to live under Alpha Shane's thumb any longer," Montgomery added.

Jordan stirred the milk and cocoa together. "I'm sure Angela would love that."

Montgomery's gaze sharpened. "Is she still troubling you?"

"Nothing new since the last full moon," Jordan said. "But I doubt she'll leave me alone."

"If you can handle Rhys, you can handle her," Thorn said.

Montgomery flinched, a haunted expression crossing his face. "I think I'm going to head back to bed."

Jordan stepped toward him but halted when Thorn placed a hand on her shoulder. "Do you want some company?"

"No, I want to be alone," Montgomery said. He turned away. "I'll see you two tonight."

"Good night, Montgomery." She held still, watching Montgomery retreat into his room. When the bedroom door shut, Thorn's grip on her shoulder relaxed. She turned to look at him, eyebrow arched.

Thorn shook his head. "Let him make the first move." He pulled her in close for a one-armed hug. "He'll come back to us when he's ready."

"You sure?"

"He did when he lost Christine." But there was a slight downturn of one corner of his mouth, as if he wasn't certain about it himself. "Just be patient."

She sighed and leaned against him. "I will. It's just hard."

"Tell me about it." He pressed a kiss into her hair. "We should go back to bed. Need company? I can sleep with you. And I do mean sleep. Nothing will happen if you don't want it, despite the last crack I made."

She looked him up and down. "I don't think that would be a good idea right now, as tempting as it is. It might send the wrong message to Montgomery."

"You're right." Thorn sighed. "I should go settle on my lonely couch. You think you'll be okay?"

"I'll be fine." She picked up her mug.

Thorn nodded. "See you in the evening then."

Jordan padded toward her bedroom. She closed the door, making sure it didn't creak as it came to rest in the jamb, then sat on the bed and lifted her mug to take a sip. She spat out the gritty, still-cold chocolate. With a dramatic grunt, she flopped onto her back, arms spread out. "So much for helping me go to sleep." she told the ceiling.

14

____

Thorn let out a heavy sigh as Helen closed the security door behind him, leaving him alone in the hall leading to Marcus's office. Office was too kind a word for what it really was. Part stronghold, part panic room that could be isolated from the rest of the building, it was the place Marcus pulled the strings of his empire as well as a hiding place from those who would threaten him.

He hated being summoned like he was one of Marcus's flunkies, even if technically he was one. Eventually, when he grew tired of this charade, he'd move on. He had lost track how many conclaves he had been in before. When he stopped to think about it, he had lost track of how many conclaves he had _ruled_ before.

But he wasn't ready to make an enemy of the Elder or Rancho Robles yet. Right now, his usefulness outweighed his annoyance, and Thorn had every intention of keeping the balance tipped in his favor. Besides, there were interesting things he wanted to keep an eye on personally. So when summoned, he responded to the Elder like a dog responding to his master's tug on his leash.

Why were all his metaphors so steeped in canines lately? It had to be Jordan's influence. He smiled. Now there was a wolf who could be a future Alpha. He saw it. Mac saw it. Alpha Shane saw it. Angela, the presumed next Alpha of Black Oak, definitely did, given how she went out of her way to provoke a fight every time they were in the same zip code. And Elder Marcus was probably planning to manipulate the hell out of it. Even the Wolf, if Mac had interpreted Jordan's dream correctly, saw it. About the only one who was unaware of her potential was Jordan herself.

Which was probably why Marcus was having him spy on her and Montgomery. At first it was concern over his child, and worry that the werewolf would stir old loyalties, which was ridiculous to Thorn. Montgomery had been loyal to his father, Alpha Cooper, not Alpha Shane. Jordan had made it clear over and over that she wanted nothing to do with the Black Oak Pack.

He reached the carved doors and knocked. He bounced up and down on his toes, waiting for the command to enter. Of course, Marcus was taking his time to usher him in. It was a petty show of power. But if Marcus wanted to play games, Thorn had the inclination to indulge him for now.

Finally, he heard the quiet 'enter.' Thorn pushed the doors open and walked to the desk with the laptop. Marcus sat behind his desk, dressed in an immaculate three-piece suit, the picture of a CEO of a Fortune 500 company. In some ways, the Conclave was. He wasn't just ruling over the vampires but managing the resources it took to keep them hidden in an increasingly technological world. Given Marcus's age, Thorn found himself wondering how much longer he could keep it up.

Thorn walked to the point halfway between the desk and the door. He bowed from the waist, a precise forty-five degrees.

Marcus acknowledged him with a nod. "Kelly," he said. He waved to the chairs in front of his desk. "Have a seat."

Thorn schooled himself not to grind his teeth at the use of his given name. He stepped forward and went to the indicated chair, aware Marcus was studying him closely. The man was paranoid and had a mind like a steel trap. "What did you wish to see me about?" Thorn asked. As if he didn't already have a good idea how this conversation would go.

"The chaos wolf and my son," Marcus said. "I would like an update on their status and your opinions about how they are coping."

"They're doing as well as can be expected," Thorn said. Time to play some verbal chess. "Jordan is coping well with her transformation. She is still trying to determine exactly where she fits in with the Black Oak Pack."

Marcus frowned. "I thought she didn't fit in."

"Just because she isn't part of the pack doesn't mean she isn't interacting with them," Thorn said. No need to mention the dream and Montgomery's interpretation of it. Not until they were certain how correct she was. "Alpha Shane's daughter is intent on reminding her she's below the pack's omega. But Jordan is developing a friendship with one of the young males and a few of the females."

"Are you sure it's only friendship?"

"Positive. If any of them have any romantic feelings toward her, she doesn't appear to reciprocate."

"Is that because of her feelings for you and Montgomery, or because she's not attracted to them?"

"Both, I believe. But she seems to be firmly on our side. If any of them are trying to seduce her away, literally, it's been a spectacular failure."

"Hopefully that will continue," Marcus said. "And what of Montgomery?"

"He is doing as well as can be expected. He no longer wakes up screaming nightly." He was down to once a week. "His main difficulty now will be making up with Rosanna. She refused his first overture made through Jordan."

"That is her right. And not something I can interfere with."

"I don't think he wants you to. But I don't think he's ready to face up to Rosanna just yet. Even though he's aware he's not responsible for her famulus's death, she does blame him. And that's enough to trigger his guilt over Christine."

Marcus shook his head. "I wish he'd let go and move on. I was hoping the werewolf would be more helpful in that regard."

Thorn shrugged. "He told her about some of what happened after the incident with Rhys. She's asked a few questions since then, but Mac's reluctant to talk. There's not much that can be done until he opens up."

"And has he opened up to you?"

Thorn shook his head. "I'm staying at his place. Jordan, he, and I are all sleeping separately. I've counseled Jordan not to attempt anything until he makes the first move. He has denied Rhys doing anything beyond kidnapping him, but . . ."

Marcus nodded. From his calculating expression, Thorn guessed he was debating ordering Montgomery to talk to Jordan and him. Fortunately, the next words out of Marcus's mouth changed the subject. "What are his thoughts about the recent killings?"

"He believes a werewolf is involved. He does not believe it was Jordan."

"Montgomery is too emotionally close to her to make that assessment."

Thorn arched an eyebrow. "But I'm not?"

"You are sleeping with her also."

"On your orders." What Marcus didn't need to know was he would have been even without the request to keep a close eye on her and Mac. "But I'm keeping a clear head about it."

"See that you do," Marcus said. "And what is your belief? Is Jordan responsible for Sabrina's famulus's death?"

Thorn shook his head once, a decisive motion. "No. She doesn't have the maturity yet to pull it off. If she had, her reaction would have been to call us for help instead of leaving the body out in the open."

"What about her working with Black Oak, or someone in the pack?"

His second shake was more emphatic than the first. "Montgomery thinks Alpha Shane has too much of a sense of honor to perform that kind of sneak attack. He'd prefer head-on, out in the open combat. Most of the werewolves consider Jordan to be an immature pup or a traitor. Right now, she's being bullied by Shane's daughter in particular. I really don't see them working together."

"That is my general assessment also, Kelly. However, not everyone shares it."

"I've heard the rumors already starting up." Sometimes he thought vampires thrived as much on gossip as they did on blood. And of course, given the mangling of the body, all suspicions would turn to the werewolves. "Montgomery doesn't think this is the act of a chaos wolf."

"Alpha Shane is responsible?" Marcus's brow lowered. "Why does Montgomery believe that?"

"He thinks Alpha Shane's grip on his territory is slipping," Thorn said. "He feels Jordan is proof enough, let alone that Rhys changed her in his territory, literally under his nose, and he didn't know she existed for what, a week? That would attract interest from other chaos wolves looking for a safe place to settle or would-be Alphas looking to take over an existing pack. His daughter hasn't kept quiet about her plans to take over, and she's impulsive enough to attack without considering the consequences. Either way, Shane is losing his standing among the packs for not having a better grip on things."

To Thorn's amazement, Marcus sighed. "That is all we need. A new ambitious Alpha turning their attention to the vampires in their new territory."

"There is another option," Thorn said. "Hunters."

Marcus snorted. "There are no hunters in Rancho Robles. I

would be aware of them the moment they stepped foot over the city limits."

"Are you certain? Sir," Thorn added belatedly.

Marcus glared at him. "I personally drained the last hunter that infested this city forty-two years ago when I ascended to Elder of Rancho Robles. There are no hunters here."

Says the man who wouldn't have the first clue about how to turn on a computer, let alone perform a web search. Thorn suppressed the urge to twitch his mouth, making sure his thought didn't make it anywhere near his expression. Instead, he kept his features mild and apologetic. "Of course, sir. My apologies for the insult."

Marcus maintained the stare for a second after the apology. "Keep a close eye on both Jordan and Montgomery, but especially Jordan. Even with her tenuous connection with the Black Oak Pack, she may learn something without realizing what has fallen into her lap."

"So, you do believe Alpha Shane has something to do with this?"

"When it comes to that werewolf, I don't put anything past him."

15

———————

"Did you hear about David?"

That was the question asked over and over, although it was never directed at her. The gathering of the Conclave meant a gathering of the Family. Very few Family went out in public, and when they did they did, it was in the presence of other vampires. They were as much a status symbol as they were servants and bodyguards. So, at this emergency meeting of the Conclave, at least one famulus of each vampire was present. And when famulus were present without their patrons, rumors flew thick and fast.

"He was found dead, ripped limb from limb, like an animal attack."

"She was the last one to see him alive."

"Do you think she has something to do with it?"

They didn't have to look in her direction for Jordan to know who the "she" was.

"All right," Reginald, Marcus's most senior famulus and de facto person in charge, called out. He stood at attention, looking like a butler of a manor house sent straight from central casting. "Everyone gather around."

Jordan joined the loose knot of about twenty people. While no one looked directly at her, no one stood too close to her either.

"You've probably heard rumors that David was killed two nights ago, the victim of a mauling at Mount Ponderosa." His expression was grave, gaze hard. "The rumors are true." He fixed Jordan with a hard stare. "The official record will state he was killed by a bear, and the animal has yet to be located."

Jordan dropped her gaze, unable to meet his stern expression. *Way to look not guilty.*

"Also, be aware Mount Ponderosa has been reclaimed by the werewolves. It is no longer considered safe territory for our patrons to hunt in safely."

An older woman raised her hand. "Was a werewolf involved in the killing?"

"As I said before, it was believed to be done by a bear. That is all I will say on the matter." He looked over the audience. When no one else challenged him, he continued. "We have one other piece of business." He turned from the crowd to a side room and called out, "If you would join us, Margaret. Margaret has just sworn to be famulus of Elder Marcus. Please make her welcome."

Jordan bit back a gasp as the blond woman stepped into the main area. *Molly!* Her tight black dress wrapped around her torso but left her arms bare. The V-neck plunged a half inch below her cleavage, leaving her skin to be the platform for a golden pendant shaped into the Family logo. The hollowness of her cheeks was emphasized by her pale skin. She had lost at least twenty pounds. But Jordan had no doubt as to who she was.

Her mind flashed back to three months ago. The building panic when she had gone home to find the police had taped off the apartment. The denial flooding her as the body bag was wheeled out after being asked who lived in the apartment. Sitting in the police car, numb as they were driven to the station to give statements and wait for Family to arrive. And the crushing guilt when she looked at her roommate at the reception after the funeral. Now she stared into the eyes of Molly Griffiths, her friend since high school and one of her last connections to her human life.

Molly's gaze swept over the room, then fixed on her. Jordan swallowed, her stomach dropping. How much did Molly know? Obviously, she was now aware of the existence of vampires, but what about werewolves? Was she told the truth about Darren's death? And had she heard the stories about Jordan?

Someone bumped her shoulder, moving past her. Jordan joined everyone in forming a receiving line. She drifted to the end of it, watching as each person introduced themselves and gave their patron's name. Molly focused on each new face but occasionally glanced down the line. Her eyes met Jordan's for a heartbeat. Then she looked away. The knot in Jordan's stomach grew tighter and tighter. Four people stood between them. Then three. Then two. Then one.

And then they were face to face. Jordan looked down, guilty thoughts tumbling through her head. She should have tried harder to reach out to Molly. Every night, she planned to call her again, to send another email. Montgomery wouldn't mind if she promised to be discreet. But she always found an excuse or something else to focus her attention on. Besides, Molly hadn't returned her earlier attempt to make contact. Tomorrow night, she promised herself. Every night.

"Jordan?" She looked up. Molly stared at her with wide eyes. "How?"

"I serve Montgomery Cooper. It's a long story."

"Montgomery Cooper, my patron's son." Molly looked her up and down. If she was the same Molly Jordan knew, she'd be piecing together bits of rumor and scraps of conversation. She'd probably been told stories of the infamous werewolf famulus. Molly reached out and took her hand. "I want to hear it."

Jordan nodded. "We can talk about it later," she said, as if they were planning to go to lunch.

"Definitely."

Reginald's voice broke in. "Jordan, a word, please."

She gave Molly's hand one last squeeze and followed Reginald into the side room. She walked past him and spoke the moment he pulled the door shut. "I'm sorry I deviated from the traditional introduction. Molly and I know each other from high school, before I was bitten."

"That's not why I wanted to talk to you, although I appreciate you explaining the situation." He drew in a deep breath. "I wanted to get your opinion, since you're the closest thing we have to an expert. How bad is the situation with the werewolf killing?"

"Bad," Jordan said. There was no point lying about it. "Alpha Shane insists there is no chaos wolf in the area, despite having missed one being here only a few months ago. If it's someone from Black Oak, I don't think he'll admit he doesn't have full control of the pack. But if someone seeks vengeance, or tries to defend themself, he'll use it as an excuse to attack the Conclave."

"Your assessment is the same as mine. Elder Marcus will do whatever is necessary to protect the Conclave. As a famulus, you will be expected to be loyal to your patron, no matter your personal feelings or desires regarding the pack."

"In other words, if open war breaks out, which side will I choose?" She looked him full in the face. "My loyalty is to Montgomery. The pack has done nothing but harass me since they found out about me." She crossed her arms over her chest. "Is that what you wanted to hear from me?"

"Not me, Jordan. My patron. I've only had to watch you to know where your loyalties lie."

Jordan bowed her head. "Thank you, Reginald." She paused for a moment. "I'm sorry about what happened to your son," she whispered. The previous meeting, she had finally put together why he and David smelled so similar. Neither were willing to acknowledge each other as such, and gossip quickly filled her in on why. Reginald, before taking his oath as Family, had had a dead wife and a living son. Out of desperation, he had taken a well-paying job, which led to him becoming Marcus's famulus. While he rose through the ranks and gained power, he had not wanted David to have anything to do with vampires. When David discovered what his father really did for a living, the headstrong teenager had run to the first vampire he could find. Apparently, Sabrina had been a good patron, but Jordan guessed this was not the life Reginald had wished for his son.

He inhaled sharply but didn't respond. He would likely have been the one who had briefed Marcus about the attack. She watched Reginald return to the main gathering, moving as if he had aged ten years in ten minutes. She followed at a respectful distance. Almost all the others watched her, with the exception of Molly. Reginald clapped twice for their attention. "The meeting is over. Please take your places outside."

Jordan, with the rest of the Family, headed to the exit. She looked over at Molly before she stepped out the door. Their eyes met. She looked frightened. Jordan wanted to run to her, to hug her. Instead, she remained rooted to the spot. It would be seen as a break in protocol worth reporting, and she was already in enough trouble. She had given away the fact they were more than acquainted with each other. But what held her back the most was that she wasn't sure Molly wanted her affection.

They lined up against the wall in the hallway. Jordan pretended not to notice there was extra space on either side of her. The doors to the meeting room opened, and the vampires walked toward the elevators. As each one passed, their famulus fell in step behind them. Jordan also pretended not to notice the vampires glaring at her as she passed.

Thorn stepped into the hall. He looked at Jordan, nodded once, and then continued on. Not sure what that meant, she almost missed Montgomery until he was passing by. She stepped in place behind him, trailing after him as a good famulus was supposed to. Once they were out of the building, he slowed his pace to match Jordan's. He glanced at her. "Are you okay? You look pale."

"I feel nauseous." Jordan swallowed. "You saw that Marcus has a new famulus?"

"Margaret? Yes. I administered the oath."

"I know her."

"Really? Who is she?"

"Molly. My friend. Darren's girlfriend," she added at Montgomery's blank look.

There was a hitch in his step, but he kept walking. "I thought she moved out of town with her family."

"So did I. I didn't know she was back."

"You weren't in contact with her?"

Jordan shook her head. "I tried to email her. She didn't respond."

"I'll drive," he offered. "You don't look like you're up to it. How much does she know about you?"

"We were both in shock at the police station. And I ran out after the funeral, so we never had a chance to talk."

"Did you tell anyone you knew her?"

"I blurted it out in front of the group when she recognized me. And I told Reginald I know her." She bowed her head. "I'm sorry. I wasn't thinking."

Montgomery patted her shoulder. "It's okay. I'll inform Elder Marcus the two of you know each other from before but haven't been in contact for a while, and that Molly was probably aware of werewolves before he claimed her." He frowned. "Or maybe she claimed him."

Jordan frowned and looked at him sharply. "What do you mean?"

"Some people, when they learn about the existence of the

supernatural, become stalkers. They aren't hunting vampires or werewolves to destroy them, but to become them."

Jordan's eyes twinkled. "So, you've got obsessed fans."

"Something like that. Some of them do become Family, but we try to discourage them, make them believe it's all an elaborate roleplaying game."

"And if they can't be discouraged?"

"We silence them by whatever means necessary."

Jordan shivered. That could have been her fate if she hadn't taken up Montgomery's offer of help. "So, Molly's choice was join or die?"

"Most likely." Montgomery shook his head. "I'm sure Marcus has done his due diligence. He always has any potential Family member's background checked. Likely, he's aware of your connection. Still, we should bring it up to him so he doesn't believe we are deliberately withholding information."

Jordan swallowed. "Is there a way I can talk to her?"

"Arrangements can be made. It's not unusual for different Family groups to get together to discuss their duties. Or plan working on things together. I'll make the request tonight."

"Thanks." Jordan shook her head to clear it. "You were saying something about Thorn coming over later?"

"Yeah. He wanted to talk about how best to handle Rosanna."

"It would be a good idea to get some outside input." Jordan paused. "You know, he's been spending a lot of time with us. How about asking him to move in?"

"Remember what I told you about him when we first met?"

"Flavor of the week. But he's been sleeping on our couch almost nightly for the last three months. I thought you might want to make it official."

"Why is he on your couch and not in your bed?"

She sat back in the seat, not sure how he'd take it. She didn't want to push, but he deserved to know what she and Thorn had decided. "Because it wouldn't be fair to you for us to move forward if you're not ready."

His shoulders stiffened. "I need more time."

"And we're willing to give that to you. For however long you need."

16

Jordan walked up to the gates of the Black Oak Pack compound, head held high and senses alert. Montgomery's car was twenty yards behind her. After the treatment it had received last time, she didn't want to leave it on pack grounds. Plus, it would be easier for her to make a fast getaway if she didn't have to crash through a gate. Jordan shook her head. She was a guest, she reminded herself. That should afford her some protection. Or she hoped so.

She was about to hit the talk button when Sentry Rodriguez shuffled out of the guard shack. He stopped opposite her. "What do you want?" he grunted.

This was a lot less friendly than when she had showed up alone here the first time. But she kept her expression polite and neutral. "I'm here to see Talespeaker Diana." He eyed her with the exact same expression he would have if he had bitten into a lemon. Jordan lifted her head a fraction higher and pulled her cell phone from her jacket pocket. "Should I call the Talespeaker and tell her I'm at the gates but being kept from our meeting?"

His expression didn't change, but he opened the gate. Jordan dipped her head and passed through. "Thank you, Sentry

Rodriguez." She walked on and did not look behind her as the gate clanged shut.

Jordan continued at a steady pace. She made sure her back was ramrod straight and her head upright for the observers she knew had to be there. She hadn't mastered the art of moving quietly as a human on a path, let alone slipping unnoticed through the foliage as a wolf. She jumped at the crunch and snap of dry leaves. Maybe she was lucky and Maria or Tran were stalking her, intending to jump out and startle her.

Snarls ripped through the night. Standing in the middle of the path, she looked for a tree or boulder. Spotting one of the larger oaks off the path, she dashed over to it, placing her back against it as her eyes swept the space in front of her. She spotted one set of green eyes shining on the path where she had stood. A second, third, and fourth set quickly joined it. They ranged in a loose semicircle, closing in on her, starlight glinting off bared fangs.

Jordan pressed her lower back against the bark but leaned her head and shoulders toward the approaching pack. "How dare you," she snarled. She focused her attention on the white female closest to her. Of course it was Angela causing trouble. "I'm here as a guest of Talespeaker Diana."

The white wolf leaped at her. Jordan snapped her arm up to protect her neck. She should have shapeshifted to offer her throat the protection of a ruff of thick fur before her little speech. She screamed as fangs sank into her forearm. She kicked at the werewolf's belly as she was knocked over. The female werewolf grunted and let go of Jordan's arm. Jordan rolled, trying to get back on her feet.

Something landed on her legs, pinning her in place. Angela stood on all fours and shook her head. Jordan grunted, the air knocked from her when two more paws added weight on her lower back. She wasn't going anywhere now. Jordan wrapped her arms over her neck to protect it as best she could. She closed her eyes, desperately trying to find the focus to shapeshift between the pain and the fear and the noise.

A new, louder roar shook the air. Then the weight on her back and legs were gone, as if blasted off by the concussive force. She lifted her head, brushing some of the debris out of her face.

"What's going on here?" Alpha Shane thundered. The wolves whimpered and lowered their heads, ears flat and tails tucked between their legs as he snarled at them. "She's here as a guest and you attack her? Where is your honor?"

The two gray wolves backed a few steps away. The white wolf lifted her head and closed her eyes. Her muzzle drew up in a grimace of concentration. The wolf melted away, leaving Angela crouching there. She rose to her feet in one smooth motion, unconcerned about her nudity. "Honor?" she spat. "She's a chaos wolf. She willingly consorts with multiple vampires. She's the one without honor."

Jordan's hands curled into fists. Before she could get to her feet, Alpha Shane stepped between them. "Enough, Angela. She is a *guest*," he said, emphasizing the word. "If you're lucky, she won't demand too much in reparation for your rudeness." Turning his back to the angry werewolf, he bowed to Jordan. "Chaos Wolf Jordan Abbey, my deepest apologies for this attack on your person. Please allow me to escort you to the main house to dress your wounds." He offered his hand.

Jordan curled her lip as she eyed him. Why was he acting so . . . polite? Was this some sort of trap or test? A glance at Angela gave her the answer. The blond was apoplectic with rage, vibrating in place, hands clenching and unclenching. Alpha Shane followed Jordan's gaze, locking eyes with Angela. After a few more seconds, Angela wrenched her face away and leaped, transforming midair into a wolf, and hit the ground, tail tucked as she ran with long strides. The other two werewolves followed on her heels.

Alpha Shane shook his head. "You still have so much to

learn," he murmured, watching his daughter run. Jordan wasn't sure if he had directed his comment to Angela or her. Then he looked at Jordan and offered his hand again. "So, chaos wolf, are you going to come with me, or will you let your pride refuse this small offer of assistance?"

She looked down at her arm. Several punctures and deep gashes scored her flesh, dripping blood. Now that she acknowledged the wound existed, it began throbbing with her pulse. She cradled her arm close to her chest as she took his hand with the other. "Well, since bleeding all over your forest would be rude, I'll take you up on your offer of first aid."

Alpha Shane let out a deep rumble as he helped her to her feet. Jordan stiffened. Had she offended him? No, wait, was he chuckling? "Come this way, chaos wolf. Let us get you fixed up before your meeting with the Talespeaker."

She followed Alpha Shane. She was surprised at how quietly the large man moved. Her feet crunched against the gravel, but occasionally Jordan made out the scrape of a stealthy paw on dried foliage. Either Angela and her minions hadn't strayed too far away, or Alpha Shane had his own spies watching their progress. If the Alpha noticed, and she was sure he did, he said nothing, as if the burst of conversation earlier had drained away his words and he was waiting for the well to refill.

He led Jordan into the house. Instead of taking her to his office or the main living room, he guided her into an area she hadn't been before. They passed a few doors before he opened one. The bathroom, done in a warm beige accented with dark wood, was larger than some apartments Jordan had seen. Alpha Shane gestured her toward the toilet. "Have a seat. Juan, Maria, bring me the first aid kit."

"They aren't here, Alpha Shane. I've got it." Pamela Henricksen stepped into the room, clutching a hard plastic blue and white box with a red cross on the lid. She looked at Jordan and made a tutting noise. "What happened?"

"Angela happened," Jordan grumbled.

"Angela took it on herself to greet Ms. Abbey when she entered the grounds," Alpha Shane said as he switched places with Pamela.

"That girl," Pamela said, making more disapproving noises. She opened the box and pulled out the medicated pads. "Your daughter is becoming more and more unruly by the day."

Jordan didn't resist as Pamela lifted her wounded arm. Or at least she didn't until the antiseptic hit the open wound. "Ouch!" She tried to pull her arm away from the stinging sensation but was held fast.

"Hold still, Jordan." Pamela swabbed the wounds. "You don't want this to seal with dirt inside it. It'll take you forever to heal properly."

Jordan twitched at the sting as Pamela probed the wounds. "There. Your arm should be back to normal by the end of the night. But it still should be bandaged."

Alpha Shane grunted as Pamela dug out the roll of mesh wrap. "Pamela, please escort Ms. Abbey to Talespeaker Diana. She is waiting at the Great Oak."

Pamela placed the absorbent pad on the still-oozing bite and wrapped the mesh around the arm to hold it in place. "Yes, sir."

His eyes shifted to Jordan. "And Chaos Wolf Jordan Abby, I apologize again for my pup's actions. I will see to it she is properly punished." Without a further word, he turned and walked away.

"Gracious as always," Pamela muttered. She let go of Jordan's arm and patted her shoulder. "Come on. Let's not keep Talespeaker Diana waiting."

17

———

Pamela led Jordan to an oak-lined trail leading away from the house. Jordan walked beside her. The pain had subsided to a dull ache, but not nearly as bad as the first time she had been bitten by a werewolf. They were three quarters of the way to the clearing with the large oak when Pamela broke the silence. "You're quiet today. Do you need something for the pain?"

"Huh?" Jordan jerked her head up. "No, sorry. I just feel like I'm not supposed to be here."

Pamela snorted. She stopped and turned around to face the way they had come. "Because the Talespeaker specifically asked for you, you have permission to be here tonight. But Billy doesn't. Come on out, boy. I know you're there.

Jordan tilted her head and flared her nostrils, snapping alert. *Idiot! What made you think you're safe now?* Using scent over sight only came naturally when she was in a wolf form. Until Pamela had pointed him out, she'd had no clue Billy was there. Pamela's words were confirmed when Billy stepped out from behind a tree.

Jordan fixed him with a glare. "I really don't like male werewolves stalking me."

"Sorry," Billy said. "I heard you and Pamela talking. I wasn't meaning to eavesdrop. May I come along?"

Pamela looked at Jordan, eyebrow arched in question.

Jordan shrugged. "I don't have a problem. I'd rather know where he is since I've already been stalked once tonight. Is anyone else with you?"

Billy shook his head. "Nope. Pack's honor."

Jordan snorted but didn't comment about what she thought their honor was worth.

"We'll talk about this later, Billy." Pamela turned away from the young werewolf and resumed walking. "I'm sorry. Pack manners aren't what they should be. You're here as Talespeaker Diana's guest and have been poorly treated. But I don't think that's what's bothering you."

"That's not enough?" She scratched the back of her head, figuring out how to say it without insulting anyone. "It's the killings going on. The accusations."

Billy trotted up to walk beside her. "Do the leech—" He cut off the word and amended it at Jordan's side-eye. "Vampires. Do they think you did it?"

Jordan nodded. "Elder Marcus could vouch for my whereabouts and they'd still think I was guilty."

"That's why you can't trust vampires," Billy said. "They'll always be prejudiced against you, no matter how loyal you are to your ma—patron."

Jordan stiffened. Billy had been about to say 'master.' To the werewolves, she was a slave. And to most of the vampires she was too. They just had prettier words for it.

"What are they actually saying, Jordan?" Pamela asked.

"They think it's someone Alpha Shane can't control or might be secretly egging on. Or it's me. There's talk about another chaos wolf being in the area, but I think it's mostly to make me think they don't suspect me. What about the police? Do they have any thoughts about it?"

"If anyone was reported missing, I could look into it officially," Pamela said. They stepped into the meadow. "So far, the vampire bribery machine is working overtime. No reports of anyone missing, and the few bodies we have are designated animal attacks outside of our jurisdiction. And as long as they disguise what's going on, nothing will be done."

"Even if it didn't look like a werewolf did it, they'd still find a way to blame me." Jordan shrugged. "I assume the pack thinks the same about me?"

Billy looked at Pamela and arched an eyebrow.

"Yeah, that's what I thought," Jordan said as they neared the meadow with the giant tree in the center. "But if not me, and it's definitely not me, then who?"

"Why, one of your vampire allies, of course." Talespeaker Diana stepped forward from where she was waiting by the tree.

Jordan wrinkled her nose. "But what would they gain?"

"Besides the death of a werewolf? That'd be enough for them." She sighed and patted the trunk of a branch so old and heavy it rested on the ground. "Come, child, it's time for another story." She looked at Pamela and Billy. "You've heard this many times before. No need to bore you with another retelling."

Pamela nudged Billy back toward the trail. "We'll keep an eye out for Angela."

The Talespeaker arched an eyebrow in Jordan's direction. "Angela?"

Jordan raised her arm, displaying the bandage. "It's a long story."

Diana sat down and smoothed her hands over her thighs. "I do like to listen to stories as well as tell them."

Jordan shrugged and lowered herself to sit crisscross on the ground at her feet. "Not much to tell. Sentry Rodriguez let me in. I was barely halfway to the house when I heard Angela and her goons crashing through the underbrush. They weren't being subtle about stalking me."

Diana smiled small and tight as she shook her head. "She takes after her father. Then what happened?"

"I knew I wasn't going to make it to the house, so I put my back to the nearest tree. I reminded her I was here as a guest, but she attacked me anyway. Didn't have the chance to shapeshift, so I tried to defend myself. Alpha Shane showed up before Angela tore out my throat."

"Good. He needs to see the trouble his daughter is stirring up." She reached out and patted her shoulder. "You should be healed up just before it's time to leave."

Jordan toyed with the edge of the bandage. "Can I ask a question? Angela kicked my ass earlier this week and then Alpha Shane all but sicced her on me. This time he's upset. Why?"

"Because you're an invited guest and should be treated with respect. Or at the very least, not attacked on sight." Diana shook her head. "What Angela did could be seen as a legitimate reason for a demand of retribution. A literal pound of flesh of prey, or from her."

Jordan wrinkled her nose, swallowing down an acidic taste in the back of her mouth. "Ugh, I think I'll pass."

"If you wish," Diana said. "My personal opinion? I'd like you to do it. The girl is too proud and has no use for traditions that aren't to her advantage." She sighed. "I'm sorry. I didn't intend for this to happen when I invited you here."

Jordan shrugged, a teasing smile on her face. "So, make it up to me by telling me a story."

Diana grinned. "Fortunately, I have one in mind. Take a seat, child." As Jordan leaned back, supporting her weight on her hands, the Talespeaker cleared her throat. "After Gaia cursed the Wolf for her sins, the Wolf left the forest and wandered, learning how to live in her new human body. At first she only transformed at the fullness of Luna, for she did not know she could concentrate and shapeshift whenever she pleased. She had no thick fur to keep her warm in the cold of the night, no swift paws to chase her daily meal, and no sharp fangs to defend herself from those who attacked her.

"Thus she was naked, weak, and hungry when she came across a man. For since the cursing of the Wolf and Bat, men had killed both when they could be found. The Wolf cowered, afraid the man would know her for who she was and she would not be able to defend herself. The man only saw a frightened woman lost in the territory patrolled by fearsome predators. He brought her to his fellow men living in the caves in the hills. He and the others taught her the ways of men—of hunting with spears and dressing in skins and eating plants they pulled from the ground. Although her sense of smell was dimmed, her sight was keen, and she grew into a fine huntress in the manner of humans, gaining her own status among the man pack. But the one prey she refused to hunt were wolves, for fear she might kill her brethren.

"In time, the Wolf and the man fell in love, and she took him as her mate. She bore him one fine boy-child. This puzzled her, since before she had borne her litters in fours, fives, and sixes. It troubled her greatly until one night she snuck out of the cave with her man-pup. She traveled a distance from the caves so she would not be spied upon. Kneeling in the dust, the Wolf cried out to Luna, begging her to answer her plea.

"Luna, ever wise and merciful, descended from the skies, white with radiance both beautiful and terrible. The Wolf trembled and abased herself, her child clasped in her arms. 'O merciful Moon,' she pleaded. 'I am so afraid with worry and fear. I have borne the man offspring, but only one pup issued from my womb. I fear that there is something wrong since he is without brothers or sisters.'

'It is the way of man to bear their children singly, or doubly once in a great while. There is nothing wrong with your womb. Now rise, Wolf. Show me the child.'

"Still afraid, the Wolf did so. Luna passed a hand over the

child. The expression on her face, though beautiful, grew sorrow-ful. 'It is as I feared. Although he is innocent and the man's blood runs through his veins, he shares in your curse, also being part Wolf.'

"The Wolf cried out in horror. 'What shall I do? My mate does not know I am his hated enemy. He will slaughter both myself and my son.'

'Hide him away in the time of my fullness, as you do yourself,' Luna counseled. 'In time, you will both learn how to control your shapeshifting and thus be able to protect yourself. But until then, the truth of what you are must be kept from those who would destroy you.'

"The Wolf did as she was told, hiding herself and her son away during the full moon. She learned that Luna was correct, for the man-child became a roly-poly wolf pup during that time. Over the years, the Wolf birthed three other children by her human mate, all of whom shared in the curse. Together they formed the First Pack. Under the care of the Wolf and following the sage advice from Luna, they hid themselves during the full moon, but were otherwise counted among the men as gifted hunters.

"The Bat also roamed the earth, outcast from his kind and from man. The Bat tried to hide amongst them, much as the Wolf did. To gain their favor, he would protect them during the night from attacking animals, but he would also indulge his hunger during those dark hours. Quickly, men would question why so many healthy people would die of a wasting sickness. Or they demanded to know why the Bat avoided the sun. He was driven off from the human settlement, but not before he had beguiled one of the men's daughters. She followed him, declaring her desire to be with him, and he took her as his mate. During the consummation, he shared his blood with her, sharing his curse as well. Together they wandered the night to slake their thirst.

"Eventually, they came across the man pack that the Wolf and her pups hid among. The Bat recognized his former friend, and the desire for revenge burned as hot as the sun. He sent his mate into the settlement to seduce the firstborn of the Wolf.

"The mate of the Bat came to the son of the Wolf dressed in all her finery. Slowly she beguiled him, gaining his trust and his affection. The Wolf, not knowing the Bat could share his curse as she had, did not burden her children with the knowledge of her former friend. So while her son was unaware of what the mate of the Bat was, he did know she was beautiful and told him all the things young men wished to hear. After several nights, she lured him to the woods with the promise of taking him as her mate. Instead, she attacked him and drained him of his blood, which the Bat replaced with his own.

"When the son of the Wolf returned to his mother, she smelled the blood of the Bat coursing through his veins and despaired. But for the love of her son, she stayed her claws and helped him hide amongst man. She herded prey to him so he did not feed on the men around them. In desperation, the Wolf went on a pilgrimage to consult Sol so her son might be freed from the Bat's curse. She scaled the highest mountain and climbed the tallest tree. From that vantage point, she howled the secret name of Sol to gain his attention.

"The air grew hot around her. She leaped from the tree as it burst into flame. The grass beneath her feet scorched, and the springs and rivers boiled. Before her stood Sol in his flaming glory. When he turned his fiery gaze on her, she abased herself, first kneeling like a human supplicant and then shifting to her wolf form, exposing her throat and belly, tail tucked between her hind legs. Her fur was blasted by waves of heat as he spoke. 'Speak, cursed Wolf. Why do you seek my presence?'

"The Wolf cowered. 'My son has exchanged the curse laid upon me by Luna for the curse you laid upon the Bat.' She dared to lift her head to look into his eyes, even though the light threatened to blind her. 'He is innocent of the crime the Bat and I performed. Please, restore him to what he was.'

"Sol gestured to the blasted ground surrounding him. 'Can the forest fire return the tender green to the scorched leaves? So is my word. I can no more withdraw my curse from the Bat's chosen companions than I can restore cool water to the lake or call down snow on the mountain.' The heat in his voice was not of anger, but of sympathy. 'Return to your home, little Wolf. Teach your children better the danger of trusting the Bat and his children.'

"'No!' the Wolf howled. 'There must be a way to free my son from this curse!'

"Sol looked at her with pity. 'There is but one way to free one who shares the Bat's curse.' He whispered the way into her ears and gave her a gift of the necessary tool. She whined, ears going flat as she heard what she must do. He stroked the fur on her back and sides to comfort her. Then he returned to his place in the sky, leaving the earth burned for miles around. The Wolf discovered her once-white fur had been burned as black as coal by Sol's nearness, and she bore black fur ever after.

"The Wolf returned to her man-pack to sorrow and devastation. When the Wolf returned, the animals she had captured for her son were dead. Soon after she left, the people had begun to sicken and die. Not even her mate and youngest child were spared. All the sick and the dead shared one common symptom —two small wounds on the throat. The marks puzzled the elders and healers, but the Wolf knew what the wounds meant.

"When night fell, she abandoned the man-pack to search for the Bat and his children. Searching the woods, she found the Bat, his mate, and her son. As the three fled, the Wolf captured her son. She used the branch that Sol had tempered in his fires, thrusting it through his chest as he begged for mercy. The stake pierced his heart, freeing him from the Bat's curse and releasing him into the waiting arms of death.

"The Bat's mate hissed and attacked the Wolf. The Wolf freed her from the Bat's curse as well. The Bat, maddened by the loss of his two companions, declared enmity between their children. Any child of the Wolf he came across, he would destroy.

"And that is why the Children of the Wolf shun the Children of the Bat. Because of the Bat, the Wolf was forced to slay her firstborn to free him from his curse."

Jordan listened, losing herself in the story. She loved the way Diana told her stories. It reminded her of when her grandmother read from the big book of *Aesop's Fables* at bedtime. But this one turned her stomach. Diana's stories always contained a warning. Sometimes they were subtle threads in the myths she chose to tell. This one wasn't anywhere near subtle. And the longer she listened, the more nauseous she grew. She swallowed down her bile and spoke. "May I ask a question?"

Diana smiled. "At least this time you waited until I was finished. What do you want to know?"

"Are we certain the Bat ordered his mate to seduce the Wolf's son?"

"Of course he did," Diana said. "Why else would she?"

Jordan spread her hands in a question. "Why was the Bat so angry they both died? Even if he had ordered his mate to do so, maybe he'd be happy at the loss of a rival for his mate's affections."

"He was angry at the loss of his mate," Diana said primly. "The loss of the Wolf's son was no more than the loss of a pawn."

Jordan picked her next words carefully. "The story said he was angry at the loss of his companions. Plural." She looked up at Diana, watching her expression carefully. "Maybe the Bat considered him more than a pawn."

"You mean he cared for him." Diana's nose wrinkled. "There are versions of the tale that claim she wasn't his mate, but he considered her as his daughter," she admitted. "There are also versions where it wasn't the Bat who declared enmity between their children, but the Wolf."

It was just like she suspected. "So, you're telling the version you like best."

"No," Diana corrected. "I'm telling you the version that imparts the best lesson."

"I think I understand," Jordan said. "You're telling me a story about how any relationship between werewolves and vampires ends in betrayal and death. We've had this conversation before. I don't understand why we're having it again now."

"Because now there are deaths, Jordan. And you are a target. Your trust in vampires needed to be addressed. Look at what happened to your patron. He was lost to us—not when he begged for the curse of the Bat, but when he took a vampire for his lover. Do you understand?"

Jordan took a deep breath and then nodded. "I think I've got it." She looked at Diana with a bitter smile. "So, am I lost to you as well? Or is Billy here to tempt back to the true path of being a werewolf?"

"You are young and still learning. But you dance on the edge of a knife. One misstep, and you will be lost. If you had been raised a werewolf among a pack, you'd have been destroyed for your actions the night you proved yourself a werewolf but chose to leave with the vampires."

Jordan spoke around the lump in her throat. "So, what's keeping you from killing me now and being done with it?"

Diana met her level gaze with an equally hard stare. "It is not my place to name your enemies. You should be intelligent enough to figure them out without me confirming or denying them."

"But that would be a hell of a lot easier." Jordan threw up her hands. "Instead, let's keep Jordan in the dark and punish her for making mistakes she wasn't aware she could make." She stood up.

"Let's also not correct anyone else in the pack who's picking on me." She spun around on her heel and tromped away.

"Where are you going, pup?"

She spun back to Diana. "Home," she snapped. "I don't care if I'm disrespecting you or insulting a long-standing tradition. If you aren't willing to speak plainly, I'm done for tonight."

She stomped out of the grove. As Jordan came around the first curve in the path, she spotted Pamela and Billy leaning against a tree. Out of the corner of her eye, she watched Pamela nod to the young man as she passed. Billy pushed off the tree and walked alongside her, not saying anything.

They walked in silence for a minute before Jordan glared at him. "So, are you here to tell me I've fallen for vampire propaganda and the pack hasn't treated me that badly?"

"No, I'm here to escort you back to your car and make sure nobody tries to pull anything on you again," Billy said. "And for the record, I agree with you."

Jordan winced. "You overheard it all?"

"Yeah. You weren't exactly being quiet." He sighed. "Look, one of the things you have to understand is the pack cares for its own. They will always choose Angela over you because you're not a member. But if you become a member of the pack, she'll be corrected if she oversteps."

Jordan sighed. "Has anyone considered that her bullying me won't make me eager to join the pack anytime soon?"

"I tried to explain it to Alpha Shane, but he doesn't get it." He shook his head. "Probably the difference between being born and bitten."

"I'm just trying to figure out the differences between being human and werewolf, let alone the nuances." She looked at him out of the corner of her eye as she peeled off the bandage. "Billy, be honest with me. What do you think about me being with the vampires?"

The corner of Billy's mouth twitched. "I'm not the best person to talk to about this. I mean, I think you're too good for them."

"Okay, back it up a step then. What're your feelings about werewolves hanging out with vampires?"

"You mean the Wolf and Bat story you were told about us being blood enemies?" He snorted. "It's an excuse and nothing more. Can I ask you a question?"

"Yeah."

"Are you and the vampires still . . ." He raised his eyebrows.

"Yes," she said. Maybe not since Rhys, but the relationship hadn't been called off. "We are." She frowned. "Um, you won't get into trouble because you didn't manage to seduce me to the pack side?"

"Nah," Billy said. "Alpha Shane knew it was a long shot an—"

"Wait." Jordan rounded on Billy, fists on her hips. "He ordered you to flirt with me?"

"No, it wasn't anything like that." He held up his hands, palms out in defense. "He noticed I was looking at you the first night and asked me to be friendly to you. The flirting was my idea. Besides, I got involved with someone afterwards."

"Really?" She grinned, glad for a change of subject to something positive. "Tell me, who's the lucky girl? Just please tell me it's not Angela."

"Oh, hell no!" Billy laughed as they resumed walking. "Actually, it's a lucky guy."

"Oh. Then tell me about the lucky guy. Is it Juan? I thought Tran was dating Maria."

His next words were quieter. "He's not in the pack."

Jordan paused. She matched his volume without thinking. "You're dating a human?"

"Yeah. It's not uncommon. Most werewolves end up with a human mate if there's not another pack nearby."

"So, it's serious? You think he's your mate?"

"I don't know. I hope so. I mean, Mark's told me he loves me, and I love him."

Something about his nervous tone made her whisper her next question. "Does he know about you?"

Billy looked around, sniffing the air carefully. He nodded, an almost imperceptible vertical jerk of his chin.

Jordan bit her lower lip. For all their bravado, the werewolves were just as interested in keeping their existence hidden as the vampires were. Billy was not just breaking a rule, he was breaking *the* rule. He had to trust her to reveal this to her. She had a hundred questions. What would Alpha Shane say? Would the pack approve of the relationship? Did he plan to make Mark a werewolf? And what had been Mark's reaction? She kept the questions behind her lips. If it had been safe for Billy to discuss, he wouldn't been so cautious before he spoke. She smiled at him. "I hope I get to meet the man who supplanted me for your affections. He's got to be one special guy."

"Thank you," Billy said. He glanced around before whispering in her ear. "It's hard enough to find happiness with what we are. If you're happy, I hope you hold onto it for all it's worth."

They walked in silence until they reached the sally port of the main entrance. Jordan paused, hand on the gate, looking around for Sentry Rodriguez. The werewolf was nowhere in sight, but she assumed he was listening in. "Hey Billy," she said. "If you need to talk to someone, feel free to call. I can usually do coffee in the early afternoon. And Montgomery's pretty cool about me doing things on my own after dark if there's no Conclave meeting scheduled."

Billy smiled. "Thanks. Same goes for me, if I can get away." He stepped back as the rolling gate opened enough for Jordan to pass through. "Have a good night."

"You too, Billy." She walked off the compound, not even twitching as the gate boomed shut behind her. She had been given a lot of things to chew over.

18

―――――――

Jordan entered the apartment without announcing she was home. She slipped her jacket off and hung it on the peg by the door. She walked over to the living room and flopped face first on the couch.

"Dramatic much?" Montgomery asked. She hadn't even seen Montgomery sitting in the recliner. She didn't raise her head at the thump of his book hitting the coffee table. "What happened?" he asked.

"Nothing," Jordan said, her voice muffled by the cushions.

"Liar," Montgomery responded. "I can smell blood on you. Your shirt is torn and dirty. And you know better than to shift while wearing clothes. So, who did you get into a fight with?"

"Who do you think?" She rolled onto her back and crossed her arms over her chest. "Angela," she huffed. "Didn't even make it to the second bend in the road before she ambushed me."

Montgomery's jaw dropped. "She attacked you on the grounds?"

"Within five minutes of me getting there. Alpha Shane charged to my rescue. Talespeaker Diana told me Angela is acting without honor, blah, blah, blah." She crossed an arm over her face, as if blocking the memory from her sight. "Don't get me wrong. I appreciated the help since I was getting my ass handed to me by her and her two goons. But I wanted to take her out on my own and not have to depend on being rescued."

"Another three-on-one situation?" Montgomery shook his head. "Jordan, we've talked about it before. You're nowhere near able to fight off three at once."

"Who's fighting three people?" Thorn stepped in from the kitchen with two mugs of blood. He handed one over to Montgomery.

"Angela attacked Jordan again," Montgomery explained.

Jordan swung herself into a sitting position as Thorn sat down.

"Again? She's done it before?"

"She and her two lackeys were the ones who ran me off of Mount Ponderosa," Jordan said. "How do I get her to stop?"

"You have to fight her," Montgomery said. "Something fair. No ambushing, no ganging up. I have no doubt that under those conditions you would win."

"I don't know."

"Hey," Thorn nudged her shoulder. "You killed a chaos wolf on your own. This won't be a fight to the death." He turned to Montgomery. "This won't be a fight to the death, right?"

"In theory it shouldn't."

"*In theory!*"

Thorn patted her shoulder. "Nothing to worry about. After Rhys, Angela'll be a walk in the park."

Jordan rolled her eyes. "Speaking of walk in the park, remind me to walk Rex later."

"You're changing the subject," Montgomery said. "You'll have to face Angela at some point. It would be best if you had a plan in place before she attacks you again."

"You said I should fight fair, but now you're making it sound like I should set up an ambush myself."

"I said you'd win a fair fight. And nothing so devious. Just have an idea of what you'll do if she attacks you someplace you don't expect."

Jordan exhaled. "So, you're saying I should live my life paranoid?"

"Not paranoid, just cautious," Thorn said.

"Things will be better when it becomes clear who the next Alpha will be," Montgomery said. "Or more accurately, when Angela finally figures out you don't have any interest in ousting her from her position of heir presumptive." He shrugged. "Or when she chooses her mate and has a pup or two. That'll help her settle down."

Jordan shook her head. Why was it men always thought a woman marrying killed her ambition? "That reminds me, I do have a question. What about same-sex relationships? We've only really talked about mates in terms of having children."

"Most don't frown on them, although there are some arguments they should at least try to have a pup to keep their bloodlines going. There have been packs with Alphas whose mates were the same sex. Or humans who were made aware but not changed for various reasons."

"About the only combination I haven't heard of is a vampire and an Alpha," Thorn added.

It fully clicked into place for Jordan. "That's the reason you left Black Oak."

Montgomery nodded, his eyes going distant. "It was easier for me to fit into Christine's world than her into mine."

"You must have really loved her." She leaned forward. "Tell me what she was like. Please."

Thorn rested a hand on her back, as if trying to pull her back from the topic. "You don't have to if you don't want to, Montgomery."

"No, it's okay." Montgomery leaned back against the chair, staring up at the ceiling. "She was beautiful. Not just her long blond hair and bright blue eyes, but her spirit as well. One moment she could be as gentle as a kitten, the next as fierce as a bear protecting her cubs. She didn't stand for any insults to her or those she believed did not deserve them. There was a strength to her that . . . I can't put it into words. If she had been a werewolf, or even a human, there would have been no objections to our relationship. But she was a vampire." He paused and sighed. "She loved me just as fiercely as I did her. I'm certain Elder Marcus was just as thrilled about me becoming a famulus as my father was. Neither could dissuade Christine."

She'd expected hearing Montgomery talk about Christine would evoke a pang of jealousy. Instead, she reached for his hand to squeeze it, aching for him. From the pain in his voice and the slump of his shoulders, it was clear he was still in love with her. "You miss her."

"Yeah," Montgomery admitted. He stared at them with hooded eyes. "After our first night together, I had to go to her grave. I always go there when I need to think things out."

Thorn smiled, a small, rueful thing. "Jordan, I wasn't kidding when I said Mac was freaking out."

"Oh, I admit it freely," Montgomery said. "After Christine passed, Thorn and I had the occasional tryst. But it was never something other than . . ."

"Scratching an itch?" Thorn suggested.

"Yeah, something like that, although I wanted to put it a more elegant way. But the night with the three of us, something changed."

Jordan put her head in her hands. "You too? Thorn said something similar. Please don't tell me I have a weird pheromone that makes any vampire I sleep with fall in love."

Thorn barked a laugh. "Nope. If anything, the werewolves probably think we're the ones with the pheromones."

Jordan's cell phone buzzed. At the same time, Montgomery and Thorn began squirming, reaching around to pull their cell phones out of their back pockets. Almost mirroring each other's movements, they swiped their screens. Jordan blinked at the message on the screen while Thorn and Montgomery frowned. "Did you guys just get—"

"Notification of a mandatory meeting of the Conclave tomorrow? Yes," Montgomery said.

"Mandatory?" Jordan glanced up from her screen. "I thought all Conclave gatherings were mandatory."

Thorn wiggled his hand back and forth. "There are different levels of mandatory. You're supposed to be there, but if you miss now and then, you're okay. But if you miss one you've been told to be at, you answer directly to Elder Marcus and better have a damn good reason why."

"So, what would make this one so important?"

"Something's up," Thorn said. "Last one he did was to announce you had been turned, Mac."

Montgomery shifted in his seat. His eyes focused somewhere in the distance. "That's not a good sign." He glanced at the clock. "We should get some sleep soon. We'll all need to be there tomorrow night."

"That reminds me," Jordan said. "I was planning to go out and run some errands this afternoon. Should I reschedule?"

"No, I don't think there's any reason for you to," Montgomery said as he rose. "I'll see the two of you in the evening."

"Sleep well, Mac." Thorn and Jordan watched him disappear into his room. When the door shut, Thorn shook his head. "Still running."

Jordan sighed. "Anything we can do to help him?"

"Not until he reaches out to us. You look tired. Go get some sleep. I'll clean up."

She arched an eyebrow. "Not going to ask if you can join me in my room?"

"You've made it clear we need to get things sorted with Montgomery before you're sharing a bed with anyone. I'm respecting your choice."

Jordan walked over to him and kissed him on his cheek. "Thanks for understanding."

Thorn patted her shoulder. "Get some sleep, Jo."

After grabbing her jacket, Jordan retreated to her room. Once in her pajamas, she flopped on her bed. She stared up at the ceiling, grabbing her pillow and clutching it to her chest. She should follow Montgomery's and Thorn's advice and get some sleep. But all she could do was keep thinking about Angela standing over her, jaws wrapped around her arm. Molly staring at her, no expression on her face. A set of yellow eyes glowing against void-black fur burning into hers.

She thumped the pillow above her head and sat up. She needed someone she could talk to. Get some of this straightened out. But who? Montgomery would be the first choice, but he was dealing with his own issues. He didn't need hers as well. Same with Thorn. Pamela would suggest all her problems would be solved by joining Black Oak. Billy she could talk to, but she wasn't sure he'd understand what she was going through.

She drummed her fingers against her stomach. Maybe she was looking at this from the wrong perspective. Or maybe she needed an outsider's perspective.

Jordan stood up and went to the closet. She grabbed her jacket and reached into the pocket. She pulled out the scrap of paper and tapped out an email to her former teacher. She could talk to him about her worries about Molly if he agreed to meet with her. The rest, she'd figure out on her own.

19

—————

Brian snorted as he crossed the street that marked the boundary between werewolf and human territories. He could have taken a car to Rancho Robles, but he wanted to run, to revel in the power in his muscles. Running from Alpha Shane with his tail tucked between his legs didn't count. He needed to reassert himself as a top predator. His ears still rang from Angela cursing and stomping. "You were supposed to warn me if anyone was coming!"

"Hey!" he'd snapped. "You said it'd be fun to harass the vampire-loving chaos wolf. You said nobody'd care."

"How was I supposed to know my dad knew she was on the grounds?"

"You're always talking about how you're going to be the next Alpha. If your challenge of your father goes like it did tonight, it'll be one of the shortest rules ever." He turned away from her.

"Where the hell do you think you're going?" Angela bellowed after him.

"I'm getting a beer," he said. He was sure they had taken the chaos wolf to the main house. No way in hell he was going there and having a second confrontation with Alpha Shane while she was around.

Angela stamped her foot. "Get the hell back here, Brian!"

Brian glared over his shoulder and raised his right hand, extending his middle digit. He barked a laugh at her outraged shriek as he leaped and shifted mid-air, landing running. He'd sped away, jaws parted in a canine grin as Angela's angry sputtering faded into the darkness behind him.

His plans were to run to the hollow tree and grab his clothes, get dressed, and go get beer. He'd left some cash and a change of clothes in the tree just over the fence so he could leave whenever he got the urge without having to go back to the main house. He always made sure to steer clear from areas that vampires frequented, and humans had no idea predators moved among them.

He set off at a leisurely lope, mind drifting from Alpha Shane to Jordan. The chaos wolf was easy on the eyes. She had to be lonely spending all her time with the vampires. He really should apologize to her, make her understand the blame lay with Angela. Maybe he could talk her into abandoning the leeches, since Billy had screwed it up royally. She didn't have to join the Black Oak pack. They could run off and claim their own territory, found their own pack. Yes, it was what the other chaos wolf, Rhys, had tried to do, but he'd be gentlemanly about it.

He inhaled deeply. The scent of stale exhaust lingered in the air. No trace of the musk of dogs or cats could be found. A squirrel had run through the trees recently. There was a human somewhere in the area. He hoped he hadn't been spotted. Alpha Shane got annoyed when Animal Control showed up to ask if there were any large dogs in the area and lectured everyone over and over about not being spotted.

His lips curled back in disgust. A skunk had urinated somewhere nearby. In fact, the scent was growing stronger as he got closer to . . . He bolted to the hollow tree where he kept his clothing. The source of the urine smell was the hollow. He stuck his head inside to grab his backpack in his jaws and figure out how badly his clothing stunk, and how bad he'd smell to humans.

The mechanical hiss was his only warning. Liquid fire sprayed into his eyes. He yelped and reared back, hitting his head. It wasn't skunk musk shooting into his face, but mace. He pawed at his muzzle, whining as he tried to wipe the burning sensation away. Frantic for any relief and not caring what Alpha Shane would say, he shifted to rub at his eyes with nimbler fingers.

Pain lanced through his flank half a second before the crack of the rifle shot exploded in the night. The Gaia-damned human had shot him. He turned in the direction the sound came from and lunged. He'd teach that puny human a lesson it would remember for the six seconds remaining in its life.

He made two painful strides when fire exploded in his chest. He gasped, trying to suck in a breath. A second bullet impacted his hind leg. It melted under him, and he fell face first into the grass. Whimpering, he tried to drag himself along on three legs. His shot leg wasn't itching with his usual accelerated healing. Nor were the wounds in his chest. He dragged himself a yard and began coughing up blood. Silver. He had been shot with silver. Gagging, his breath whistling in his throat, he continued to scrabble away. If he could get to help, they could pull the silver out of him and he'd heal. It would take months, and there'd be pain and scars, but he'd live.

Heavy footsteps trod toward him. Something slammed into his back, pinning him to the ground. What little air he had gusted out of his lungs. He let out a weak whine and made one last attempt to wriggle free. He died from a silver slug to the base of his brain without hearing the deafening thunder of the rifle.

Montgomery stepped into Eleganza Discreta and walked to the counter without so much as a sideways glance at the customers. "Hello, Karen," he greeted the woman by the register. I'm here to see Rosanna."

"Yes, sir. She told me to expect you." She stepped around from the counter. "She said she had an unavoidable errand and asked if you would please wait in her office."

Montgomery nodded, schooling himself to show only a bland response. He had scheduled this appointment and was told this was the first night they could meet. 'Unavoidable errand' translated to making him wait because she could. Without a further word, he headed to the doors marked "Employees Only." He passed by several racks of deceptively simple but very expensive dresses before stepping through the door.

The rich woods and fabrics fell away to beige walls. He walked into an office with a desk, piles of even paper resting in the inbox. On the cork board mounted to the right were notes and licenses and a calendar held in place by plastic pushpins. He sat down on the plastic chair in front of the desk and waited.

It was ten minutes before the door from the sales floor open.

The *pok pok pok* of heels striking linoleum echoed toward him. He rose as his sister-in-blood stepped into the room. "Hello, Rosanna."

She didn't acknowledge his greeting as she swept around her desk. "You finally deigned to meet with me, Montgomery."

Montgomery. Not *fraternello*, her nickname for him. No humor in what would have once been a chiding joke about how long he had been away. "Rosanna," he said as he turned. He bowed slightly and took his sister-in-blood's hand to give it a polite kiss. "It is good to see you."

Rosanna eyed him, skeptical lines creasing her forehead. "Is it, Montgomery? You have made no attempt to contact me since you sent your bitch here with your peace offering. Is your famulus accompanying you?"

Montgomery kept the wince firmly inside his gut. "She relayed to me your refusal. Given what was said, I thought it would be best if she were not present." He pulled the box out of his jacket pocket. "I am here to ask your forgiveness personally."

Rosanna looked down at the box. "Montgomery, I worry your judgement is biased when it comes to your famulus. You care too much for her."

"And you didn't for Bridgette? I'm sorry she died. But that was not Jordan's fault."

"Of course it is not her fault. But had you done what you were supposed to, handed Jordan over to the werewolves, Bridgette would be alive. The bastard who attacked her would not have been hunting for your bitch in the city. She would have been Black Oak's problem. They were the ones who were properly prepared to handle it."

"You blame me for it." Montgomery's hand swept in the direction of the Hotel Cataluna, as if it could be seen through the walls. "You're leaving out something. Marcus didn't order me to hand her over, which was more than within his capability. If anything, he backed my decision to keep her." He narrowed his eyes. "Or are you blaming him for turning me? Or Christine for taking me as her famulus and her lover?"

"I could take this whole fracas as far back as the Wolf and Bat themselves," Rosanna said in frosty tones. "But it would not soothe the rage in my breast nor slake my thirst for vengeance." She took a step closer to Montgomery. "She is a danger to us all. What is it they call her? A chaos wolf? An apt name. She sows chaos and dissension wherever she goes. But then you do like that type."

His phone pulsed with an incoming call. Montgomery slipped his hand in his pocket to still the vibrations, his attention focused on Rosanna. "Meaning?"

"Christine, rest her soul, was not the most obedient of children. Otherwise, she wouldn't have taken you as a lover. Between her and Thorn . . . I would not have expected him to follow Elder Marcus's orders to spy on you."

"His what?"

"You didn't know?" Rosanna's smile turned vulpine. "Thorn has been reporting to our sire about your private actions. That is part of the reason he has cultivated his relationship with you. He does the same with me, of course, but I figured out the reason for his attentions long ago." She paused. "Did you believe he actually cared for you?"

Those words struck like a precisely aimed stake to the heart. How many times he had asked Thorn to stay longer, but Thorn begged off flashed through his mind. The times he was "too busy" and had to "work late" were prefect opportunities to report in to Marcus. He swallowed the lump in his throat. "Rosanna, you asked for the fangs, and here they are. What else do you want from me?"

"If I believed Marcus would allow it, I'd have you present me her hide before the entire Conclave." Rosanna's voice was calm and controlled. "I will settle for seeing her with the Black Oak Pack where she belongs—or turned into a vampire so she truly is one of us." Her gaze turned steely. "And I am not the only one who shares that opinion."

Montgomery locked his gaze onto hers. "I find neither of those acceptable. It appears we are at an impasse."

"For the moment, we are," Rosanna agreed. "The only reason you stand where you do is because Marcus is supporting you. He's not besotted by the little bitch, but Alpha Shane's frustration at her antics amuses him. It will not always be so. And when you lose his favor, you will find yourself with very few friends." She arched an eyebrow. "Is the bitch servicing you in your bed worth it?"

Montgomery swallowed a hiss. His words were clipped. "What I do with Jordan is my own business."

"Why did you really come here, Montgomery?"

"I came here to speak to my sister, whom I've missed. I came to offer my sympathies, since her favorite famulus is dead, and to offer what comfort I could."

"I have told you what you could offer me, Montgomery Augustus Cooper. And you will not comfort me in the way I desire." She placed her hand on the box with the fangs, sliding them toward her. "I will accept this token, consider it *weregild* for the death of my famulus, and cease public demands for forgiveness. Unless you have further business to conduct with me, I request that you leave."

Montgomery stiffened. Ceasing demands for forgiveness wasn't the same as granting it. He nodded once. "I take my leave of you then and will trouble you no further. Farewell, Rosanna Lombardi."

"Farewell, Montgomery Augustus Cooper," she said. "But do not think this is over."

He turned and walked out of the office, straight-backed and gait stiff, ignoring the employees and customers watching him weave among the displays of clothing.

The night air hit his face in a cool wave but didn't push away his worries. *Of course Rosanna is still angry.* If the situation had been reversed, he'd be furious. She had the knowledge to aim for his weak spots with an accuracy that made most marksmen jealous. It didn't mean it wasn't true. Thorn wouldn't . . .

No. Deep down, he knew. Thorn would.

His phone vibrated again, reminding him of the missed call. Montgomery pulled it out of his pocket and squinted at the screen. He swiped, hit the voicemail icon, and lifted it to his ear.

"Hey," came Thorn's voice. "Wanted to tell you and Jo I have to deal with something that came up at the shop, so I'll be spending the day here. Let me know how it went with Rosanna. See you tomorrow night."

He sighed as he lowered the phone. This was the third call this month he had received from Thorn about "problems" at the office. Whenever he asked Thorn what the exact issues were, he always had an answer. Paperwork. State forms. Inspections. Just specific enough to present as a problem needing his attention, but not saying what the exact issue was, and just enough to put Montgomery's suspicions off. Until now.

He looked at the entrance to the Hotel Cataluna. He could walk in and chat with Richard. Slip into the conversation a question about whether he had seen Thorn lately. Tonight, even. Or he could head down to the parking lot and walk a circuit, look for Thorn's hybrid car before he got into his SUV. With a sickening clench in his stomach, he decided he didn't want to tonight.

He resumed walking down the sidewalk to where he parked. Maybe he should discuss it with Jordan.

No, Jordan had enough on her shoulders dealing with the Black Oak Pack. And he wasn't sure she would have a clear view when it came to Thorn. As a famulus, her loyalty should be to him. As a woman, well, there had always been flirting between them. He would have to sit down and talk with Jordan.

But first, he needed to have a talk with Thorn.

21

Emma Chase walked toward the exit of the community center, trying to stifle a yawn. A lot of her associates, herself included, would mercilessly tease a famulus who had trouble staying up late at night. Except those people hadn't spent the last two hours pounding on a CPR training dummy. Or at least that was her excuse for why she wouldn't attend the stuffy meeting Reginald had nightly to keep Marcus's Family up to date. All she wanted was to go home to the Hotel Cataluna and climb into her warm, waiting bed. And she would do so, with her patron's dispensation.

"Done for another two years," she muttered to herself. Normally she would never leave the security and luxury of the hotel. CPR certification required her to attend a class in person. Since Marcus considered it a point of pride to have certified phlebotomists as part of his Family, she didn't argue against it. It kept her out of the immediate group of people he fed from. While Marcus's average female famulus lasted four years, she had been in his service for ten years. So, it was worth the hassle of traveling from the Hotel Cataluna to the community center and taking a class every year or two, even if this time she'd forgotten to wear casual shoes.

As she reached the exit doors, she paused. Emma glanced to either side but didn't spot anyone. She had spent too much time around predators not to recognize when she was being sized up as prey. She whipped around, reaching for the mace in her purse.

She almost laughed in relief. It was her teacher behind her, holding out a paper card. "Ms. Chase," he said. "You forgot your documentation. You wouldn't want to have to retake the class, right?"

She took the card, a sheepish grin on her face. "Oops. Thank you." Marcus insisted everyone working in the Blood Bank have their paperwork in order. It made it easier to bribe state officials to look the other way if something went wrong.

Her instructor nodded and opened the door for her. "I'll see you next class."

Emma smiled as she walked through the exit. *If I'm still here.* While Marcus valued her training, she was still a famulus. If he decided his hunger was more important than her skills, there would be nothing to stop him from drinking from her. The question was if he'd slake his thirst fully or leave her enough to live.

She hustled across to where her car was waiting under a streetlamp. Her three-inch heels made an echoing *pok pok pok* as she hurried along. Berating herself again for forgetting her gym shoes, she pulled her keys out of her purse, flipping through them to find the right one.

A hand clamped over her mouth. A body pressed against her back. She bit the hand and stomped on her attacker's instep. There was a shriek of pain as the hand released. She bolted, running across the parking lot as fast as she could. She had to make it into the building. She could find her teacher, hide in a room, call either Marcus or the police, and hope one of them made it to her in time. She reached the doors and pulled the handle.

The doors remained shut, locked.

"No, no, no!" Emma screamed. She pounded on the glass doors, hoping her teacher heard her. The reflection of her attacker came closer.

Her forehead slammed against the glass. Her vision went white as hands grabbed her upper arms from behind. She kicked out, trying to plant her feet as she was dragged away from the door and into the bushes next to the building. She jerked, but the grip was implacable iron. "Please, let me go," she begged. "I won't tell anyone. My boss will pay you whatever you want—"

Hot pain sliced across her throat. She gagged, coughing up blood. Her free hand went to her neck, trying to keep the blood from spilling out of the wound. She gagged and dropped to her knees. *Please*, her eyes begged as she fell onto her side. She couldn't get any air in or out, and there was blood everywhere, so much blood. Even being around vampires, she had never seen this much.

A booted foot nudged her in the shoulder. Gagging, she looked up into the face of a stranger. "Sorry it has to be like this," he rumbled, kneeling beside her. He reached down and grabbed the blood-slicked pendant that marked her as Family. "But now you're no longer their slave." He snapped the chain. "You're free."

"Hey! What's going on?"

Her vision was going dark, but she recognized the voice of her CPR instructor. A set of footsteps ran toward her as another ran away. Something thumped down beside her head. Another set of hands pressed against her throat. "Call 9-1-1!" he shouted. "Hang in there, Emma, you're going to be okay."

No, I'm not was the last thought she managed before her breath gurgled out of her throat one last time.

22

———

It felt odd to Jordan to be at Rancho Robles Community College without a backpack weighing her down. Elias could only meet with her during his free time between classes. She double checked her to-do list on her phone, deciding she could squeeze it in between walking Rex and getting ready for the gathering of the Conclave. Montgomery and Thorn wouldn't be upset with her meeting with her old teacher.

If you believed that, her inner voice scolded, *you wouldn't have kept the meeting a secret from them*. But wasn't Thorn always telling her it was better to ask forgiveness than permission? Except, the small voice inside argued, it probably doesn't apply to Family.

She walked from the parking lot to the Liberal Arts building over the tree-lined path. The unease in her stomach roiled with every step she took. She was halfway to her destination when she figured out why. It was the path she had walked three months ago.

The sun, which had been slanting toward the western mountains, blinked out. She grabbed the metal of the streetlamp as her knees went weak. Instead of the afternoon, it was dark as night. She looked around as stalking footsteps thumped behind her. No, not footsteps, but the thudding of paws—the same pounding she'd heard the night that Rhys bit her.

Then the light flooded back in. Jordan pressed a hand against the post. Her breath gusted in and out at a rapid clip. She forced it to slow as she pushed down the panicked nausea rising in her stomach. "I'm safe," she whispered. The words were only half convincing even though it was the truth. "He can't hurt me. He's dead."

When her breathing returned close to normal, she pushed away from the lamp. Her first few steps were shaky, but the farther she walked away, the more her confidence returned. Still, she glanced backwards as she continued down the path, unable to shake the sensation of being followed.

She passed by the exterior doors of classrooms to step into a hallway. Inside, the space between doors was smaller. She passed by several with name plates and paper signs. She stopped at one of the ones with a plate and knocked on the door.

A voice floated back through the door. "Open office hours are at 11:00 a.m."

"Mr. Campbell," she called back. "It's Jordan Abbey. We have an appointment?"

"Ah, Jordan. Give me a minute." She could make out the shuffling of papers and footsteps behind the closed door. Then it opened to reveal Elias. "Sorry about that. I forgot we arranged a meeting."

"If this is a bad time, we can meet later," Jordan said.

He smiled "Not at all. I was so busy preparing lessons I forgot what time it was." He held the door wider. "Please, come in."

She stepped into the office, although office might have been a generous word. The size of the space reminded her of the changing rooms of Eleganza Discreta. The desk and bookshelves taking up most of the wall space did nothing to help the cramped sensation. Elias swept some papers on the desk into a haphazard pile. "Take a seat," he said, gesturing at a wooden chair. "Can I get you some coffee?"

"Sure. Cream only," she said.

"I'll be back." He stepped out of the office, pulling the door mostly closed.

Jordan looked around the room. There were several stacks of books, some of which she recognized as being on the syllabus for the world lit class she had dropped out of. One title caught her eye, and she found herself tracing the spine. Odd. He had copies of *The Vampire: His Kith and Kin, An Annotated Shakespeare, Carmilla,* and *Jane Eyre* all shelved together. *Or maybe not so odd after all,* she thought as she spotted the end of a necklace chain similar to hers peeping out from under a paper. Curious, she lifted the paper to study the pendant on the broken chain. The circle pierced by a wedge with a drop hanging from it matched the one she wore. The symbol of a vampire's trusted servant. Elias was Family?

The door rattled, and Jordan lowered the paper. Her ex-teacher stepped into the office and handed her a paper cup. "Thank you," she said. She took a sip as he sat down. The coffee tasted stale, and the undissolved powder passing for creamer tickled her nose to the point of sneezing. For half a second, she wished she was in the student lounge with its overpriced coffee shop, even if it meant passing by where she had been attacked again.

"So, Jordan," Mr. Campbell said. "What have you been up to since you dropped out of my class?"

She frowned, touching her pendant to make sure it wasn't tucked into her shirt. Maybe he hadn't noticed her necklace yet. "Well, I moved and got a new job, Mr. Campbell."

"You're not my student anymore. Call me Elias. And tell me, where did you move? Is it part of the reason for the new job?"

"Not exactly," Jordan said. "You heard what happened to Darren Fraiser?"

"The dog attack a few months ago? Yes. It's a tragedy what happened to that young man. Was he your boyfriend?"

"No. He was dating my roommate Molly." She looked down at the coffee cup and twisted it, watching the liquid swirl back and forth. "After what happened to him, we didn't want to stay in that apartment. She moved home, and I had to find a new place to live. And I got fired from my job, so I dropped out to deal with everything."

"That was a lot to handle in a very short time, Jordan. I understand why you needed a break from my class."

She took a sip and made a face. Despite the powdered creamer, the coffee tasted bitter. "I ran into Molly a few days ago. She and I are—will be—working together again and it's . . . awkward. I was hoping I could talk to someone who could help me figure out how to handle the situation."

Elias shook his head. "I'm a literature professor, Jordan, not a counselor. I'm probably not the best person to offer advice." He leaned forward in his chair. "Is there anyone close to you that you can talk to?"

"Yeah, kind of." Jordan sighed. She'd have to tread carefully to explain this. He hadn't acknowledged her necklace or said anything about her Family, so she didn't want to ask about his until she got a better understanding of the situation. "I made some friends just before Darren's attack happened. One of them offered me a room at his place until I could get my feet under me."

"And it became something more?"

Heat flushed her cheeks. She stared down at the coffee cup again. "Yeah, you could say that." Three months later, she still wasn't certain what their relationship was. Montgomery was retreating emotionally. Thorn at least was more teasing than pushing. But what was she? Girlfriend? Roommate? At least they supported her with the vampires and the other Family.

Then there was the tension with the werewolf pack. She'd

have to figure out how to handle Angela without bringing down Alpha Shane's wrath. But she was sure he'd always pick his daughter over the mouthy chaos wolf who defied him at every turn.

The question she didn't dare ask was how much longer she'd be able to put up with the stress. How long before she snapped? Returning to her old life would never be an option, no matter how much she wanted to during the loneliest parts of her day.

"Jordan, is there a problem? Do you need help?"

Ugh. He thought she had gotten herself into an abusive relationship. She shook her head. "No, it's nothing like that."

"Then why the hesitation? What are you so unsure about?"

She tapped her fingers against the paper, figuring out the best way to phrase it. "I made a lot of choices very quickly. At the time, I thought they were the right ones. Now that I've had a little time to breathe, I'm not so sure."

"If you decided to move out from your friend's place, what would stop you?"

A city of bloodthirsty vampires looking for any excuse to kill me. "I made some promises. Promises some people wouldn't be happy if I broke. Not Mon—my friend, but some of his friends and family."

"I think I understand." He paused, assessing her expression. "What if I told you I could help." He stared into her eyes as if he were searching for something. "That if you decided to leave, I know ways to keep you safe."

Her eyes went wide. He believed she was in an abusive relationship and was ready to ride to her rescue. "I think I've accidentally misled you, Mr. Cam—Elias," Jordan said. "I'm happy. I really am. I've got a job working as a personal assistant that pays very well and leaves me lots of free time. Montgomery is a great guy. But running into you and Molly got me thinking about how much things have changed. I stopped talking with her, and I feel guilty."

"You saw her recently? Have you spoken with her?"

"We ran into each other unexpectedly the other day as part of our jobs. We're trying to sync our schedules so we can get together and catch up."

Elias nodded. "And what about school? Are you planning on coming back?"

"I intend to. I'm not ready to yet. I'm still figuring out some things."

"I see." He looked down and shuffled some papers on his desk. "I do hope you reconsider. You were a bright student, and I think you have a gift. I would hate for your potential wither away to nothing. I can help you if you decide you need it." He twisted his wrist to glance at his watch. "And I'm sorry, Jordan, but I have to get ready for my next class."

She was being dismissed. Why, when he had been offering help a moment before? Did he consider her a lost cause because she didn't accept his aid? "Of course," Jordan said. She rose, gathering her purse. "Thank you for seeing me, Mr. Campbell."

He gathered several books and a laptop. "I'll walk you out."

There wasn't anything more to say. They walked in silence down the hall, Jordan a pace behind him. They split into separate directions after stepping outside the building. As she headed toward the parking lot, she mulled over the meeting.

She had wanted advice about Molly, but seeing the Family pendant threw her off her game. He had to be Family, with that piece of jewelry on his desk. She hadn't met all the Family members, just the ones who were the public aids. And, she suspected, some were used as an accessory. Not all Family members were treated well. Was that why he was offering her a way out?

Then why hadn't he identified himself. Jordan wasn't hiding her necklace. Surely he had seen it. And he must have heard his patron talking about her.

Or maybe he had found the necklace on campus and was

going to hand it over to the lost and found. Either way, she couldn't ask about it now. Or for advice about how to handle Molly. And unless he reached out to her or she ran into him at a gathering of the Family, she probably wouldn't have a chance to again.

She dropped into the driver's seat and let out a heavy sigh. At least she'd walked past the lamp post without having another panic attack.

The drive home was uneventful. She hoped getting back into the apartment would be too. She managed to only make a soft, metallic jingle as she put the keys back into her pocket. Her footsteps pounded in her ears as she tried to walk quietly into her bedroom. Thorn had told them he would be working late and staying at the tattoo shop, so no one was sleeping in the living room. Montgomery's door was still shut. She slipped into her room and closed the door with a click. Her chest heaved, heart thudding. The rush reminded her of the time in her sophomore year when she had snuck back into her house to meet up with her then-boyfriend Scott at a party being held by a senior whose parents were out of town.

There was a knock on her door. Her stomach dropped into her shoes. What she had forgotten was how her parents had confronted her about her little excursion the moment she'd climbed back in her window. "Yes?" she squeaked.

Montgomery opened the door. "Oh good, you're dressed," he said. "Did you see Reginald's email?"

"No," Jordan said. "I haven't checked it this afternoon." It was the truth, although her stomach twisted around the foundational lie.

"Elder Marcus has moved up the time of the meeting by about an hour. Do you think you'll still have enough time to run your errands?"

She did some quick mental math. He had no idea she had left

the apartment and returned. "I don't think so, even if I leave now. I'll have to do them tomorrow."

Montgomery nodded. "Okay. Be ready to go then. Oh, that reminds me. The keys aren't in the bowl."

She slipped her hand in her pocket and pulled them out. "I must have forgotten to put them back yesterday," she said, handing them to Montgomery.

He took the keys. "At least one of us knows where they were," he said with a bemused smile. "I was starting to worry I was losing my mind."

Jordan laughed as Montgomery closed the door. He stepped away, and she exhaled her tension. She had gotten away with it.

23

———

Victor Claddan stood outside the entrance to The Row's Blue Tiger Brewhouse, acting like he was waiting for his ride-share to show up. He kept an eye on the crowd and traffic, as if watching the cars go by. He would kill for a drink, but not one from the bar.

He didn't have his famulus go to the blood bank for him. Unlike most of the young ones, and some of the old ones these nights, he preferred to do his own hunting. Predatory instincts were dulled through drinking from plastic bags. Besides, blood pumping warm from a neck was much better. And if he wasn't able to bring down his prey, well, that's why he didn't allow himself to get too attached to his famulus.

He looked around, trying to spot any other vampires. He didn't spot any. Good. No amateurish competition lurking around the club scaring off his dinner. Everyone was probably hiding from the big bad wolf rumored to be hunting Family members.

He snorted. There had been warnings about werewolves hunting out in the woods where no civilized vampire would be. So out he went hunting without any concern. He wasn't Family, but a full member of the Conclave. No werewolf would dare attack him. The only werewolf in town was Montgomery's pet. She had the potential to be a threat to him. Not only had she seen him hunting where he technically should have asked permission first, but also he had attacked another vampire's property, namely her. There hadn't been any repercussions so far from either Marcus or Montgomery. And if she was the one who'd killed the famulus, well, he had been a weak human. She'd find it much harder to kill a vampire. She had only been able to knee him in the groin because he had been caught off-guard. If she tried it again, he'd have a wolf-skin rug as a new display piece in his bedroom. A famulus, especially a werewolf famulus, would not be allowed to get away with any infraction. If Montgomery whined about it to his sire, he was sure he could convince Elder Marcus he was in the right.

That was for later. This night, this moment, was for hunting.

He watched people coming out of the bar, scanning for his next meal, ignoring the growling in his stomach and the urge to let his fangs descend. Most of his potential prey were stumbling down the street in pairs. Those he discounted immediately. It was too difficult to take down two people at once without drugs, and he didn't like fighting the sluggish feelings as he disposed of the bodies. A young woman standing near the entrance piqued his interest until she stumbled to the curb and climbed into a waiting car. After several more groups of people headed off into the darkness, he finally spotted his meal. Men in general weren't his preferred prey, especially middle-aged men. But he was hungry, and his options and time were limited. He had fed on his famulus the night before, and she needed time to recover. He did not want to have to replace one so soon after overfeeding on her predecessor.

This man staggered down the street, away from most of the other people. He followed him at a discreet distance. It was hard not to gain on him with how often he paused to lean against a lamp post before weaving his way on.

Victor eventually caught up with his prey. They walked side by side. Victor hoped the man wouldn't object when he placed a guiding hand on his elbow. But before he could touch him, the man looked at him and slurred "Stu! Howyah doin?" His prey put an arm around him. "Thersh an afterpartah down tha stree. Wanna go?"

"Hell, yeah. Let's go." Half supporting, half guiding him, Victor walked his meal down the street. This was the easiest hunt ever. Victor kept scanning the upcoming side streets and buildings for a good place to duck into. They were heading away from the bars and toward the closed businesses. Those were a little too public for feeding, although it amused him to imagine Rosanna's outraged expression if a corpse were found in front of her high-end display windows.

His prey stumbled past the stores and ducked into the underground parking lot. *Even better.* There was a delicious irony to having dinner below the structure the Elder Vampire of Rancho Robles owned. While not against killing, Elder Marcus was getting squeamish about having blood spilled on his well-manicured grounds. Now he had to get close enough to his prey to put the bite on him in the blind spots the security cameras wouldn't cover. Most of the parking slots were full, but there were no people walking around. Marcus's security would recognize what was happening and wouldn't interfere.

He leaned in, fangs bared, ready to get his first drink. A fist landed in his throat. He gagged and reared back, snapping at air. When he got his vision back, the man stood at the ready, all signs of blurriness and unbalance gone. His prey's breath didn't smell like alcohol, but his clothes did. Hissing, Victor charged, reaching for his throat. His prey moved with more coordination than he'd give a sober man credit for. The not-drunk man reached into his coat and lifted something to his sternum.

The stake pierced his chest. Searing pain shot through his being as his vision went dark. The trap had been sprung neatly. The hunt had been too easy. He hadn't realized he was the prey.

24

Montgomery looked around the broad space that served as a conference room for a smaller convention. This wasn't Marcus's private office, where he spent most of his time when meeting his sire, but the meeting room he used when he wanted something witnessed by the entire Conclave. Mostly it was used when initiating a new famulus, but on occasion it was used for important announcements. A low stage took up the back third of the room. It was tall enough to allow Marcus to stand a head above them. Another subtle reminder of his position of power over those gathered. A podium perched in the center, six inches from the edge.

He watched as Thorn made his way through the group toward him. As the blue-haired vampire passed by Rosanna, she glanced in Montgomery's direction. Their eyes met and her smile widened. She nodded, a small, precise movement. He looked away from her, keeping an eye on Thorn's approach out of the corner of his eye. "Hey," he said, trying for friendly, but managing a neutral tone.

"Hey," Thorn said. "Quite the gathering, huh?"

"Yeah." He leaned in closer to Thorn. "Any idea what it's about?"

Thorn's trademark flippancy was nowhere in his voice or expression. "Scuttlebutt is one of Marcus's Family is dead."

"What's unusual about that?"

"They aren't usually the victim of a random throat cutting." Thorn slashed three fingers across his throat.

"Another one like David?"

He nodded. "And given the entire population's here, I'd say there's more than a grain of truth to it. Don't be surprised if Jordan's name gets mentioned."

Montgomery's voice dropped an octave. "Do you think—"

"Easy, big guy. Jordan and Emma may not have gotten along, but I don't think for a moment Jordan shredded her. They"—he jerked his chin toward the room—"may not."

Montgomery looked around the room again. The last time there had been so many vampires in one place had been when Jordan was presented. No, it wasn't. He counted heads, index finger twitching with each number to confirm his impression. The entire Conclave wasn't present. He nudged Thorn. "Do you see Hannah Banks?" he asked in a low voice.

Thorn shrugged as he scanned the room. "Her sire wanted to speak personally to her. She left last night after informing Marcus she was going. She's probably halfway to St. Augustine by now."

Montgomery made a face to hide the twist in his stomach at the evidence that Thorn was so intimately aware of Marcus's doings. "It must have been important if her sire called her across country. How do you think she went? Car or train?"

Thorn looked over the last of the arriving vampires. "Probably had her famulus drive her. Although I have no idea how she'll tolerate being in a stuffy trunk during the day. Hope a cop doesn't pull her over and ask to search the vehicle." He scanned the last of the arriving vampires. "How about Victor Claddan? You heard anything about him?"

"No, I haven't." He shared a look with Thorn. "He's always been a jerk, though. Maybe he's trying to prove to Marcus he's independent?"

"If he is, he chose the wrong meeting to skip." Thorn tilted his head, frowning. "You okay, Mac? You seem a little off."

He was about to answer when the murmurs around them died down. The Elder of Rancho Robles stepped into the room, drawing attention to himself with his mere presence. He didn't step to the podium, but instead came to the edge of the dais, leaving him several inches taller than the tallest vampire present. He looked over the assemblage, noting who was present and who was not before he addressed the crowd. "I have called you all here to discuss a growing situation." Marcus's grave expression deepened. "Several members of our Family have been killed over several nights."

A low murmuring swept through the gathered vampires. Montgomery stiffened as several sets of eyes glanced in his direction. Thorn had been right, again. Another famulus dead, and they were already linking Jordan to it.

"Their deaths are being passed off to the mortal authorities as animal maulings or other violent attacks." Marcus paused, glanced to the side of the dais, and frowned. "However, we believe we have come across the true cause."

A quiet murmur passed through the crowds. It wasn't due to the Elder's words. Reginald, face white as a sheet, stepped from behind the curtain. He stood ramrod straight, arms stiff at his sides. His hands trembled slightly. "Does he have a death wish?" Thorn whispered.

Marcus turned and frowned at his famulus. "Yes?"

Reginald crossed the floor and whispered into Marcus's ear. Marcus straightened up and looked at him, eyes narrowed and lips pulling upward, revealing the tips of his fangs. "Bring them to the room. I will be there shortly."

Reginald bowed and left. His damp hair was plastered to his neck.

Marcus turned his attention to the room again. His fangs were still down as he addressed the Conclave. "The situation has changed and requires my immediate supervision. I ask you wait here. I will return as soon as possible. Montgomery, if you would join me, please."

All the eyes in the room focused on him. He stepped toward Marcus, and Marcus raised his hand. "No, Rosanna. You are not needed."

Rosanna stared at Marcus, hands clenching into fists. Her glare shifted to Montgomery and then to the floor, shoulders stiffening.

Thorn nudged him forward as the other vampires broke into small groups, discussing what was going on. He followed Marcus out of the room.

"I am requesting your famulus join us, Montgomery. We may need her talents."

Montgomery frowned. What would Elder Marcus want with Jordan? Then he saw what was on the other side of the door and understood why.

25

―――――――

Jordan stood in the corner of the room, back to a wall for the false sense of security it gave her. The Family were gathered in the antechamber, as they did for most of Marcus's meetings. Rumors had wrapped thickly around her the moment she stepped into the building. She looked around the room. Most vampires had at least one famulus here to carry the information back to the others. All of Marcus's she could recognize were here, including Molly. There was one exception. The rumors, when boiled down, had three pieces of fact she couldn't deny.

Jordan had been seen threatening Emma Chase.

Emma Chase was now missing.

Elder Marcus wanted answers.

Jordan didn't like how the math added up.

All the other Family gathered in small knots of twos and threes, chatting. Occasionally they tossed a look in her direction. She didn't bother protesting, trying to defend herself, or convincing anyone of her innocence. After all, she was the big, bad wolf. They wouldn't believe her.

Someone in a security uniform came over and whispered into

Reginald's ear. Reginald stepped back from the guard, color draining from his face. Then he turned to look at Jordan, eyes wide. He blinked and the impassive mask dropped into place. His gaze snapped away, and he whispered something to the guard, then walked to the door leading into the meeting chamber, every motion sharp and controlled.

The murmur of conversation faded to nothing as the door opened and shut. There was an underlying energy, a tension between everyone, a collective breath being held. Reginald never opened that door, never stepped onto the dais. Interrupting Marcus was tantamount to signing your own death warrant.

A collective inhale echoed when Reginald stepped back into the room. He clapped his hands once to gain their attention, not that he needed to. Every eye was fixed on his ashen, grim face. He looked around the room, stopping when their eyes met. "Jordan, if you would join me, please."

She wasn't sure if the ringing in her ears was due to sudden nervousness or if it was the buzz of renewed conversation. She wove through the crowd without brushing against anyone. Or more accurately, the crowd stepped out of her way, giving her a clear path to Reginald. His expression was unreadable, but his pulse quickened at his throat. "Come with me, please."

He didn't lead her into the conference room or into Marcus's office as she expected. Instead, she followed Reginald into a side room she hadn't seen before. Marcus and Montgomery stood in front of a table, speaking quietly. On the table was—

Jordan gasped. Her hands clamped over her mouth to try to catch the noise. A vampire lay on the table, a stake plunged into his chest. It was the same vampire who attacked her the other night.

"Jordan?" A hand landed on her shoulder and squeezed. She shifted her gaze from the table to Montgomery. "Did you hear what I asked?"

"No." She shook her head. "I'm sorry. What was the question?"

"We need you to identify who killed Victor," Marcus said.

Victor. The jerk who had attacked her was named Victor. Trying to recall the details of their confrontation, she almost missed what Montgomery was asking. "Do you think you can shift and identify any scents on him?"

They wanted her to sniff the corpse? Her skin crawled. It made sense from a purely logical view. She could sift through the scents well enough to identify the killer in her lupine form. From an emotional point of view, she wanted to puke. She wasn't sure she'd be able to step close to the body, even with a duty to perform. She looked to Montgomery. "I'll try." She closed her eyes and focused as he withdrew his hand.

Jordan drew in a deep breath and turned her focus inward, trying to find the center of her canine instincts. She became more and more aware of her physical form. Her bra dug into her back. Her jeans were tight on her hips. Her blouse slid over her shoulders. But nothing changed. No prickling of her skin. No fur, no fangs, no claws. She opened her eyes and hung her head. "Sorry. I don't think I can right now."

"A pity," Marcus rumbled.

Montgomery replaced his hand on her shoulder. "She's still learning control. These aren't ideal circumstances for her to shift."

Marcus raised one eyebrow. "She did it in front of a larger audience under much more dire circumstances."

"Which she knew about going into." Montgomery gestured to the table. "She wasn't shocked unexpectedly by a dead body."

The slight flaring of Marcus's nostrils was the closest she had seen him come to snorting. "Is there anything she might be able to tell us?"

Jordan straightened her shoulders at the scorn in his voice. She pushed away from Montgomery and walked to the body.

There was little blood, which surprised her. He might have been asleep if it weren't for the piece of wood protruding from his chest. She closed her eyes to focus on her sense of smell and block out the phantom sensation of the two vampires' eyes on her. She might not have the keener senses of the wolf, but she could pick up something, she hoped. She inhaled deeply several times. Then sneezed.

"Anything?" Montgomery said.

"Not sure. Maybe . . ." Jordan pinched the bridge of her nose and rubbed her nostrils before risking another inhalation. There was a familiar sting. "Was he a drinker? Because all I can smell is alcohol . . . an ale of some sort, I think."

Marcus and Montgomery looked at each other. "It'd interfere with her sense of smell, drown out other scents" Montgomery said. "Don't we have video of the murder?"

Reginald shook his head. "The cameras in the garage were broken. They were scheduled to be repaired tomorrow," he added with a note of apology in his voice.

She edged closer to the body, studying the stake. Jordan held her hand above it without touching, curving her fingers like she was going to grab it. She flexed her fingers twice, studying the shape they made compared to the wood. "There are some gouges in the wood. They look like they might be claw marks."

Marcus's gaze snapped to her. "Are you absolutely certain?"

Montgomery leaned down to study them. He straightened up. "Definitely werewolf. Besides, when was the last time you heard of a bear strolling into the heart of Rancho Robles carrying a stake?"

Marcus crossed his arms over his chest. "This is not the time for humor, Montgomery."

He bowed his head. "I ask your forgiveness, sire. But at least Jordan is cleared."

"Is she?" Marcus studied her. "A stake might be not the preferred choice for a werewolf, but if she wasn't able to shift, she'd use whatever weapon she had at hand. And, of course, she is aware of how effective a stake would be."

Montgomery shook his head. "Then why would she say she didn't know who the killer was instead of naming a false murderer to throw us off her track?"

She bit her lip to keep the words 'I'm right here, guys' from spilling out. If it were Montgomery and Thorn, she'd have snapped at them without hesitation. The one time she had sassed off in front of Marcus, she had been warned never to do it again. This wasn't the situation to press her luck.

"Because she's telling the truth," Montgomery continued. "Besides, Victor was killed sometime this evening? She's been with me since sundown. And once we got here, she was with the other Family."

Marcus looked at his famulus. "Is that correct, Reginald?"

He nodded. "I saw Jordan come in and spotted her throughout the evening. I did not see her interact with anyone." He paused. "It would have been extremely difficult for her to have killed him."

"But not impossible?"

Reginald looked at Jordan and then away. "No. However I don't think she did it."

Montgomery looked at Marcus. "Is it enough of an alibi?"

"For me, for this particular murder? Yes. But I doubt others will accept it, given her history." He focused his eyes on Jordan. "You're sure you cannot sense anything that would identify the killer?"

Jordan shook her head and looked to the ground. "No, sir." There was a scent, something beneath the alcohol. It was vaguely familiar, but nothing she was confident enough to voice to the Elder. She'd talk to Montgomery about it when they were alone. Maybe hashing it out with him would help her place it.

"In that case, there is nothing more to be done at the moment," Marcus said. "The rest of the Conclave will be informed." He looked to Jordan and Reginald. "You will return to the Family and say nothing of this. They will be informed by their patrons."

Reginald bowed his head, Jordan a fraction of a second behind him. Both silently turned and left the room. She didn't bother saying the obvious as they walked back to the other room.

The quiet murmur of conversation died away when they stepped into the room. "There has been an incident," Reginald said. "Your patrons will be informing you about what happened shortly."

"Does this have anything to do with David's killing?" Molly asked.

"Yes, Margaret," he said. "But there is nothing more I can say at the moment. Please, hold your questions for your patrons."

Jordan could feel eyes scrutinizing her. The unspoken question hung heavy in the air. What did she have to do with it?

Which, she realized with a sinking sensation in her stomach, was what all the other vampires would be asking as well.

26

The moment the door shut on Marcus, Montgomery, and Reginald, the room broke into a buzz of conversation. There was nothing more gossipy than a gathering of curious vampires. Thorn included himself in that group. All of them had shared the rumors about werewolves attacking Family. And all of them were now discussing various theories with anyone willing to listen. Most of those theories were centered on Jordan.

"Any ideas why Elder Marcus called Montgomery to him?" Solomon Adams asked.

"No, not a one," Thorn lied.

"Maybe he's teaching Montgomery the proper way to deal with a rebellious famulus," he said.

Thorn's teeth ground together. "Jordan isn't rebellious. She's still learning."

"Perhaps. But with her wolf blood, Montgomery's biased in her favor and will let her get away with things he shouldn't."

Thorn rolled his eyes. "You were turned in the 1900s. You think it's scandalous women wear skirts revealing their ankles."

"Mark my words, Kelly Henderschott. Montgomery Cooper and his famulus will be the cause of the downfall of Elder Marcus."

"You also think television will cause the downfall of Elder Marcus."

"Technology will make it harder for us to hide," Solomon said. "Right now, I'm more worried the werewolves will get us first, especially with two of them accepted in our midst. Especially if Elder Marcus is favoring him over Rosanna."

Thorn opened his mouth to point out Montgomery was a vampire when Marcus and Montgomery stepped back into the room. Montgomery drifted through the crowd toward him. His eyes met Thorn's, and he gave the slightest shake of his head.

Marcus resumed his place on the dais. "I had originally gathered you here to inform you Emma Chase had been killed." He continued speaking despite the murmur running through the crowd. "The situation has escalated. Reginald has just informed me Victor Claddan was found with a stake through his heart."

The room went absolutely still. "So, it's not a werewolf doing it?" came a female voice from the back of the room.

Marcus shook his head. "It has not been confirmed. The stake had deep grooves in the blunt end that could match a werewolf's claws digging into the wood. I will be reaching out to Alpha Shane, but since he has already denied involvement in Sabrina's famulus's death, I do not expect him to take any responsibility for this either."

"The Black Oak Pack aren't the only werewolves in the area," cried a female voice. The crowd parted to reveal Rosanna, standing erect with arms crossed over her chest. "What about Montgomery's famulus?"

Thorn, out of the corner of his eye, watched Montgomery stiffen. "What about her?" Montgomery asked.

"Jordan was seen threatening Emma, was she not?"

"She lost her temper," Montgomery said. "It wasn't a threat."

"So she told you." She gestured to the crowd watching with rapt attention. "Speaking of which, can you tell us where she was earlier?"

Montgomery stared at her, his expression as flat as his inflection. "She was with me this evening before we arrived."

"All of this morning?" Rosanna purred. "Or only at dawn in your bed?"

Montgomery's eyes narrowed. "I'm not going to dignify that with an answer."

"Enough, you two," Marcus chided. "There was a witness to Emma's slaughter. A male was seen running from her." He addressed the rest of the crowd. "Are there any other questions?"

"Where was Victor's body found?" someone yelled.

Marcus's expression went stone solid. "Inside the parking structure beneath Hotel Cataluna."

An animated hum rose among the assembled vampires. "They had the temerity to destroy a vampire in the heart of Conclave territory?" Rosanna cried out above the rest. "How dare Alpha Shane—"

"We do not know for certain it is Alpha Shane," Marcus countered. "Nor can we accuse Montgomery's famulus. It could be another chaos wolf is in the area."

"Which would still be Alpha Shane's fault."

"Enough!" Marcus glared at Rosanna. The woman glowered back and then dropped her gaze. "I called you all here to inform you of the situation, not to debate fault. And I will not place blame until we have incontrovertible proof." He glared at Rosanna, waiting for her to make another statement. When she didn't, he continued. "Remember, be cautious, be safe. Until such a time as the threat is over, do not hunt if it can be avoided. Now go, and may the Bat's wings enfold you in a protective embrace."

As the crowds dispersed, Solomon spoke again. "I told you,

Kelly Henderschott. Montgomery Cooper and his famulus will be the downfall of Elder Marcus."

Thorn couldn't find it in himself to disagree with Solomon. "If that is the case," Thorn said, studying Rosanna's angry expression. "They might be the downfall of us all." He nodded once and headed in Montgomery's direction.

Montgomery stood by the dais, speaking with Marcus. The elder had stepped off the low stage and stood eye to eye with his brood. As he got closer, he could make out the last of Elder Marcus's words. "Given the situation, I would like you to give some serious thought to moving back here. It's escalating from Family to vampires. You might be the next target."

It was Marcus's usual ploy to regain control over his child's life. Thorn allowed himself a mental smirk. Montgomery had been turning down offers like this for the last ten years. But to his surprise, Montgomery drew in a deep breath. "I'll consider it."

Apparently, Montgomery's noncommittal answer was as good as an acceptance to Marcus. "I will order that your old quarters be prepared."

Montgomery bowed his head. "I'll reach out with my plans once I've made a decision."

"Take your famulus back to your apartment," Marcus said. "I'll look forward to your call." He turned and walked away.

Montgomery looked after him and then spun on his heel and left.

Thorn followed. "Bravo, Mac," he said once they reached the hall. A few vampires were walking toward the elevators, Family trailing behind them, wanting to make it to their homes before dawn. It was empty enough for him to be comfortable speaking freely. "I never thought you'd actually have the balls to lie to his face about moving back."

Montgomery's voice was flat as he stared straight ahead. "I wasn't lying."

"Wait. You're actually thinking about doing it?"

"Not the old rooms I shared with Christine," Montgomery said. "But yes. It might be better for us all if I moved back in."

"Why? You remember what it was like." Thorn swung around in front of him, grabbing Montgomery's upper arm. "Under twenty-four-hour surveillance? Marcus overseeing your every movement?"

Montgomery shook his arm free. "Is it any better than having someone I'm sleeping with reporting my every move to Marcus?"

Thorn's stomach dropped.

"What?" Montgomery snapped. "You didn't think I figured out why you've been staying at my apartment? Easier for you to spy on me?"

He smiled even though he felt the blood draining from his face. "Spying is such a strong word . . ."

"So, you're denying it, Kelly?"

He had used his real name. That was not good. "No, I'll admit it, Mac. Montgomery," he amended. "We were worried about you. Marcus asked me to keep an eye on you, nothing more."

"Before or after Jordan?" Montgomery's gaze pierced Thorn like a stake. "How far back?"

Maybe he could deflect. Or at least put it off until they were in a more private setting. "You really want to do this in public?"

"Answer the question."

Thorn sighed. "When Christine died."

Montgomery stiffened. "I see." He took a step closer. "I want you and your things out of my apartment before sunrise tomorrow. And today you can find somewhere else to sleep."

"Mac, it's not like that . . ."

"Yes, it is. I trusted you. Just as much as I trusted Christine. Hell, I turned to you for comfort after she died. I thought you were just watching out for me. I didn't listen to the voice that tried to tell me you had other reasons."

A dozen lies he had prepared for this situation sprang to his mind. To Thorn's surprise, he discarded them all for the truth.

"Yes, I was reporting to Marcus. He was worried about you and wanted to have someone keep an eye on you. Someone to make sure you didn't do something stupid. But he never ordered me to sleep with you."

"So, I guess sex was just a bonus for you."

"Don't act like you didn't enjoy it. You were perfectly happy with me bouncing in and out of your bed. You never said you wanted more."

"You never offered more. You didn't start regularly hanging around until Jordan appeared." He paused as if considering a new idea. "Is that why you're staying? I'm not letting you into my bed, but you'll climb into hers while you're waiting? One-stop shopping?"

Thorn narrowed his eyes. "We've done nothing since that night, and you know it."

"Not for lack of you asking her. Or did you think I didn't hear?"

"We were discussing the best thing to do. After we decided it wouldn't be good, we'd double-check we were still on the same pa—"

"Bullshit." Fangs down, Montgomery took a step closer. "What's really going on?"

Friend or not, he wasn't going to let a vampire who hadn't passed his first century threaten him. "Fine. I'll tell you what I think's going on." He stepped into Montgomery's space, his fangs down. There was no growl in his voice, but silky steel laced through every word. "I think you're using being captured by Rhys as an excuse to push us away because you feel guilty. You think you betrayed a woman who has been dead for almost thirty years. Or something more happened while you were captured by Rhys. Either way, you're punishing yourself."

Montgomery's body stiffened. "Don't come back tonight. Or ever again. My famulus will return your property to you." Before

Thorn could react, Montgomery spun away and barked into the room where the Family waited. "Jordan!"

Thorn turned away, walking toward the stairwell. He had no desire to be trapped in an elevator with Montgomery and Jordan. Mac needed time to cool off. He did too. Otherwise, they both might do something they would eventually regret. The problem was, Thorn reflected, he already had.

27

Jordan stood by the door to the hallway, listening to Montgomery and Thorn's conversation.

"Is your patron breaking up with his boyfriend?" Gloria asked.

Jordan shifted her weight from one leg to another as she bit her lower lip. "Sounds like it."

"Ah, Jordan. Good. You're still here." Jordan and Gloria turned from the door to face Reginald. He watched them with his normal inscrutable expression, mask firmly back in place. "Gloria, you're wanted upstairs to man the phone system."

Gloria curtsied. "Yes, sir." She scampered toward the other side of the room.

Reginald turned his attention to Jordan. "It's best you don't listen to them argue in such a public place. Or at least try to make it look like you're not spying."

His tone had been more instructive than chastising. Jordan bowed her head. "Yes, sir. I'm sorry."

"You don't have to apologize to me, Jordan. You aren't doing anything I haven't done. Just try not to be so obvious about it." He waved his hand, dismissing the subject. "I actually wished to speak to you, but our summons delayed it. You've been granted permission to meet with Margaret tomorrow night. Details will to be sent to your email. Your patron has been informed, of course."

"Thank you. Please pass my gratitude on to Elder Marcus." Not that Elder Marcus would care if she said it. Actually, given her reputation, he'd care more if she *didn't* say it.

"Jordan!" a voice snapped. She and Reginald turned to the door. Montgomery stood there. His expression was strained as he gestured toward the hall.

She nodded to her fellow famulus. "Again, please express my thanks to Elder Marcus. I will email you confirmation when I arrive home." She inclined her head in a bow and turned to join Montgomery. He turned on his heel and strode toward the elevator. She followed him at the prescribed half a yard behind and listened for any footsteps trailing them. Although a few grimly amused faces watched their progress, she couldn't detect anyone actively following them. When they reached the elevator, she ventured the question as she hit the down button. "Thorn?"

"Will not be joining us," Montgomery answered. "I do not wish to discuss it any further at the moment."

His words were his standard code for 'ask me when we're alone.' But the level of ice in his voice made her fight the urge to shiver. She glanced at his face and wasn't surprised at the expression of neutrality covering it. She looked away. *Not here, not now,* she told herself. Once they were alone, probably back home, he'd open up to her. Maybe. She hoped.

She bit her lip as they rode down to the lobby, silence as thick as a thermal blanket covering them. Any hope she had for an unobtrusive exit was dashed when the elevator doors opened. There were several vampires in the lobby. All of them turned dark looks on Jordan as she followed Montgomery out of the lobby. The one exception was Rosanna, who looked at her brother with a small, vicious smile. Had she witnessed the fight between him and Thorn? Or was the gossip chain that fast?

She expected something to indicate that a body was found earlier in the garage—a car parked askew, bloodstains on the wall, or perhaps yellow police or caution tape marking off an area. There was nothing to indicate a murder had taken place, nothing to scare the mortals in the area. Montgomery walked to his car as if they were leaving after any other meeting.

"Aren't we checking out where Victor was attacked?"

"No. By now, too many people will have been there. The scent will be too muddied unless you think you can shift."

"I don't think I can." Jordan hung her head again. What else would go wrong this night? "I'm sorry. I failed."

Montgomery's shoulders slumped. "It's not your fault. You're still learning. Given the shock of the situation, we're lucky you didn't spontaneously shift."

At least he was willing to talk to her about something. She started the car. "Home? Or is there anywhere else you want to go?"

Montgomery's jaw shifted back and forth. "Home. For now."

Jordan wasn't sure if he meant he might ask her to go somewhere else on the drive, or if she was to consider their apartment home only for the moment.

They pulled out into traffic in silence. Jordan kept quiet, wanting to concentrate on traffic. Even though the sun had long gone down, the area was a beehive of activity. People were still driving to the movies, to pick up children, to go to the bars, or for a late dinner. She did glance over to her right at stop lights. Montgomery stared straight ahead, stone faced. His eyes shifted, meeting hers, before he turned his head away.

The silence stretched through the entire drive. Montgomery was out of the car before she set the break in the parking spot at the apartment building. But once they were inside, she wouldn't let the awkwardness continue. "Montgomery, what happened?"

"Didn't you overhear?"

She bowed her head. "Some, but not all. Look, if it's something I did—"

"No. It's not your fault at all. Something that's been simmering under the surface between me and Thorn finally came to boil." He shook his head. "Remember what I warned you about when we all met?"

She frowned, quiet for a moment. "Something about him seeing me as a flavor of the week?"

"I didn't pay heed to my own warning. I always wondered why he was so supportive of me after Christine died. And why he was staying with us."

"And you found out why?"

"He's been ordered by Marcus to spy on me," Montgomery said.

"No." Jordan shook her head. "No, he wouldn't." Her defense sounded weak to her own ears. "How long? Since I started living with you?"

"Long before that. Since Christine died, at least." Montgomery shook his head.

Jordan's jaw dropped as she did the math. "Thirty years? You think he's been spying on you for over thirty years?"

"Which is the same as a week for most vampires."

But not for you. Thirty years would have been the sum of his existence as a vampire. "Maybe he was ordered by Elder Marcus, but he wasn't staying with us because he was ordered to." She hated how uncertain the last two words were.

"I don't know," Montgomery said. "He doesn't normally spend more than four or five with me before he heads off to his next conquest. The fact that he's been practically moved in for the last three months should have alerted me that something was wrong."

"Yeah, but you wouldn't have been kidnapped by an insane werewolf any of those other times." She paused, pulling together the phrasing she wanted. "You think he might actually love you?"

"If he does, he has a funny way of showing it."

"I'm not following, Montgomery. Exactly what did Thorn do wrong?"

"We had an agreement. We were going to be up front with each other about what was going on. I kept my side of the deal. I thought Thorn was."

It clicked into place for Jordan. "Except he was meeting with Marcus?"

"Yeah. I knew he was called in from time to time. We all are. It's one of Marcus's ways to keep an eye on things."

"So, what's the difference?"

"Marcus specifically ordered him to keep an eye on me."

"You think he ordered him to sleep with you?"

"I . . . I don't know. All I'm certain of is I trusted him and told him things I'd rather Marcus didn't know. And I have no way of being certain he didn't repeat them to Marcus." He shook his head. "I trusted him. I . . ."

"Love him," Jordan finished.

Montgomery jerked, then looked away from her. "Is it that obvious?"

"You wouldn't be hurting so much if you didn't." She reached out to squeeze his hand. "What triggered the fight?"

"Marcus has suggested I move back to the Hotel Cataluna, and I'm considering it. I used to live there with Christine," he said. "I moved out after her death, but Marcus asks me to come back every so often. Normally I say no. He doesn't accept no as an answer."

"Why'd you move out?"

"Too many memories. Not enough autonomy. I wanted to feel like I was able to handle things on my own, not have them handed to me on a silver platter, pardon the joke. Prove that although I was the son of the Elder of Rancho Robles, I was my own person. But if there's a werewolf stalking vampires and

Family . . ." He shook his head. "It might be the safest for the both of us."

"You think you might be a target?"

"I'm more worried about you," Montgomery said. "Marcus saying he believes your alibi won't keep some of the other vampires from thinking you had something to do with it. Whoever this killer is, they know too much about how the Family operates."

"And," Jordan added with a sigh, "I'm known to have had a conflict with each of them recently. Including Victor."

"You did? When?"

"A few days ago. He was the one hunting near the Cataluna who didn't recognize me."

"Damn, it, Jordan." Montgomery sighed. "About the only thing that could clear you is for you to be killed and the murders to continue."

She shook her head. "I think I read a mystery book like that once."

"Do you remember who did it by any chance?"

Jordan swallowed. "It was the person the protagonist believed with all his heart couldn't have done it."

Montgomery shook his head.

"So, Thorn wanted you to move back also?"

"No, he seemed to be against it. But if he's been lying to me the whole time . . ." He shook his head. "I have one assignment for you to do tonight."

"What do you need done?"

"I need you to help pack up Thorn's things and arrange to return them to him tomorrow before your meeting with Molly."

Jordan swallowed. "Are you sure you don't want to wait a night or two? Talk to him after you've both had a chance to cool off?"

"No. The sooner it's done, the better."

28

A bell tinkled as Jordan stepped into the tattoo parlor. A woman with hair dyed a shade of red most often found on cardinals rested her elbows on the counter, thumbs tapping at her phone. She looked up and smiled, teeth flashing as brightly as the light glinting off the ring piercing her right nostril. "Hi. Welcome to the Wilted Rose. Do you have an appointment?"

"Not exactly." Jordan lifted the duffel bag a few inches. "I'm here to drop this off for Thorn."

"Oh. You must be Jordan. The boss said you were coming in. He wants to talk to you." She pushed up. "Wait here," she said and walked around a counter and through a curtained door.

Jordan looked around, studying the different pictures of completed tattoos and sketches. She traced her fingers over a line drawing of a howling wolf and a swooping bat. For all the time they'd spent together in Montgomery's apartment, they weren't aware of much about Thorn's life outside, or of his past. Montgomery put it down as most vampires considering it rude to ask about a vampire's past. They either volunteered the information, or they didn't. Maybe that was why they were addicted to gossip.

The red-headed woman popped her head out from between the curtains. "He can meet with you now. Follow me."

Jordan followed her through a room divided into three curtained cubicles. High-pitched buzzing and low conversation floated past the fabric. The employee stopped at a door and knocked on it. At Thorn's muffled "send her in," she opened the door and gestured Jordan inside

The door opened on Thorn getting up from a chair. "Thanks, Charla." As the woman nodded and closed the door, he crossed the space to wrap Jordan in a hug. "Hey, Jo."

She sighed and relaxed into the embrace. "Hey Thorn."

He pulled back to squint at her. "You look like hell. Didn't sleep well?"

"Yeah." She sighed, hefting the duffel bag. "Brought your stuff."

"Thanks." Thorn grunted. He took the bag from her and led her to a chair by the desk. "How's he doing?"

Jordan shrugged as she sat. "Upset. Tense. Snappy. But no nightmares."

"At least there's one good thing." He dropped the bag on top of his desk before leaning against it. "I'm sorry to put you in this situation."

She sank further into the chair. "Montgomery told me his side. I want to hear yours. What happened between you two?"

"Mac discovered something I was ordered to do a long time ago."

"So, you were ordered to sleep with him."

"As well as to spy on him and report back to Elder Marcus. Which came after we slept together for the first time. But he won't believe anything I say."

Jordan crossed her arms. "I'm not sure I should."

"Fair enough, but I can give you a reason to believe I'm telling the truth." He met her eyes without any of his usual trademark snark. "I haven't slept with anyone else since the night you shifted in front of the Black Oak Pack. And you may not be able to smell as well as a wolf while human, but your sniffer is good enough to pick up if I've been skin to skin with anyone else."

She hummed softly through her nose. "That may be true, but staying away doesn't really help your case. Especially if you're reporting everything to Elder Marcus"

"I know it doesn't look good. I care about Mac. I really do. I'm too old to call it love but . . ." Thorn shook his head. "I only told Marcus the minimum to keep him happy. And never anything damaging to Montgomery in the long run.

"So how do we convince Montgomery?"

"That's not the problem, Jo. The problem is he trusted me. Probably more than he should have. I'm sure he thought I was being upfront with him about everything."

"And you weren't. And you aren't with me either."

"Jordan, think about your past friends. Right or wrong, how many times was there something you held back because you believed telling them would cause more problems?"

Of course there was a situation her mind immediately went to. Something she'd have to face shortly. After she left here, in fact. "Yeah."

"Add the weight of decades of holding it in. Most of us vampires are tied in so many emotional knots we'd send any psychiatrist screaming out of their office."

Jordan frowned. "Still doesn't make it right," she said. "Look at it from his point of view. You helped him through the roughest time of his life. Now he's thinking all of it was a lie."

"I know. I should have told him then. And it may be too late now for him to listen to me." He shook his head. "I've seen him upset before, when Christine died. I've never seen him direct any of it at me. And I deserve it." He frowned. "Aren't you going to ask me if I was reporting on you?"

Jordan shrugged, an efficient lifting and falling of her shoulders. "With everything I've been told about Elder Marcus, I assumed that was a given." She drew in a deep breath. "So, what does this mean for us?"

"It's up to you. I'm aware this puts you in an awkward situation with Mac. And I can't say he'll forgive me any time soon."

"I'm his famulus," she said. "And more importantly, I think he needs my support right now."

"I can't disagree." He sighed. "And I'm glad you said that. As much as I didn't want you to."

She sighed. "Can't you talk to him? Just get together somewhere private and hash this out?"

"He's not willing to listen to me. And I can't say I blame him." Thorn paused. "You're meeting with Molly tonight? I should let you get going."

She slumped. "Another thing I'm not looking forward to."

"Why? You said you wanted this meeting."

"I do, it's just . . ." She rested her elbow on her knee and her chin on her fist. "I want what I can't have. I want to be able to get together with her and watch movies on a couch. Order a pizza and gorge ourselves. Be able to send each other stupid texts about how our day is going."

"You want my old friendship back," Thorn said. "You want your human life back."

His gentle tone made her stiffen. "No, or not exactly. Things can't be the way they were before. Too much has changed, between us both becoming Family and me a werewolf. And by now she'll know about Rhys and why he killed Darren." Her voice became small. "And I didn't tell her."

"Oh, Jordan." Thorn slipped off the table and crossed the room to her. He rested a hand on her shoulder. "You weren't in a position to share that with her, ever. If you had told her, Marcus would have ordered you both killed. Her for being in possession of information about the supernatural. You because it would have been seen as a betrayal of your oath as Family." He squeezed his hand. "It may be hard for you to understand, but by lying to her, even a lie of omission, you saved her life."

She leaned into his touch, soaking up the comfort he offered. "I don't think she'll see it that way,"

"I hate to say it, Jo, but she's also keeping secrets from you. Think about it. As Marcus's famulus, she has to be familiar with everyone in the Conclave—all the vampires and their Family, as well as all the werewolves she'd need to be aware of. And you'd be high on the list of two of those. She didn't exactly reach out to you first."

"But she hadn't taken the oath yet."

Thorn waggled his hand back and forth. "At Marcus's level, the oath is more of a public formality. Since Marcus was willing to introduce her, he was certain of her loyalty. Otherwise, she'd have been a meal. Or disposed of quietly another way."

A shiver ran down her spine at his words. "I can't believe you're so matter-of-fact about murder."

To her surprise, his expression sagged. She had seen him be serious on rare occasions, but now he leaned forward as if bearing the weight of millennia on his shoulders. "You're not used to being with a long-lived vampire. Mac's practically a baby. Live over five centuries and see how your outlook shifts." He rested both hands on her shoulders, staring into her eyes. "You don't have to do this, Jordan. You don't have to face her."

Jordan closed her eyes. It would be easy to back away, go curl up in a corner and hide, take the out he was giving her. "No." She opened her eyes with a slight shake. "This isn't about closure for her. It's about closure for me."

A warm, approving smile spread across Thorn's face. The humorous gleam was back in his eyes. He stroked his thumb under her chin. "That's my girl."

Part of her glowed under Thorn's approval. And his touch, however brief it might be. "We still haven't solved what to do about Montgomery."

"You let me worry about Mac." He kissed her forehead. "Come here any time you need to, day or night. My door is always open to you."

"Thanks." She leaned against him for a moment and then pushed back. "I should get going. Otherwise I'll be late."

Thorn nodded once. "I'll check in with you tomorrow night. And Jordan, even though she was your friend, now she's Marcus's famulus. Be careful."

29

———————

This evening when she came into the Hotel Cataluna, instead of heading to the private elevators at the end of the lobby, she went to the restaurant. Not the attached high-end fancy restaurant where a steak cost as much as she made a day at her old cashier job, but the one catering to those on a budget. Designed to draw in people staying at the hotel and shoppers passing by, it had several large screen televisions tuned to different sporting events. The casual atmosphere wasn't in keeping with Marcus's classy style, but as Thorn had pointed out, he had to pay for his fancy art collection somehow.

She followed the hostess to a corner table. Although she wasn't a fan of football, which was what was playing on the screens now, Jordan found herself watching them instead of keeping an eye out for the person she had come to see. Arriving before her friend reminded her of the first days when she and Molly had moved into the apartment, before she met Darren. The memory sent an ache through her. Jordan, usually making it home first, cooked dinner. Molly then ran in from class to shower and eat before her campus job began. Because time was so tight, she'd plop herself down opposite Jordan and began eating. Odds were fifty-fifty she'd say hello before the third forkful.

She glanced away from the screens to keep an eye on the entrance. A second later, Molly stepped into the room and scanned the tables for her. For a second, the old memory appeared to be playing itself out. Instead, Molly walked across the room, all poise and polish. In other words, very much the famulus of a high-ranking vampire she was. "Jordan Abbey," she said with a formality at odds with the surroundings. "May I join you?"

She ignored the way her breath caught at the stab of pain. "Of course." Montgomery had warned her that her friend would act differently. At the same time, it hurt she was being treated like a foreign dignitary instead of a friend. "I thank you and your patron for allowing the meeting," she said, completing the formal request.

Before they could continue, the waitress scuttled over to their table. "What can I get you ladies?"

Jordan glanced at the menu. She wasn't really hungry, but they needed the camouflage. "Black cherry soda and the chicken nachos."

"The usual," Molly said, handing her menu to the waitress. The waitress nodded and hustled off.

Jordan arched her eyebrows. "The usual?"

Molly shrugged. "Sometimes it's easier to come down here than have food delivered from the kitchen."

"You have a usual?" She should have guessed. While they were the vampire's daylight servants, their time in the sun was minimal. Compounded with regular blood loss, most Family members gained a pale cast to their skin. There were no visible bruises on Molly's neck or wrist, but they may have been on her elbows, hidden under the mid-arm sleeves.

Molly shrugged. "I was kept separate from anyone but

Marcus's Family while I was taught the rules. I didn't think about you being in the area until the introduction last night."

"Yeah, last I heard you were at your parents." She wanted to ask how much Molly had been told about her, but the waitress returned with several plates. Jordan's soda and nachos were placed in front of her. Molly only had a coffee cup. She lifted it and took a deep drink. Jordan's nose wrinkled as she smelled the cream and whiskey in it.

Molly scowled at Jordan. "Something you wanted to ask?"

"How—" Jordan glanced around. The word came out sharper and louder than she had intended. "How did you become, well, one of us?" she asked in a much softer tone.

Molly looked down and twisted her coffee cup. Jordan recognized her friend's tell. Molly was trying to decide the best way to deliver something she considered bad news. "They found me about a month after it happened," she said without looking at Jordan. "I don't know how, or if I did something to give myself away." She looked at Jordan from under her brows. "Did you tell them?"

"I had to give them your name, since you were in . . . the apartment. But I kept you out of it as much as I could." Jordan guessed the rest of the story. It was probably something like what she went through. "They gave you a choice?"

Molly sighed, her expression grim. "Cake or death. It was funnier when we watched that comedy special." There was little humor in her voice. Molly's fingers strayed to the gold links of the bracelet on her wrist. They lightly stroked the matching charm, the fang piercing a circle above the ruby stone. "It's not as bad as I thought it would be. I'm one of fourteen women. He only takes my blood once a week, and the rest of the time I'm free to do whatever I want, as long as I don't leave the building. It's kinda boring, actually."

Jordan relaxed. Her experiences didn't match the nightmares

Jordan had imagined about Molly being forced to submit both blood and in body. "Did you tell him you knew me?"

"Once I saw you the other night, yeah. Your patron . . . um, Montgomery. Does he know?"

"Yeah. I was upset and he asked me." Jordan tilted her head. "Marcus is okay with it?"

Molly shrugged. "He doesn't discuss those types of things with me."

"Yeah, I guess he wouldn't." Marcus struck her as one who wouldn't have deep discussions with his food. She drew in a deep breath, preparing to ask the question she was dreading the answer to. "How did you become Elder Marcus's famulus?"

Molly looked down at the coffee cup again. "I was in the cemetery one night. Visiting . . ." Her voice faded for a moment. "He knew who I was, what had happened to Darren, and what I had seen." She shivered again.

Jordan swallowed. Exactly how much did Molly know about the night Darren had died? "What did you see?"

"Darren in the middle of the room, mangled. And what I thought was a big, gray dog until it ran out on its hind legs and crashed through your window." Both women shivered. Molly continued her story. "Instead of killing me, Marcus offered me a choice. I could become his famulus and live, or I could die then and there." She bit her lower lip. "It wasn't much of a choice."

"Yeah, I can see." Jordan paused, trying to come up with the best words for her next questions. "Are you . . . I don't know how to put it." Happy wasn't the right word. Nor was content.

Molly twisted her cup again. Her mouth opened and shut a few times before she answered. "I'm . . . okay. I really can't put it any way but that." She pulled out her cell phone from her purse and checked it. "I'm afraid I'm wanted upstairs. I should get going."

Jordan nodded, wondering if he was observing through a hidden camera, or if some of the customers were quietly reporting events in real time. *Probably both.* Just because Marcus had allowed a meeting didn't mean he wasn't controlling it. That was why Molly was leaving after having just arrived. It couldn't be she didn't want to be around her.

Both women rose from the table and exchanged an awkward, stiff hug. "Maybe we can make this a regular thing," Molly said.

Jordan smiled with her mouth only. She had gotten a nose full of Molly's perfume and was trying to suppress a sneeze. "Sure. We'll have to do it again sometime," she said, a pang stabbing deep in her chest. They were both lying to each other—and themselves.

"I'll be in touch."

Jordan watched Molly turn and go, a weight settling on her heart as she sat back in her seat. That was when the server swung by, her smile plastered in place. "Would you like me to box your plate to go?"

Jordan looked down. The nachos were untouched. "Yeah," she said, pushing the food toward her.

"I'll be back with your bill."

"Thank you." Jordan sat back, eyes wet with unshed tears. She was lying to Molly as much as Molly was lying to her. She knew it, and she suspected Molly did too. But it wasn't until she got to the car that the stomach-knotting questions crossed her mind. How long would Molly last as Marcus's famulus? And when she did die, would it be Jordan's fault?

30

The knot in Jordan's stomach didn't unclench during the drive to the apartment. Instead, it settled in her gut like a permanent part of her anatomy. It grew heavier as she rode up the elevator. It reminded her of the queasiness she'd felt the day her first quarterly report card from her freshman year of high school was scheduled to arrive in the mail. That lump hadn't dissolved until hours after her parents' questions about how she planned to pull her grades up to pass the semester.

She stepped into the apartment, carrying the box of leftovers. The scent of chicken and sour cream didn't help the nausea. "I'm back," she called out as she stepped into the kitchenette.

Montgomery appeared in the doorway as she opened the refrigerator. "How did it go?"

She placed the nachos on the shelf and turned to Montgomery. The door swung shut with a soft thump as she walked to him. She wrapped her arms around him, hiding her face against his chest.

He didn't push her away, but it took a moment for him to embrace her. "Jordan? Did something happen?"

"No." She hugged him tighter. "Give me a minute."

Montgomery patted her back like an awkward teenager not sure what to do with his hands. "Did something go wrong?"

"No." She pulled away and looked up at him. "We talked about what happened to her. She's basically a pretty face for Marcus to feed from. She can't leave the hotel for even the smallest reason. Everything is brought to her. She's living in a gilded cage, waiting to die."

"That's how most older vampires handle their affairs. A lot of vampires use their Family for blood as well as daylight errands. But Marcus likes to keep the ones he feeds from protected. Or at least that's how he sees it."

She tapped her fingers against the countertop. "It just kinda hit me while I was listening to her describe what she has to do. It's all stuff you've never asked of me."

Montgomery shrugged. "It's different for each famulus and patron. What is he asking her to do?"

"I think he's just drinking her blood. She didn't say she was having to sleep with him."

"That fits Marcus's style. He tends to collect beautiful young women for food. He doesn't deliberately kill them, but accidents do happen. When they grow older, he finds them places in the hotel to work. He rarely kills outright unless he has a reason to. He's gentler with his Family than a lot of others I know. Some consider it a weakness."

Jordan shivered. "I don't get it."

"Get what?"

"No matter how much I try to imagine it, I can't picture you or Thorn doing that." She noted the slight twitch of Montgomery's lips at the mention of the other vampire's name. "The killing. I've seen you both drink blood, but I can't picture you attacking someone at random on the street."

"Every vampire deals with the urge to drink blood in a different way. For me, I had so much practice with shapeshifting and controlling the wolf urges, it wasn't hard for me to apply it to the bloodlust. Also, the fact I prefer animal blood is a big aid." He looked away and sighed. "As for Thorn, I think it's a game for him to see how far he can seduce someone and feed without being noticed," he continued, heading into the living room.

Jordan followed. "There's another thing. I've always wondered why Thorn is the only vampire I've seen who doesn't have a famulus."

Montgomery sat on the couch, eyes going distant. For a moment, Jordan debated if it had been a mistake to say Thorn's name. Whether Montgomery was remembering or his name brought pain, she couldn't say. "I don't think I've heard him talk about having a famulus the entire time I've known him." His tone was one of instruction, one she hadn't heard from him since the night she'd tracked him to the cabin. "Having Family used to be a sign of status among vampires. Only Elders and high-ranking blood-children would have them, or they'd be gifted by the Elders to someone who had performed a great service to the Conclave. But it became necessary for vampires to hide and deal with humans during the daylight hours. While claims of illness and bribes help some, more and more younger vampires started taking on Family. Some, however, honor the original tradition and will not take one."

"Hard to believe Thorn does anything traditionally," Jordan murmured as she perched beside him on the edge of a cushion.

"Okay, maybe it's the wrong word to use when it comes to Thorn." He shrugged. "Given the lifestyle Thorn choses to lead, a Family member would be more of a hindrance than a help." He paused, turning to face her a little more. "Speaking of which, did you talk with him?"

Jordan nodded. "Yes. I dropped off his things."

"That's not what I asked."

Jordan sighed and leaned back into the cushions. "I talked with him. He's . . . worried about you."

She didn't think it was possible for Montgomery's expression to become more closed off. Somehow, he managed to tighten his features further. "He has a funny way of showing it."

"You kicked him out. Publicly, I might add." She shook her head and twisted, resting her weight on her hip. "And he knows you're angry. He's giving you the time and distance you wanted."

"I don't want distance from him. I wanted him to deny it."

"And you warned me about him from the start. 'Flavor of the week.' Remember? Why didn't you think he was spying on you?" Montgomery shifted his weight to get off the couch. She rested a hand on his. "I'm not saying you're stupid or should have known better. I want to understand where your head's at."

He remained balanced for a second. Jordan was about to withdraw her hand when he slumped, leaning into the cushions. "I thought . . . no. I hoped he . . ."

"Loved you," Jordan finished.

"Yeah." Montgomery stared down into his lap.

And what about me? She grimaced inwardly. *Stop that.* This wasn't about her, or at least not at this moment. "So, what are you going to do next?"

"Do next?" Montgomery shook his head. "There is no next."

Jordan blinked. He wouldn't fight for Thorn? "But you said you love him."

"Just because I love him doesn't mean I can trust him."

31

Thorn sat in the leather chair across from Marcus's desk, forcing himself to stillness. Marcus hadn't said anything when he entered the chambers. The elder vampire studied several papers, picking them up from one pile, reading them over, and then placing them face down in another stack in an open folder. The precision of the actions put Thorn on edge. Marcus had a reputation for appearing to not pay attention to his target before he unsheathed his fangs and attacked. It was his favorite tactic to put people ill at ease. And Thorn had to admit, with a grudging admiration, it was working. But not showing any reaction irritated Elder Marcus to no end.

Marcus lifted the second-to-last page, scanned it, and spoke. "Care to explain the little display in the hallway last night, Kelly?"

Thorn twitched as Marcus put down the paper. Dammit, the Elder had gotten under his skin. Using his given name just added salt to the wound. "I didn't notice you in the hall," he said.

He picked up the last page. This one he didn't read. His eyes focused on Thorn's. "Between the witnesses and the security cameras, I have a complete record of what happened."

Thorn spread his hands. "I told you Montgomery was smart. He finally put two and two together."

"It took him long enough. What do you think tipped him off?"

"He had a meeting with Rosanna between the time I met him and last night. She's still angry with him. I wouldn't be surprised if she outright told him."

Marcus nodded once. "And what steps have you taken to regain his trust?"

He steeled himself for the coming reaction. "I have moved out. Jordan returned my things earlier this evening."

Disbelief dripped from Marcus's voice. "You're regaining his trust by leaving him alone?"

"I'm giving him time to get past his first rush of anger," Thorn countered. "He needs time to calm down and remember this is what vampires do. We don't trust each other implicitly or completely. Remember, Montgomery was a werewolf. He still thinks in terms of the pack, or at least the idealized version since he never really experienced firsthand that their internal politics are just as nasty as ours."

"And you are sure this is the right move?"

"He won't listen to me right now, especially if I keep pushing. He will listen to Jordan, and she's worried about his emotional health. If nothing else, she'll confide in me and keep me updated."

"Until she figures out you're using her for information."

Thorn waved a hand in an expansive gesture. "I was one of her first friends after she was bitten. Her emotions will cloud her logic some. Maybe enough to have her persuade Montgomery to take me back. Or at least resume our friendship."

"This sounds like it will take some time."

Thorn leaned back. "What's time to an immortal?"

"Still, I'd like to have you closer to him. Or perhaps I should order someone else to cultivate a close relationship to him, or to his famulus."

A wave of jealousy and territoriality flashed over him. He tamped down the emotions. If he'd reveal how attached he was to Montgomery and Jordan, he would hand Marcus yet another weapon to use against them all. "Anyone attempting to seduce him, especially this close to our public blow out, will make him suspicious. I'll handle it. You have to let me do this in my own way and my own time if you want him to trust us at all."

Marcus glared at him. Thorn returned the stare with a neutral expression. "You had better, Kelly, for your own sake."

Thorn kept his face still. Marcus didn't make naked threats. Something had him rattled. Surely it wasn't that Montgomery had figured out he was a spy. "Is there anything else, sir?"

"Yes." Marcus lowered the last page, tilting it so Thorn could see. It was a photograph, a selfie judging from the angle of the hunch of the blond's shoulder. He had seen that woman's face last night when Montgomery had placed a Family necklace around her throat. There was no mistaking the brunette, even if her hair was slightly longer than she wore it now. Jordan and Molly looked younger and full of hope for a bright future he was certain didn't include vampires or werewolves. "My researchers didn't turn up a connection between my new famulus and Jordan Abbey. I want you to look into why, and how deep their association goes." He placed the photo on the stack, closed the folder, and pushed it toward Thorn.

Thorn's eyebrows lifted. "Montgomery doesn't trust me, and you want me to go poking into his famulus's past? Are you sure that's smart?"

"You do not need to be concerned if I'm being smart or not. I have given you your assignment. Now see it through."

Thorn rose. He picked up the folder and tucked it under his arm. "Have I failed you before?"

"No," Marcus admitted. "Don't let this be the time."

Thorn nodded. "I will report in as soon as I make any progress." He headed to the carven doors.

Once back in the small lobby, he spent a few minutes flirting with Helen before continuing. Thorn kept up the devil-may-care appearance until he reached the elevator. Once the doors closed, he leaned against the walls and looked at the folder with the same level of caution as if he were handling a snake. This was the first mistake he'd ever heard of Marcus's security making. It was the first sign he wasn't holding the territory in an omnipotent fist. And the moment that fact began to filter across the city, it would be the beginning of the end for him. Maybe the end was a decade away, but vampires were, for the most part, patient creatures. Someone would use this to their advantage in a bid to take over eventually.

The questions were who would make the first move and who would survive the fallout. And to his surprise, he found himself hoping Montgomery and Jordan made it through with him unscathed.

32

Jordan pushed the grocery cart across the parking lot to the green SUV. Out of habit, she glanced to the west. Long shadows were starting to meld into the dark of night. She fumbled the keys out of her pocket and hit the fob. After the ubiquitous warning beep, the trunk popped open.

As she lifted the two bags of groceries over the tailgate, an authoritative voice cut through the air. "Alpha Shane said you're not allowed to hunt in this territory."

Jordan stiffened, one canvas bag slipping the last few inches to thud into the trunk. She really hoped it wasn't the one with the eggs in it. After fighting the grocery cart with the frozen wheel for the last hour, she did not want to go back into the store. She looked over her shoulder to snort in Angela's direction. "I'm buying groceries. While they call it bargain hunting, it's not the same thing, and you know it."

Angela crossed her arms over her chest. "You're procuring food without permission that might have gone to feed the Black Oak Pack," she stated. "Same thing."

"Seriously?" Jordan slammed the trunk shut and swung around to face Angela. "You're comparing buying a microwave burrito with bringing down a full-grown deer? Besides, this is the city, not the woods. It's Conclave territory. I have every right to be here, while you're only allowed in at the sufferance of Elder Marcus."

Angela bristled. The woman took a stiff-legged step toward her. "We're claiming it back from the leeches, like we should have a long time ago."

Jordan stretched taller and squared her shoulders. She growled low. "I'd so like to see you try."

Angela's eyes flashed as she bared her teeth. Jordan mirrored her expression. She was tired of the constant harassment and the unique interpretations of the rules. Jordan's toes flexed inside her shoes, seeking better purchase. Her fingers curled into claws. Her skin itched as fur threatened to burst forth from her follicles. Angela stood still, watching and waiting. Jordan tensed, teeth bared, ready to leap and shift, hoping to get her fangs into Angela's throat before the other werewolf did the same.

She jumped as a hand landed on her shoulder. "Ladies, ladies," said Thorn in a calm voice. "This is not the time nor the place to air your dirty laundry."

Angela's eyes narrowed. Her body tensed, hostility splitting between Jordan and Thorn. "This is none of your business, vampire."

"She's my friend," Thorn said. Jordan glanced out of the corner of her eye at him. His voice was calm and his expression serene, but the hand on her shoulder gripped harder. "That makes it my business, pup."

Angela's lips peeled from her teeth. Her fingers curled into fists and then opened, as if she had already shifted and released her claws. Thorn had obviously hit a nerve. Just like Angela had been poking at hers. Shame and realization cut through the anger, lowering the intensity to something she could leash. Thorn was right. Marcus would be displeased if she fought, let alone shifted, in full view of mortals. Alpha Shane wouldn't agree with the weak argument Angela put forth, but of course he'd side with his daughter. And more importantly, Montgomery and Thorn would be disappointed in her. It was a trap, and she had blindly walked into it. "Angela, just go," she said in a quiet voice. "If Alpha Shane has a problem with me grocery shopping, have him lodge a formal complaint with Elder Marcus."

Thorn's hand squeezed again. This time the motion was gentler, approving. He stepped up beside Jordan, mouth opening to say something. What came out was a pained grunt as the crack of a rifle echoed through the air. His grip on her shoulder tightened and then released as he staggered away from her and collapsed to his knees. Angela squawked and dropped to the ground. Tires squealed as a gray sedan tore out of a parking spot.

Jordan turned and reached for Thorn. He was holding his shoulder. The stench of hot metal, burned flesh, and blood tainted the air. "Go!" he urged through clenched fangs. "Sic 'em, Jordan."

Jordan bolted away, targeting in the sedan. Angela sprinted in the same direction. She glanced at Angela out of the corner of her eye as she caught up, but Angela didn't threaten her. For the moment, her enemy had become a packmate as they hunted their prey.

They raced across the parking lot toward the car. But the sedan was faster. It pulled out of the lot and disappeared into traffic before Jordan could read the license plate. Jordan's nose was flooded with the scent of jasmine and gunpowder, drowning out the scent of whoever had stood there. Broken glass glittered in the spot the car had pulled into.

She and Angela backed away from the broken perfume bottle, gagging. "You let him get away!" Angela snapped as soon as they were able to draw a clear breath.

"I was making sure Thorn was okay!"

"If you hadn't hung back, the shooter might have taken a second shot at you, and we'd have caught him!"

"You're the Alpha's daughter. You're as much of a target as me!"

"Yeah, but I don't hang around leeches."

Jordan fisted her hand and then forced it open. Angela was provoking her again. At least this time she had caught on much earlier. "Are we going to continue fighting?" Jordan asked. "Or are we going to report what happened?"

Angela snorted. Jordan wasn't sure if it was in derision or from trying to clear her nose of the cloying perfume. The she-wolf spun on her heel and marched away. She looked back over her shoulder to call out, "We're not done, chaos wolf."

"Of course we're not." Jordan sighed as sirens approached in the distance. "Damn it!" In the sweep of instinct to hunt their attacker, she had forgotten Thorn. She dashed back to the car. A splatter of blood painted the side of Montgomery's car. More blood smeared the door handle. Blue hair pressed against the inside of the passenger seat window.

The sirens grew louder and higher in pitch. Jordan jumped into the driver's seat. Muscle memory made her put on the seat-belt before she started the car. "How bad is it?"

Thorn had bundled up the hem of his T-shirt and pressed it to his shoulder. The gray fabric was turning a rusty brown. "I'll live," he grunted and then hissed. "Get me to the Cataluna, now."

She cranked the engine and yanked the transmission into gear. "Montgomery's is closer—"

"Cataluna! Now!"

"Okay!" Her knuckles were white from her grip on the steering wheel. The hand gripping the steering wheel trembled as the rush of adrenaline drained from her system.

They had made it a block away from the parking lot when two police cars, lights flashing and sirens blaring, raced past her in the opposite direction. "Someone reported the gunshots."

"Keep driving," Thorn growled. He leaned against the

passenger window, eyes pressed shut. "Marcus can clean this up later."

Most of her attention remained on the road, trying to drive normally and not attract attention. Every block or so she'd glance at Thorn. She didn't like how pale he was, or how the tips of his fangs poked out from under his upper lip.

His eyes popped open, sclerae solid black—a predator's gaze. Now she understood the fear the doe she'd stalked the other night had experienced. "Thorn?"

The vampire hissed. The answer couldn't be more clear. Thorn wasn't here right now. Instead, a hurt and hungry vampire stared back at her like she was the finest cut of filet mignon. He needed blood, and the sooner he got it, the better.

She did some quick calculations. Cataluna was twenty minutes away, if all the traffic lights were with them. They were ten minutes away from Montgomery's home if every light stayed green and twenty-five if they got stopped at each one. If the predatory gleam in his eye was any indication, he wasn't going to last ten minutes.

Jordan pulled into a parking structure. Most of the employees had left, leaving it abandoned for the moment. She swallowed and shut off the engine, then turned to face Thorn and bit back a gasp of shock. While she had seen feeding vampires before, she had never seen Thorn with his game face on, as he called it. "Thorn?"

His focus snapped to her. There was no sense of his warm, humorous personality behind those flat coal-black eyes. He growled, overhead lights glinting off his fangs. "Thorn," she said, hoping she could reach him. "You need blood. You can feed from m—"

He tackled her. Her head slammed against the window. His hand grabbed her hair and yanked, twisting her chin away from her neck. He bit down, fangs breaking skin, and began to feed.

Jordan's breath froze as sensations and images flooded her. A sharp pain in her neck from being bitten. Screaming in agony, thrashing on the ground, bones breaking and reforming, wing membranes splitting and wrapping around shortened claws to create hands. Diving from the sun into the blessed darkness of a cave, the scent of charred flesh filling the air.

Sweat broke out over her skin. She shivered. Her eyes tried to focus on the dashboard, but the dials remained stubbornly fuzzy. Too much. He was taking too much. She pawed at his shoulders, unable to summon more than weak half-aimed slaps. Darkness rimmed the edges of her vision as her body went limp. She couldn't pull in enough air.

The suction on her neck stopped.

"Shit!" A hand patted her face, gentle at first then harder. Hands shook her shoulders much like she had wanted to shake Thorn's. "Jo! Jordan! Come on, wake up!"

Who was Jordan? Was she Jordan? Or was she just a lung desperately pumping for air in short, gasping breaths?

"Fuck!" The ring of darkness grew thicker, taking up over half her vision. She was pulled from the driver's seat and manhandled into the passenger's. The armrest of a car door dug into her ribs. Her right hand twisted beneath her back, but she couldn't summon the strength to move it. "Don't you dare die on me, Jordan. Mac'd never forgive me if I changed you."

Thorn's pleas. They were important, even if she couldn't remember why. She should care, but she couldn't dredge up the energy. Something lurched under her. But it was easier to close her eyes and focus on trying to suck in enough oxygen and resisting the beckoning unconsciousness. Even that effort was too much work, so she let go and dove into oblivion.

33

———

Jordan was floating in darkness. No, not floating. She was sinking into a soft surface. It did feel familiar, but she was too tired to remember from where. She'd remember if she could look around, but her eyelids were too heavy to struggle with.

Murmurs filled the air around her. People speaking? Like opening her eyes, it was too much effort to focus on making the noises into words. All her energy was spent on shivering to stave off the cold surrounding her.

A weight pressed down on her from chin to toes, enveloping her in warmth. "Rest, Jordan," a female voice said close to her ear.

No longer shivering, she used that energy to parse out the sounds. She could make out a male voice carefully enunciating. His volume was just below a yell. "What the hell were you thinking?"

"Mac, I told her to get me to the Cataluna—"

"You know what I mean," Montgomery snapped. "You could have lost control and killed her, which you came damn close to doing. She could have—"

Jordan never heard what she could have done. The warmth had done its job and the darkness reclaimed her.

The next time a voice brought her to consciousness, it was easier for her to make out the words. "Jordan?" a woman's voice asked. "Can you hear me?"

This time, she managed to open her eyes. The first thing she saw were blue eyes sparkling in a smiling face framed by long red hair. "Welcome back, Jordan," Doctor Beverly said. "Can you tell me where you are?"

Jordan glanced around. There was a stinging pain in her left inner elbow. She recognized where she was immediately, despite the addition of the IV pole with the drained plastic bag attached to it. "My room. Montgomery's apartment."

"Do you know who the Elder of the city is?"

"Elder Marcus, assuming Thorn hasn't attempted a coup yet."

The doctor, trying not to smile, extended her arms, placing her hands by Jordan's. "Grab my fingers and squeeze. Any tingling anywhere? Blurry vision?" Jordan shook her head. "Smile for me."

Not sure why she, Jordan did as she asked. She winced as the needle in her arm shifted, feeling like it was about to tear free. Beverly pointed into the corner behind her. "What is that?"

Jordan's gaze followed the doctor's outstretched arm. "Chair? Quilt? I'm not sure which one you're pointing at."

Beverly glanced at the patchwork quilt draped over the chair. She smiled. "You werewolves are damn tough. I didn't expect you to recover this quickly. How do you feel?"

Her stomach answered with a gurgling growl before she could speak.

Montgomery's head poked through the door. "Can we see her?"

Beverly sighed. "I don't know how I can stop you since you won't wait for me to come and get you." She gestured the vampire in and then turned back to Jordan. "She's not showing any signs of a stroke, despite her blood loss." She pulled the needle from her arm. "Don't let her stand up until I'm back. I'll check on Thorn."

"Thanks, Doc." Montgomery swapped places with the doctor. He grabbed the chair from the desk and pulled it to the head of the bed. "How do you feel?" he asked, repeating the question Beverly had asked.

Jordan levered herself into a sitting position, taking stock of her body's reaction. "Little tired. Kinda weak." Her stomach rumbled again.

He took her hand and squeezed. "I'm not sure who I should yell at more, you or Thorn."

She closed her eyes and wilted. "How is he?"

"He'll be fine. He's healing right now. More embarrassed about losing control than anything. Between you and him, you've gone through my blood supply for the next month."

There had already been snide comments about Montgomery taking more than he gave back. She could almost hear them if she went back for more in the same week. "Sorry."

"Don't be." He took her hand. His skin blazed with an unfamiliar heat. Or she was still cold. "What were you thinking, Jordan? Thorn was far enough gone he could have killed you."

"I know, I know," Jordan said. "He wasn't going to make it here or to the Cataluna. All I could think about was getting him out of sight."

"Your instincts were right." Montgomery sighed. "Next time, call me before you do something. At the least I can get aid to you faster."

"Okay." She sighed. "How'd I get here anyway?"

"Thorn dragged you in once he realized what he'd done. He was barely in control himself, so I called Doctor Beverly over to take care of you while I handled him."

"Can I see him?"

"Yeah. He's in the living room."

Her stomach rumbled again as she climbed out of the bed. "Why am I so hungry? I ate before I went grocery shopping—shit. They're still in the trunk."

"Don't worry about it." Montgomery held out her robe, wrapping it around her shoulders. "You're building your blood volume back up, in addition to what was transfused into you. I've got some steaks finishing in the oven. You'll need the protein." He held out his arm.

Jordan leaned on it and slowly walked into the living room. Thorn sat in Montgomery's recliner, feet raised almost even with his head. Beverly stood next to him, handing him a sports bottle. She glared at Jordan and Montgomery. "I told you to keep her off her feet."

"Relax," Montgomery drawled. "She's not a fragile human. Besides, it will be easier for her to eat sitting up. Tell Marcus I overrode your sound medical advice if something goes wrong."

"If you say so." The doctor shook her head. "After all, you're the expert on werewolves."

"And don't you forget it," Thorn said. He took the squeeze bottle and pulled a long draw on the straw. "How you doing, Jo?"

"I'll live. You, however, look like death warmed over."

Thorn snorted. "I'll be fine. And thanks, Jordan."

Heavy thumps banged on the front door. Montgomery looked over at Beverly. "Are you expecting any deliveries?"

The doctor shook her head. "No. You'll need to restock, but I had enough on hand between your supply and mine."

Montgomery's hand dropped to his waist as he padded to the front door. He was wearing his gun. Jordan hadn't seen him carry a weapon since the night they first met. She watched as he sidled up to the door, staying to one side of the frame. "Who is it?"

"Detective Pamela Henricksen, Rancho Robles PD." Pamela's voice was all business. "Open up."

Jordan straightened up as Montgomery and Thorn shared a look. By using her human persona as part of her greeting, Pamela was making it clear she wasn't here as an emissary of the Black Oak Pack.

Montgomery unlocked the door and opened it. "Detective," he greeted her. "What brings you here?"

"You want to do this inside or in the hallway, Cooper?"

Montgomery gestured her in and closed the door behind her. "Business then," he said. "What's up?"

Pamela stepped inside. She looked from Jordan and then to the IV pole by Thorn. Her gaze lingered for a long moment on the blue-haired vampire. Thorn raised a hand to wiggle his fingers in greeting, a sheepish smile on his face. Pamela snorted and returned her focus to Montgomery. "I got tasked with investigating a shooting that happened late this afternoon. A car matching your SUV's description was seen driving away from the scene. And I noticed on my way in there's a blood smear on the door handle. You wouldn't happen to know anything about it?"

"It depends on if you're seeking information as a detective or as part of the Black Oak Pack."

"If I'm the police?"

"Jordan was in the area when the shooting happened. She cut her hand on a glass bottle she dropped since she was rattled by the nearby gunshots, but she didn't see the shooter."

"And if I'm here on pack business?"

"Someone attempted to kill either Jordan or Angela. Thorn ended up taking the bullet."

Pamela's gaze shot to Jordan. "Is that true?"

Jordan nodded. "Angela was harassing me about 'poaching' at the grocery store. We were about to get into it when Thorn interrupted. He was pulling us apart when he was shot."

"That girl." Pamela shook her head and turned to Thorn. "How do you know you weren't the target?"

"Your concern warms my heart," Thorn mumbled.

Beverly gestured to the table. Jordan noticed a pink plastic kidney-shaped basin with red stains turning to dry brown. A metal lump covered in similar stains rested next to a set of forceps. "It didn't deform the way a lead bullet would. Unless they think a silver bullet can kill vampires, one of the two women were the target."

Pamela stared into the basin. Her lips didn't twitch from their neutral lines as she studied the silver bullet. How many werewolves took the risk and carried silver? How many vampires? Montgomery did, but he wouldn't shoot her. Pamela's words interrupted her thoughts. "Has Elder Marcus been made aware of this?"

"I'll make my report to my patron once I return to the Hotel Cataluna," Beverly said.

Pamela's eyebrows rose. She turned to Jordan, and her eyes widened. "Were you shot too?"

Jordan shook her head, but Montgomery was the one who spoke. "She's okay. Just a little faint at the sight of blood."

Pamela glared at her with the same sharp expression she had used on Thorn. Jordan, following Montgomery's lead, kept quiet. She didn't feel the icy chill of when she was almost conscious, but was still cold enough to fight the urge to shiver. She glanced down at her hands and suppressed her surprise at how pale they were. The bite wound on her neck should have healed by now, but would the bruising that was part of it? Without makeup, she wasn't disguising any of the signs a vampire had fed on her. She held Pamela's gaze, daring her to say otherwise.

After a few seconds, Pamela addressed Montgomery. "I'll report to my superiors at the police department that your car was in the vicinity but had nothing to do with the shooting. I'll also inform Alpha Shane about what you've told me."

"And I'm sure it will match what I tell Elder Marcus," Montgomery returned. "If you don't have any other questions for my famulus, I politely request you leave."

Pamela glanced at Jordan one last time. "Then I'll be on my way."

Thorn smiled at her lopsidedly. "You don't have anything to say to me?"

Pamela rolled her eyes. "Not that we haven't said before."

Montgomery escorted her to the door. Once he closed and locked it, he held up a hand for a few seconds. His shoulders relaxed. "Okay, she's gone."

"Why didn't we want her to know Thorn fed on me?" Jordan asked.

"None of her damn business," Thorn muttered.

Montgomery arched an eyebrow at Thorn's shift in attitude. "What's with you and her?"

Thorn squirmed further under the blanket. "Let's just say we've known each other a long time."

Jordan bit the inside of her lip. She'd never seen Thorn uncomfortable talking about anything. What could have happened between them that made him look like he wanted the earth to swallow him?

"Jordan," Beverly said. "Thorn's told us about what happened from when he showed up. But what happened before?"

"It's what I told Pamela. Angela confronted me in the parking lot," Jordan said. "Said I'm poaching because I was buying groceries." She didn't meet Montgomery's eyes. "I was losing control when Thorn stepped in. Almost wolfed out in public."

"Which was probably what she wanted you to do." Montgomery shook his head. "She's devious, I'll give her that."

A soft 'ahem' reminded them there was one human in the room. Beverly was packing up her medical supplies. "Now that Jordan is awake and Thorn's no longer a danger, I need to report to my patron."

"What will the report say?" Montgomery asked.

"Thorn almost drained Jordan after being shot with a silver bullet. Your famulus's quick thinking kept it from being a public disaster." She looked at Montgomery, lips compressed. "Everything else is your responsibility to report."

"Fair enough," Montgomery said. "Would you like help to your car?"

"No need. Besides, it's after sunrise. I don't need a third patient with severe burns to deal with."

Montgomery nodded. "Tell Elder Marcus I'll report in person an hour after sunset."

Beverly picked up her bag. "Let me know if anything changes, for either of them." She glanced at her watch. "I'll let myself out."

The door closed at the same time a timer beeped. Montgomery walked toward the kitchen. "That's your breakfast, Jordan. I'll be right back."

Alone in the living room, Jordan looked over at Thorn. "You okay?"

"Yeah." The infinity symbol tattooed on his neck stuck out in stark relief against his ashen skin. "Jordan, I'm sorry."

"Thorn, you don't—"

"Let me finish." She swallowed as Thorn continued speaking. "You did the right thing, pulling over, and took a big risk letting me feed from you when I was barely in control. I could have killed you. I'm sorry."

Blood loss too fast for her body to regenerate was one of the few things Montgomery had warned could kill her. She reached over to take Thorn's hand. "It's okay," she said. She squeezed his hand lightly. "I'm glad you're okay. Besides, you took the silver bullet meant for me, so I guess we're even." She closed her eyes as her energy drained out of her body.

She heard Montgomery's footsteps pad close and smelled the cooked meat. "Jordan?" he asked. "You still awake?"

"Kinda," she said. Her jaws split wide in a yawn. Part of her was awake enough to be disappointed that she was too tired to eat.

"I think you need to get back to bed," Thorn said.

Jordan looked from Thorn to Montgomery. "You guys won't kill each other while I sleep?"

Montgomery offered her hand. "Promise. Let me help you back to your room."

Jordan rose to her feet and leaned against Montgomery. She let him half guide and half carry her back to her room. "Montgomery, do me a favor?" she asked as she lay down on the bed.

He placed the plate with the meat down on the table by the bed, within easy reach of her. "Whatever you need, Jordan," Montgomery said as he tucked one of the patchwork quilts around her.

She raised her head off the pillow to meet his gaze. "Talk to him."

Montgomery arched an eyebrow. "You want Dad and Daddy to get back together?"

"Something like that. I want you guys to be friends at least. And no. I'm not telling you which one of you is Dad and which one is Daddy."

He snorted, but a smile curved his lips. "Go to sleep, Jordan."

She let her eyes shut and her head fall against the pillow as he walked out of the door.

34

———

Montgomery closed the door to Jordan's room. The handle made a soft click as it engaged, which was as loud as a gunshot to his ears.

Gunshot. He winced. This was a new mess he'd have to handle. He didn't believe for a moment Pamela would cause problems, at least not with the mortal authorities. It might make the news, but as a general comment on what the world was coming to. It would be noted in the police logs and cited in passing in a report about gun violence. He'd have his car cleaned by people who were paid not to ask too many questions about odd stains. In short, the mundane world would continue turning, unaware of what had really happened.

Right now, the bigger problem was sitting in his armchair. He stepped into the living room. Thorn was untangling himself from the IV unit. "I'll be out of here as soon as the sun goes down. Sorry to trouble you."

"It's no trouble," Montgomery muttered. "Thanks for bringing her back." He wanted to say so much more. Ask Thorn why he couldn't trust him. Why didn't he tell him he was spying on him for Marcus? It wouldn't have changed anything between them. Or it wouldn't have on his part. He still wanted Thorn in his bed. But what he said was, "You're welcome to take the couch. I'll get you a blanket." He turned to go get them, deciding now was not the time to discuss their relationship.

"Mac." He turned at his softly spoken name. There was something unguarded in Thorn's expression he couldn't remember seeing before. "Montgomery, I'm sorry. I should have told you I was reporting to Marcus."

His resolve wilted at the sincerity in Thorn's voice. "I'm not stupid, Thorn. I knew you'd be talking with him. I just hoped you'd talk to me about it."

"I wanted to. But you were hurting after what happened with Rhys."

Montgomery shook his head. "That explains the last month. But you've been reporting to him for a lot longer."

"Yeah, I have. Look, I get it. You don't trust me now. Yes, I was keeping Marcus informed about what you were doing. But I never told him anything important, anything with the potential to really hurt you. I didn't want to risk you pushing me away just when you needed me the most."

Montgomery steeled himself to ask the question he dreaded the most. "Did he order you to sleep with me?"

His stomach dropped into his shoes at his old friend's answer. "Yeah, he did." A sly smile crossed Thorn's face. "It's a good thing we had already slept together by the time he got around to it."

Montgomery twitched and snorted. This was Thorn being honest, even if he was deflecting with humor. "Yeah, I guess that is a good thing."

Thorn settled onto the couch and patted the spot beside him. "This has been a long time coming," he said as Montgomery sat. "I'm curious why it came up now."

"Rosanna." Montgomery sighed. "She put the thought into my head. Not that it wasn't there before, but she made sure I couldn't ignore it any longer."

Thorn shook his head. "Yeah, I thought so. She can be spiteful when she's hurt."

"And I hurt her. And she's mad at me for not punishing Jordan for something that wasn't her fault."

"Yeah. She and most vampires think of Jordan as an extension of you. I doubt you'll ever get back on her good side."

"There's only one good side I want to be back on," Montgomery said.

"What makes you think you were ever on my bad side?"

"Well, there was the public breakup in the Cataluna."

Thorn waved a hand in dismissal. "Don't worry about me. Be more worried about what Marcus thinks about the public display of your grievances. Actually, don't worry about it. You probably impressed him by showing you actually do have a temper."

Montgomery shook his head. "I'm surprised I haven't been called in for a dressing down."

Thorn snorted. "I'm not part of the bloodline. He wants his children to show a unified front. Especially after Nicolas went rogue. You yelling at me would be seen as part of the proper order of things, not a break in tradition that could lead to you and Rosanna at each other's throats."

Montgomery's gaze dropped. "Like me not giving her the fangs directly."

"You trusted she wouldn't be offended because Jordan was proper and polite. Can I say something, Mac? Something that may hurt?" Montgomery nodded and Thorn continued. "You're trusting. Much more than a vampire should be. You've trusted Marcus, Rosanna, me. You let Jordan go after telling her she was a werewolf, trusting she'd come back without keeping any sort of tabs on her."

"She did come back."

"That's beside the point. Anyone else would've locked Jordan up. You got lucky. And you're lucky nobody's seen your blind trust as a big enough threat to take you out."

Montgomery pulled his limbs into himself, hunching as he leaned back against the cushion. "No vampire, you mean."

Thorn sighed. "You need to forgive yourself for what happened to Christine." He turned Mac's face to look at him. "It wasn't your fault you couldn't stop those werewolves from killing her."

Montgomery shook his head. "I should have known what was coming."

"You were young and in love and believed you were safe. You should have been safe." He sighed. "I should have seen it coming, and I'll never forgive myself for not."

"I know." Montgomery looked down. "When it comes down to it, there's only three people who could have been responsible. Marcus, Shane, or—" He choked on the last word.

Thorn nodded. "Your father."

"I don't want to think he was responsible. It was enough for him to cast me out of the pack. But . . ." Montgomery looked up at the ceiling and swallowed. "You've offered before, and I wasn't ready to take you up on it. I think I finally am. Would you look into what happened?"

"The trail will be cold. But yeah, I can use some of my out-of-town contacts to find out who placed the hit on you."

"Or your in-town?"

"I wasn't going to say that," Thorn said. "But you have to be ready to accept you won't like the info I dig up."

"Yeah, well, maybe it's time I start facing up to things."

"Like me reporting to Marcus?"

"Yeah."

He placed a hand on top of Montgomery's. "You'll have to trust that I'm only telling him the bare minimum and avoid telling him anything he can use to hurt you."

"And you'll have to trust that I can handle whatever you tell me. I'm not going to do something stupid and give you away."

Thorn's lips curled into a small smile. "I guess I should tell you now that Marcus ordered me to apologize to you."

He arched an eyebrow. "Did he also include orders to get back into my bed?"

"Yeah, but I planned to do that anyway."

Montgomery laughed and pulled him in for a rough kiss. Thorn melted against him, clutching at his shirt. He pushed away far enough to look into Montgomery's eyes. "What about Jordan?"

"Jordan's probably too hungry and tired to do anything but eat and sleep. We can make it up to her tomorrow. Besides, she told me to talk to you. But I don't think she actually meant talk."

Thorn laughed deep from his belly. "You heard the woman," he said, nudging Mac's hip with his. "Let's go finish up our apologies."

35

It had been tempting to crack the door and listen to Montgomery's and Thorn's conversation. But that required getting out of bed, and at the moment, the siren call of the sheets and warmth wrapped around her kept her there. She'd have to trust they would talk to each other and make up. Jordan snuggled into the promise of warmth and shut her eyes.

Something wet nudged her cheek.

Since neither Montgomery nor Thorn were in the habit of licking her cheek, half-asleep she muttered, "Rex, no," wondering how her neighbor's dog had gotten into her room.

She reached out to push his head away and her fingers brushed over long shaggy fur. *Definitely not Rex.* Her fingers tangled in it and tugged.

The yelp snapped her to full alertness. Jordan stared into the amber eyes of a huge black werewolf. Her grip released, hand falling flat on the mattress. The werewolf growled, sending a wave of hot breath rolling over her.

Jordan balled the sheets under her fists. She wanted to growl back. It was one thing to be chased through a dream forest. The context made sense in that setting. This room was her territory to defend. She settled for gritting out her words. "You going to end this by eating me again? Because those types of dreams don't make me inclined to trust you."

Black lips covered ivory fangs as the snarl faded to a subsonic rumble. "You have been spending too much time with him," she snorted. "You won't listen to me when you're awake, so I have to get through to you somehow."

"Montgomery?" Jordan raised up on her elbows. "Look, if you're planning on lecturing me about how I should join the Black Oak Pack, don't waste your breath."

The werewolf snorted. "Really? And why should I not speak the truth?"

"Because it's not the truth." She raised up, half expecting to bash her forehead against the Wolf's chin. To her surprise, the Wolf scooted back, letting her sit upright. Jordan pulled her knees to her chest, resting her crossed arms on them. "From the moment I met Alpha Shane, he's been ordering me to do things. Doesn't ask, doesn't explain, just orders. And I'm expected to jump to and do it without thinking. I was supposed to obey him without question, although the first time we met, he told me he'd kill me if I failed to control my shapeshifting. And when I proved I could shapeshift, he assumed I'd join the pack."

The Wolf jerked her head back. "I hadn't thought of it that way," she rumbled.

She looked up into the Wolf's yellow eyes. "My relationship with Montgomery isn't perfect, but at least he has the decency to ask instead of assume."

"And if Alpha Shane asked, would you join the pack?"

Jordan considered her answer before speaking. "I don't think so. I don't think I'd be able to live with the pack. And it's not just due to Alpha Shane."

The werewolf nodded. "You'll defeat Angela when the time is right."

"And until then I'll keep getting our asses thoroughly kicked."

The Wolf snorted. "Maybe if you worked with me instead of against me?"

"How? How am I supposed to work with you?"

"You could start by listening to me. Pay a little more attention to this." The wolf tapped one claw against her nose. "And not so much to this." She lightly touched above and between her eyes.

The Wolf had a point. She should use her senses more. Or pay closer attention to her sense of smell. But she was human. It was hard to turn off her thoughts in favor of what her senses were telling her. "I'm not sure I can unless I'm a wolf."

"Not true. You've done it before."

She was about to protest, but she had. She had tracked Rhys from the cemetery where he'd abducted Montgomery to his cabin. And she had done it as a human. And didn't dogs have a better sense of hearing than humans? "What about my other senses?"

"Ambitious. Good, good." The wolf's tail thumped against the bed, shaking it. "Let's work on one sense at a time, okay?"

"Okay." This wolf may have been a projection of her subconscious, but she had the urge to apologize all the same. "Sorry for yanking your fur."

The Wolf's tail froze, ears flicking back. For a moment, she was afraid her words weren't enough, or worse, had been taken as an insult. The head lowered and she closed her eyes. A warm breath stirred her hair, and a wet nose brushed against her forehead.

Her eyes opened. She looked around, inhaling through flared nostrils. She was lying flat on her back as if she had been asleep all along. There was no sign a werewolf had been here—no fur clutched in her hand, no scent lingering in the sheets. The only scent was the steak, now cold on the plate on the table. It had been a dream, her subconscious trying to reconcile her new wolf instincts with her human mindset. Montgomery's comments about the visions of the Wolf couldn't be correct.

She stared up at the ceiling, thinking over what the Wolf had said. A low rumble echoed through the room. She bared her teeth and snarled before she recognized the noise. She shook her head. Her dream discussion had left her on edge. Why else would she think her growling stomach was a threat?

She should be worrying about the person who took a shot at her. She touched the spot where Thorn had bit her. The images she had seen when Thorn fed were nothing like she had experienced with Montgomery. But he had only bitten her once, and she had been riding high on adrenaline from fighting Rhys when it happened. Maybe it had cancelled out any mental affect a vampire's bite had.

Her stomach rumbled again. She glanced at the steak. Although it was cold, the meat did smell appealing. And despite not having fangs, she devoured it in five bites. But it wasn't enough.

Jordan eased herself out of bed, keeping one hand on the mattress. Her head didn't spin, so she assumed it was a good sign. She took a few cautious steps and decided she wouldn't be falling over any time soon. She opened the door to her bedroom.

There were no lights on in the living room. No one was sitting or sleeping on the couch. A ray of sunlight peeked around one of the blackout curtains. She made a mental note to tape it to the wall until she could get it fixed so Montgomery could move freely about the apartment during the day. The IV stand that had been hooked up to Thorn was tucked into one corner. She made another note to return it and the one in her room to Doctor Beverly.

Her stomach rumbled again, reminding her why she'd left her room originally. Jordan padded over to the kitchenette. She rummaged through the refrigerator and pulled out a plastic storage container. She popped the lid. Saliva flooded her mouth as the scent filled her nostrils. She fished the baked egg and bacon muffin out of the container and popped it on the plate.

She'd just hit the button to start the microwave when bare footsteps padded behind her.

"Should you be out of bed?"

Jordan turned to the voice. Montgomery stood there, wearing a pair of boxers. As she opened her mouth to answer, her belly made another noise. "My stomach thinks I should be."

Montgomery chuckled. "Go sit. You still look too pale for my comfort. How are you feeling?"

Jordan dropped into the chair next to the small table. "Hungry, tired."

The microwave beeped. Montgomery pulled the plate out and carried it to her. "I meant emotionally this time. You almost died twice in a ten-minute span."

"I don't think I've started to process that," Jordan said. "Or those weird visions I had when Thorn bit me." She picked up the egg and bit in, savoring the cheese and bacon mixed in.

"Visions?"

Jordan chewed and swallowed. "I guess that's what they were. It was shapeshifting from wolf to human. But my paws weren't growing fingers. I was growing . . . skin between them. Kinda like they were bat wings."

"Bat wings?" Montgomery repeated. His brow furrowed "Odd. When Christine fed off me, I never felt like I was shifting, let alone to a different animal."

Jordan took another bite. "I thought it had something to do with the adrenaline."

"Maybe." His lips twitched as if he was about to say something else. "Thorn and I were wondering if you wanted to sleep with us?"

"Huh?" she said around her mouthful of baked egg. It took a moment for her mind to catch up with the change in subject. "As fun as it sounds, I don't think I'm up to sex at the moment."

Montgomery shook, a small smile on his lips. "No, I don't

think any of us are. We wanted to know if you wanted to join us in bed."

Jordan snickered. "That doesn't sound any different. Same response."

He lightly poked her shoulder. "You know what I mean." His smile slid into a serious line. "We're all tired. We're all scared. We all need the rest and comfort."

Jordan blew out a breath. "Does this mean you and Thorn have made up?"

"Yeah, we have."

She considered his offer. He was right about needing rest and comfort. She could go back to her room and curl up in bed, but she'd relax more with the sense of others around her. "Let me finish eating this," she said, lifting the half-devoured muffin.

Montgomery nodded. He turned and walked down the short hall and disappeared into his bedroom.

She watched him retreat, chewing her last bite of the muffin. For a moment, she debated retreating to her bedroom. "So, are you finally ready to resume the relationship, like you said you wanted to?" she murmured. She got up, got a drink of water from the sink, and headed toward his bedroom.

She paused at the door. Montgomery lay in the center of the bed, resting on his side. Thorn was spooned in behind him. Montgomery lifted his head, looked at her, and lifted the sheet. Jordan smiled at him and walked over to the bed. She slipped under the sheet, spooning against him. As Montgomery tucked the sheet around her, Thorn's hand rested on her hip. As warmth encircled her and Montgomery's hand joined Thorn's, her eyes shut and she drifted off to sleep.

36

Jordan walked into the Hotel Cataluna behind Montgomery, eyes downcast like a proper famulus. What was unusual was Thorn walking behind her, taking the position of rearguard. And he didn't do anything to dispel the impression, looking around in all directions at once. She was sure tongues were wagging. This was the first time Thorn and Montgomery had been seen together since their public breakup. None of them relaxed until they were alone in the elevator.

When the door opened on the seventh floor, they were greeted by Helen. "Mr. Cooper, you and your famulus are expected," she said formally, and then looked pointedly at Thorn.

Thorn crossed his arms over his chest. "I'm going in too," he said.

The two vampires stared at each other before she looked away. "Your funeral, Thorn." She punched in a security code on a panel. As Jordan passed through the door, she noticed Helen pick up the phone and dial it.

The hallway always had a dark feeling to it, no matter how well-lit it was. Today was no exception. Perhaps it was due to the dark wood paneling lining it. More likely, it had to do with the vampire whose office this hallway lead to. Marcus exuded power even through the closed door. Although she was appearing before him as a victim and not a criminal, Jordan still had a lump of unease in her stomach.

As if sensing her agitation, Thorn rested a hand on her shoulder. "It'll be fine, Jo," he said as Montgomery knocked on the door.

Jordan glanced over her shoulder and smiled. The smile fell off her face when the doors swung open without Marcus issuing his usual order to enter. Molly, wearing a fitted, off-the-shoulder black dress ending mid-thigh, opened the door and gestured them inside.

Marcus sat behind his desk, studying the three of them as they came closer. He gave no sign of being surprised or irritated by Thorn's presence. His face remained impassive as he waved a hand to the three chairs in front of his desk. Once they were all settled, he focused his attention on the werewolf. "Jordan Abbey," he said in his deep baritone. "You were attacked last night."

Jordan nodded. "Yes, sir."

Marcus tented his hands and leaned forward to study her. "Tell me exactly what happened."

"I went out to get some groceries."

"Alone?"

"The sun was up when I left, and the attacks had all happened after dark. We figured it wouldn't be much of a risk." That assumed it was the same person who was killing vampires and Family who had taken a shot at her. Arrogance or a stupid assumption, she wasn't sure. "While I was loading the groceries into Montgomery's car, Angela Shane showed up."

"Alpha Shane's daughter?"

"Yes, sir. She accused me of poaching on Black Oak's territory."

Marcus looked at Montgomery. "Would this be considered poaching?"

"Only by the most extreme of stretches," Montgomery said. "It could be an excuse if Alpha Shane really wanted to justify harassing her in the city."

"And I have something to say about that, since the city is Conclave and not Pack territory."

"My impression is Angela is acting on her own, without official sanction from her father," Montgomery said. "The girl, from what I have observed, is rash and sees Jordan as a threat to her rank in the pack."

Marcus glanced down at his desk phone. Frowning, he pushed the lit button on it. Then he turned his focus back to Jordan. "Do you think she had something to do with the attack?"

"No," Jordan said. "She was as startled as I was. We both ran toward the shooter. Whoever it was dropped a bottle of perfume to cover their tracks. We didn't see who did it or get a license plate."

"Pity that. It would have made things so much easier." He leaned forward, hands clasped on the desk. "Montgomery, for your safety as well as your famulus's, I suggest you move back here for the time being."

Montgomery shook his head. "I've been giving it some thought after our earlier discussion. I don't think it is a wise move, sir. If Jordan is a target, we'd be endangering you."

"Montgomery, please be reasonable," Marcus said. A speaker buzzed three short bursts. Marcus touched a button on his desk. "Yes, Helen?"

"Sir, Alpha Shane is insisting on seeing you."

"Of course he is." He looked at the trio speculatively and then responded. "Send him in. Margaret, please open the door. The last thing I need is to replace it if he gouges the carving trying to open it."

Molly, paler than usual, pulled one of the doors back. Alpha Shane thundered into the room without slowing down, as if he had planned to walk straight through the barrier. He scanned the room, teeth audibly grinding when he spotted Montgomery and Jordan. "Why am I not surprised you are here?" he growled.

Jordan shrank into her chair while Montgomery met his gaze without saying anything. "Alpha Shane," Marcus said. "What brings you here?"

"You know damn well what brings me here. One of your people attempted an assassination on my daughter."

"Yes, I am aware of the shooting, although I am not certain about the target. Miss Abbey was just telling me about how it missed her by a few inches."

"She could have been the bait that lured her there."

"Really?" Montgomery's voice dripped disdain. "All the other victims have been related to vampires, and you think your daughter was the target?"

Shane stabbed his finger in Jordan's direction to emphasize his words. "It is a well-known fact that Angela and that chaos wolf do not get along. Angela has bested her in physical confrontations. This act without honor would be well within the purview of a chaos wolf."

"Jordan," Marcus said, turning to her. "Do you wish to respond?"

Jordan lifted her head from her hand. How many times did she have to tell the story? "I had no idea she was in the area. She accused me of poaching because I was grocery shopping. We were about to throw down, and that's when someone fired a bullet at us."

"You didn't contact her?"

"No. In fact, I want to know how she knew I was there. 'Cause that implies a level of stalking requiring a restraining order."

Alpha Shane glared at Jordan. "Still, it doesn't mean one of Jordan's allies couldn't have helped."

Montgomery and Thorn burst into raucous laughter. Jordan's cheeks grew red. Marcus merely arched an eyebrow at them.

"Sorry, sir," Montgomery said, elbowing Thorn. "Jordan's just as popular among us as she is with Black Oak."

Thorn stifled his laughter, and then snorted. "A vampire would be more likely to order their famulus to shoot Jordan than Angela."

"Still, it doesn't mean that my daughter—"

"Sir?"

All heads snapped round at the interruption. Helen stood at the door. Trembling, she held a box with the top flap partially open.

"What is the meaning of this, Helen?" Marcus asked in a quiet, deadly voice.

Her voice was dry and her skin ashen as she held out the box. "Sir, I think you'll want to look at this."

The thick scent of decay hit the werewolves. Jordan swallowed against her rising nausea. Alpha Shane went white, then red. Snarling, he leaped across the room and snatched the package from Helen. He opened the other flap, looked inside the box and froze. He crossed the room and placed the box gently, reverently on the table. Marcus rose, an expression equal parts horror and disgust on his face as Shane lifted a freshly skinned pelt out of the box. He held the skin in his arms, staring at it with an open mouth. A howl began in the depths of his stomach and rose in volume and sorrow.

Marcus's sharp gaze darted to Montgomery. "Could he have survived that?"

Montgomery swallowed, voice cracking. "If whoever did this had any mercy, he was dead before it was done. If not, he would have died soon after. Too much to heal all at once." He looked at Jordan. "Do you recognize him?"

Jordan swallowed before finding her voice. "Yes, it's . . . it's Brian. He's one of the ones who was bullying me."

Shane's howl faded into an angry snarl. "You caused this," he spat at Marcus. He spread the pelt across Marcus's desk, his gentle handling of the remains at odds with the harshness of his voice. "This is your doing, Elder Marcus. A vampire has violated the Treaty. You and yours will pay for this desecration."

"I did no such thing." Marcus's words were precise and sharp. "But make another such accusation, and I will. Personally."

Shane's snarl became a deeper growl. His fingers clenched, claws extending. "I'd like to see you try."

Thorn and Montgomery took up flanking positions, protecting Marcus. Jordan remained rooted. The stench of blood and death hung in the air. She wanted to close her eyes but couldn't stop looking into the holes in the pelt where Brian's brown eyes had been. Jordan forced her gaze to trail down each of the limbs. She looked at the forelegs and then at the hind. "Why are his claws missing?"

Everyone stiffened. Shane paused mid-accusation and lifted one of the forepaws for a closer examination. At Marcus's gesture, Montgomery stepped closer and studied the other one. He then looked at Marcus. "The claws appear to have been amputated at the first knuckle."

Marcus's posture stiffened. "Would they be consistent with the claw marks found on the stake that killed Victor?"

Montgomery nodded.

Jordan then witnessed something she hadn't believed possible. Marcus blanched under his dark skin. "Hunters!" he spat, packing an incredible amount of hatred and venom into the word. He turned to Shane and spoke words Jordan wasn't sure were in his vocabulary until that moment. "It appears I owe you and your pack an apology for the accusations I made."

Shane growled louder, lips lifting from his teeth. But unlike before, this aggression didn't appear to be directed to anyone in the room. "Apology accepted," he grated out. "I propose we inform our people, remind them the Treaty is still in full force, and hunt down those who did this together."

Jordan looked at Molly. She shrugged, looking as confused as Jordan felt. "What's going on?"

Montgomery held up a hand and gave the two women a warning shake of his head to keep them quiet.

Marcus shot Montgomery a disapproving glance before returning his attention to Alpha Shane. "I will make arrangements with the Conclave. Gather your pack. We will show our people this as proof and begin the hunt tomorrow night." Shane's eyes narrowed. Jordan was sure he was about to protest that werewolves did not take orders from vampires when Marcus raised his hand. "And I will see these remains"—he placed his hand on the box—"are returned to your pack with all due respect as soon as possible."

The scowl in Alpha Shane's expression relaxed into neutral lines. "I will gather what information I can and meet with you tomorrow night to begin the sweep and destroy these bastards." Without saying goodbye, the werewolf turned and stalked toward the exit.

"Good hunting," Marcus called after the departing werewolf. "This is something I'd hoped we would never have to do again." He looked at Thorn. "Have you had dealings with Hunters?"

"A time or two before," Thorn said.

"Were you any good fighting them?"

Thorn spread his hands as if about to take a bow. "I'm still here to talk about it."

Marcus hmmmed, sitting down in his chair. Then he looked at Jordan and Molly. "I'm certain the two of you are wondering what just happened."

Both women nodded.

Marcus's words were calm and measured, designed to keep them from panicking. "We have an infestation of hunters in Rancho Robles. Any disagreement between the Conclave and the Black Oak Pack will be put aside to hunt them down, starting immediately."

"Hunters are humans who are aware of the supernatural and choose to fight it," Montgomery explained. "They're made up of different types of people. Some are the 'holy men' of various religions who have decided we are abominations to be cleansed from the face of the earth. Some are victims or had family who were victims and have sworn revenge. Some think of themselves as big game hunters seeking a more challenging type of prey."

"There's an informal communication network allowing them to swap tales and exchange notes about their hunts," Thorn said. "Some take trophies, like fangs from vampires . His next words had a heavier emphasis. "And claws from werewolves."

"We've managed to stay under their radar for almost fifty years," Montgomery said. "Why now? What drew their attention?"

Marcus sighed, reminding Jordan of when a teacher was about to answer a question they thought the solution obvious to. "Perhaps a werewolf attacking multiple people and blatantly killing a human without bothering to hide his presence?"

Molly's lip trembled. Jordan stiffened. "Rhys," she whispered. When was that bastard ever going to stop causing her problems?

"The media made it sound like a run-of-the-mill attack by a dog, like a mauling made the news," Thorn said. "Any hunter worth his blessed salt would read between the lines and quickly come to the conclusion there are werewolves in Rancho Robles."

"And from there, it's a short step to discovering the Conclave," Montgomery added.

Jordan swallowed. Despite being in one of the most supernaturally secure areas of Rancho Robles, each shadow bristled with unseen menace. "How many hunters do you think there are?"

"Impossible to say," Thorn said after a moment. He rubbed his chin "This could be the work of one skilled hunter or the coordinated actions of several amateurs."

"Which is why we will work together," Montgomery said. "Whatever their emotions toward each other, either as individuals or as a species, the supernatural community unites when we are all threatened. Once the news is officially announced, vampires and werewolves will work together. Afterwards, we'll go back to fighting amongst ourselves."

"What do we need to do?" Jordan asked.

"You will continue in your usual duties," Marcus said. "Possibly, you will be asked to help track down the hunters. Part of it will depend on what information Alpha Shane is able to produce."

"If you will excuse us, sir," Montgomery said. "We should return home."

Marcus looked evenly at Montgomery. "Do you still think it is wise? Especially since your famulus was targeted?"

Montgomery shook his head. "Perhaps not, but the attempts have always happened in relatively public places."

"I'm pretty sure the hunter saw me last night," Thorn said. "If I wasn't on his radar before, I may be now. To play it safe, I'll be staying with them."

"If you insist," Marcus said. "But do be careful. It wouldn't do to lose two members of the Conclave."

Unlike Family, Jordan thought.

Montgomery placed a hand on Jordan's shoulder but didn't comment about the fact Jordan was in just as much danger as they were. "We'll be in touch tomorrow night," he said as they all rose and bowed their respects. He nudged Jordan toward the door.

Jordan followed the two vampires, waiting for the relative privacy of the elevator to speak. "How deep is this shit, Montgomery?"

"Extremely." He took a deep breath. "The last time hunters were in the area was just before I was born. Everything we've heard fits with what I was told happened. Except there's something bugging me."

"What?" Thorn asked.

"How did they know Jordan was a werewolf? You haven't shifted in the city, and you didn't think you were followed when David was killed."

"Angela was there," Thorn said.

"Yes, but until tonight, they hadn't attacked any werewolves. They'd only be aware you were a famulus if they've been stalking you."

"You think someone's feeding them inside information?"

"Not think. Know." Montgomery emphasized the word. "Why else would they try to shoot you with a silver bullet?"

The elevator doors opened. As they crossed the lobby, Jordan scanned every face, lingering on strangers.

Despite the situation, Thorn chuckled. "Looking for someone lurking in the shadows wearing a trench coat and fedora pulled low over their eyes?"

Heat rushed to Jordan's cheeks. "Sounds like silly paranoia when you put it that way."

"I wouldn't call it silly," Montgomery said. "It might save your life."

37

The doorbell ringing pulled Jordan out of her sleep. Cuddled between Thorn and Montgomery, she was tempted to ignore it. It was probably a door-to-door salesman going from apartment to apartment hoping to make a sale.

An elbow nudged her side. "You need to get that," Montgomery murmured into her ear.

Jordan didn't open her eyes. "You're on the edge of the bed."

"Sun's still up," Montgomery pointed out.

Jordan moaned and curled into a tighter ball, pulling the quilt over her shoulder. "Maybe they'll go away."

The doorbell rang three times in rapid succession.

Now it was Thorn's voice in her ear. "Nope. Not going away."

Jordan sighed. "Okay, okay." She wiggled her way over Thorn, which earned her a swat on the ass. She ignored his wolf whistle as she pulled on her robe.

The triple ring sounded again. "I'm coming," she yelled as she tied the belt around her waist and stepped into her living room. She checked to make sure everything was decently covered and peeked through the sight hole. Recognizing one of Marcus's couriers, she cracked the door open, safety chain still in place. "Yes?"

"Jordan Abbey, I've been asked to deliver this." He passed a cream-colored envelope through the door. The moment her fingers closed on it, he let go. "Make sure it's put into your patron's hands immediately." Without waiting for her response, he turned and strode away. Jordan closed the door and stared down at the envelope, tapping it against her hand.

She returned to the bedroom, where Montgomery was sitting up in the bed. "Who was it?"

"Cedric. He gave me this to give to you." She held out the envelope to Montgomery.

Thorn sat up on his elbows. "That the official announcement?"

Montgomery slit the envelope open with one finger and extracted a thick piece of paper. He unfolded it and scanned the page. "Yes. We're officially on notice that they believe a hunter is in the area, so play nice with everyone."

"Huh." Jordan plopped down crosswise on the foot of the bed. "I thought there'd be an email blast."

"There will be one of those too," Thorn said. He leaned over Montgomery's shoulder to read the letter and made a hmmphing noise. "Marcus is using formal language, even for him. He must be serious."

"What does it say?"

Thorn snatched the letter from Montgomery's hand. He grinned at the dirty look the other vampire shot him. Thorn made a big show of loosening a nonexistent tie and adjusting a pair of bifocals as he cleared his throat. His words carried some of Marcus's cadence as he read. "To all members of the Conclave of Rancho Robles: Greetings. Due to the potential infestation of hunters in our fair territory, we—" Thorn interrupted himself, reverting to his everyday voice. "He's using the royal we. Fancy."

Both Montgomery and Jordan rolled their eyes. "Go on," Montgomery growled.

"Patience, guys, patience. I'm getting to the good stuff." He readjusted the distance of the paper from his eyes and continued reading. "We hereby command any authorized or unauthorized aggression toward the Black Oaks pack to cease forthwith." Again Thorn broke character. "Forthwith. He's just showing off his vocabulary."

"Thorn," Jordan growled.

"I know, I know. Keep going." He shook the papers and resumed reading. "In addition to the cessation of hostilities, all vampires residing within the territory of Rancho Robles are required to join with the Black Oak Pack to determine the identity of the said hunter and deal with the threat immediately and with finality." He scanned over the rest of the letter. "We're to gather at the designated neutral ground tonight at 8:00 p.m., bringing along any Family we wish to have in attendance. The werewolves will be there. Blah, blah, blah." Thorn let the sheet fall from his hand.

Jordan frowned. "We're all meeting tonight to make nice and hunt the bad guy? Will we really be able to, given all the egos and grudges at play?"

Montgomery shrugged. "In theory, all issues we have will be put aside while we're chasing the hunter down. That includes Angela blatantly trying to bully you out of the area."

"Blatantly," Jordan said. "So, subtle troublemaking is still a go."

"Yup," Thorn agreed.

"As for the rest, there'll probably be a big show of saber rattling. We'll all be on the lookout for this hunter. There probably won't be any vampire/werewolf cooperative hunting parties, but if someone stumbles across information, it'll be shared."

"And the Family is allowed into the event instead of having to hang out in another room?"

"Yes. The information needs to be spread as quickly and as accurately as possible. You may be able to spot something during the day that I would miss."

"But isn't it a huge risk?" Jordan pushed herself into a sitting position. "If there's a famulus providing the hunter with information, this meeting is going to tell him exactly what we know about him."

"Yes, it is a risk." Montgomery admitted. "But it could also be a chance for Marcus and Shane to spread a little disinformation."

"We already know there's a mole in the area. That's not going to help."

Thorn tapped a finger against the letter. "But if they frame it the right way, it might reveal if it's a famulus or a werewolf passing on information, depending on how he changes his tactics."

"The thing bothering me is his tactics have already changed," Montgomery said. "Until the werewolf's death, I was positive it was one of the Black Oak Pack trying to overthrow Alpha Shane."

"So, what changed?" Jordan asked. "Other than Angela kicking my ass at any given opportunity, nothing has, either before or after David's death. I was kicked off Mount Ponderosa, but that was the night the killing started."

"We're overlooking something," Montgomery said. "Marcus has a new famulus."

"Molly?" Jordan shook her head. "No, she became Family after Emma was killed."

"No, that's when she was announced," Montgomery said. "He'd have been training her three, maybe four weeks ahead of time to determine what role she was best suited for."

Thorn nodded. "Probably closer to six. And he'd have been feeding off her too. You can't use your experience as the baseline, Jordan. Because of your situation, you were rushed through."

"But it couldn't be Molly," Jordan protested. "She's my friend. She—"

"Lost her fiancé in the mess with Rhys." Montgomery's voice was as gentle as a kitten's tread. "She's hurting and lost and angry and afraid. The perfect combination for a hunter to take advantage of."

"Think about how you felt learning the supernatural wasn't just the stuff of nightmares and horror movies and scary stories. You had our support, Jordan. She's had no one."

"And then someone shows up and tells her the monsters can be defeated, and she can have part of that revenge." Montgomery shook his head. "It's no wonder she accepted his offer."

"We're talking about this like it's fact," Jordan said. *But it couldn't be.* Molly wouldn't betray her. But the statements had a logic to them that sent a cold chill down her spine. "We were best friends. She had to know I was at risk if she took part."

"Then let's eliminate her as a suspect," Montgomery said. "You met with her the other day?"

"Yeah," Jordan said. "We met for lunch at the hotel. She said Marcus didn't want her leaving the building."

"Did you talk to her about how they met?

Jordan nodded. "She was visiting Darren's grave up in Arroyo Secco. He approached her while she was there and—"

Montgomery and Thorn's heads both whipped toward her. "She said Marcus went to the cemetery?"

"She said he gave her the choice of being a famulus, or death. She chose life."

"Jordan," Thorn said in the gentlest voice she had ever heard him use. "She lied to you."

She bristled and rumbled low in her chest. Molly was her friend. She wouldn't lie. "How do you know?" she snapped.

"Remember when he was invited to Black Oaks to witness your shapeshifting? It was the farthest he's gone from his hotel in years."

"There is no way he'd have gone to Arroyo Secco," Montgomery added. "That trip would take at least three nights—a night up, a night to meet with her, and a night to get back since he'd insist on traveling in comfort. He'd be worried about someone attempting a coup the entire time. He'd send a trusted famulus or vampire to kill her. There wouldn't be a choice offered."

"So how did she end up Family then?"

"If she's working with the hunters, there are ways. Every so often, some human enamored with illusions about the vampire lifestyle seeks us out. I wouldn't be surprised if she, with the aid of the hunter, managed to catch his eye. We try to screen them out as much as possible, but every so often, one slips through."

"And one apparently has." Thorn shook his head. "He said his background checks didn't turn up any relationship between you and her, Jo. That is a big red flag right there. Besides, your friend is a beautiful woman. Her attention would flatter his ego. The combination has always been Marcus's weakness."

"The question is, how do we discover how Marcus really met her?"

Jordan tilted her head to one side. "Can't we ask him?"

"And tell him he has a huge blind spot in his security? That his due diligence is sloppy? Reveal he's the ultimate source of the information leading to the deaths of those he's sworn to protect and govern?" Montgomery shook his head.

"I haven't lived this long taking stupid risks," Thorn said. "He'd kill us to keep us quiet, unless we bring him irrefutable proof and promise discretion about sharing it."

"The question is how," Montgomery said. "She's lied to you once, Jordan. And there's already been an attempt on your life."

Thorn frowned as he sat up. "I've got an idea. She uses email, right?"

Jordan snorted. "Of course."

Thorn arched an eyebrow. "Think you can guess her password?"

Jordan frowned, a churning sensation swirling in the pit of her stomach. "I don't know about this."

"I understand you don't want to violate your friend's privacy," Montgomery said. "But if we don't find anything there, she's in the clear."

"We're assuming this hunter is communicating with her by email," Jordan said.

"He has to be." Thorn slapped his thigh. "How else would she get information out? You said she's not allowed to leave the hotel. Phone calls could be overheard. Anyone meeting with her regularly, especially a mortal, would be noticed quickly."

"Wouldn't Marcus monitor her email?"

Montgomery and Thorn exchanged a look and then snickered. "Well, that's the thing. You know how some vampires have problems with modern technology? He's one of them. Cell phone is about as advanced as he gets, and that's only because he understands the concept of land line phones."

Her mouth dropped open. "But he's got a laptop on his desk."

Thorn arched an eyebrow. "He likes to keep up appearances. Mac, you ever seen it powered up?"

Montgomery shook his head. "Can't say I have."

"So much for you guys and your blending in. I wondered why I couldn't find any social media accounts for him." Jordan sighed. "Well, if we're doing this, let's get it over with."

Montgomery nodded. He stood up and grabbed a pair of slacks. "We'll need a reason to get you into Molly's quarters—"

"No, we won't. Get me your laptop." Jordan turned to Thorn as Montgomery stepped out of the bedroom. Concern clouded her eyes. "If she's innocent, and I do this, she's never going to speak to me again."

Thorn placed a hand on her shoulder. "If she's not innocent, and you do this, you'll be saving lives."

Montgomery returned and handed him her laptop. "Impress us with your hacking skills."

"Not much to impress you with," she said as she powered up the computer. She opened the web browser and entered the webmail URL. "I hope she's using the same mail address and hasn't made up a new one to communicate with the hunter. Then we *will* need access to her computer." She typed in the username Molly had emailed her from and paused. "I can only do this three times," Jordan said. "If I don't get her password in three tries, we'll be locked out and she'll know someone tried to get in the next time she logs on."

"Any other way you can get access?" Montgomery asked.

"Fake a subpoena? Pamela might be able to help." Jordan suggested.

Thorn shook his head. "Takes too long, even if we could talk Detective Henricksen into it."

"Okay." Jordan drew in a deep breath. "Keep your fingers crossed." She typed in the name of the lead actor of the television show they watched every Saturday, the one Molly had a crush on.

The browser loaded an error page. "Strike one," Thorn said under his breath.

Jordan hit the back button. She tapped her finger against the bezel before typing again. This time she chose the name of the cat Molly had grown up with and had left at home when she left for school. Molly still got a little misty eyed when she looked at the picture taken during her last visit home of her holding Fluffykins.

The error paged popped up again. "Strike two," Thorn said, miming a baseball swing.

"Not helping." Jordan sat back, staring at the screen. She tapped her finger to her lips. There were so many choices Jordan could pick from—the name of Molly's elementary school, her favorite type of chocolate bar, her favorite cartoon character.

Jordan gasped. Her fingers dropped to the keyboard. She knew it was the correct choice. There could be no other once she thought about it. She typed in the string of letters and hit enter without hesitating. They all leaned closer to the screen. "Come on, be right," Jordan muttered, watching the webpage progress bar.

The inbox appeared. Jordan blew out the breath she had been holding as Montgomery squeezed her shoulder. Thorn pumped his fist in the air. "What was it?" he asked.

Jordan closed her eyes. "Darren."

Montgomery put his hand on her shoulder and squeezed.

She opened her eyes and started reading off the messages in her inbox. "Mom, mom, shopping, mom, shopping, shopping . . . wait a minute." She frowned. "Lots of emails from someone named B. Vordenberg."

Thorn squinted at the screen. "You know anyone by that name?"

"No," Jordan said. "But I didn't know all of her friends. Still, the name sounds kinda familiar, but I can't place it."

Montgomery's grip tightened on her shoulder. "Open one of them."

She clicked on it. As she scanned the screen, her heart sank.

Montgomery leaned over her shoulder and began reading. "Confirmation of the information about when and where the meeting with Alpha Shane and Elder Marcus is."

"And that's not all. Passcodes. Diagrams of the meeting area. Schedules for staff and arrival times."

"Dammit," Thorn said. "Someone's setting up an ambush. If things keep going the way they are, Marcus or Shane will be dead by dawn. Any way we can tell who it is?"

Jordan shook her head. "It can be done, but it takes some time. And it's beyond my skill set."

"This is enough." Montgomery's fangs were down. Jordan didn't think she had ever seen a predatory gleam in his eyes that reminded her of a hunting wolf before. "Baron Vordenberg is a vampire hunter from the novel *Carmilla*. There is no way someone mailing a famulus using that name can be brushed off as a coincidence. Elder Marcus and Shane will be able to convince holdouts it's not an elaborate plan by the other side to take them out."

"We'll have to get to them before they go onstage to announce the hunt." Thorn said. "Last thing we want to do is reveal Elder Marcus's background checks leave a lot to be desired."

"Let him spin it however he wants," Montgomery said. "He'll probably end up claiming he did it deliberately to flush out the hunter."

"When's the announcement?"

"Letter said 8:00 p.m. About an hour after sundown," Montgomery said. "We'll have to leave just as the sun sets if we want to warn him before he takes the stage. If something happens to one or both of the leaders in a room full of vampires and werewolves, it'll be a slaughter. And the survivors won't stop until the other side is exterminated."

"Can't we call Marcus and warn them?"

Montgomery shook his head. He headed for the closet and grabbed some clothes while Thorn snagged his jeans from the floor and pulled them on. "He doesn't allow anyone direct access. He'll have his Family answering his phone. And with our luck, it will be Molly. We can't trust any message we send will get through to him. Alpha Shane will gleefully hang up on me, if he decides not to send me directly to voicemail." He tossed Jordan's jacket in her direction. "We need to talk to them. The best way to do that is in person. Go get dressed. We don't have any time to lose."

Jordan hustled back to her room, a pool of nausea welling up in her stomach. *Please let me be wrong.* She grabbed her clothes and pulled them on. *Please don't let my friend be a traitor.*

38

Jordan surveyed the area, one hand on the passenger door of Thorn's electric car. Thorn had insisted on driving to make it clear that he and Mac were a couple again by arriving together. He had also insisted on driving, claiming loudly that no one drove his sweetie. She was fine not driving since she wasn't sure where this neutral ground was. She figured they were headed to the convention center, or maybe the community college's theater. "This is where the meeting is taking place? Really?"

"Really," Montgomery said. "Fletcher Park has been a neutral meeting place since Rancho Robles was founded. I can remember my grandfather telling stories about the open-air amphitheater being built."

Jordan nodded. "So, where do we find them?"

Thorn stepped onto a paved path winding uphill between well-manicured bushes. "There's two small buildings next to the amphitheater. Marcus and Shane will be setting up there before addressing the groups."

Montgomery and Jordan followed him. The shrub-lined path twisted and turned among the trees. Despite the feral life surrounding her, it struck her as artificial. This didn't invoke the same feeling as tramping through the leaf and dirt-strewn game trails on Mount Ponderosa or on the Black Oak Pack's land. The flagpole-straight trees were spaced too evenly, their shapes too uniform to be natural. The bushes stopped at the edge of the path, not daring to encroach so much as a leaf onto the pavement. The manicured lawns glimpsed between regular gaps in the foliage were the uniform green of regularly cut grass. "I always thought the only things happening here were the summer concerts and plays put on by the county."

"That too," Thorn said. "But we get first dibs. Plus, we only do this maybe once a decade, so we usually don't interfere with any scheduled events."

"Isn't it a nightmare for security?"

"It's part of the beauty of the location. We're forced to trust each other."

"Isn't it a little too . . ." Jordan looked around. "Public for Marcus's tastes?"

"And Alpha Shane's," Montgomery confirmed. "But since neither of them are happy about it, it's the best compromise."

The greenery around them gave way to a clearing. Jordan found herself at the edge of a large semicircular depression. Five rows of blocks tall enough to sit on were molded into a curve and cut through with several sets of stairs. A raised platform used as a stage was even with the lowest seats. Five poles hung with stage lights interrupted the row of seats about two thirds down the curve. People were claiming their seats closest to the stage—one side with vampires and their Family, the other with the Black Oak Pack.

"Looks like almost everyone's here," Jordan said.

"Damn it," Montgomery said. "I hoped we'd have more time." They took the central stairway down. Out of the corners of her eyes, Jordan tracked hostile expressions turning to follow their progress on both sides. She remained focused on Montgomery's back and keeping her balance. The last thing she needed was to fall down the stairs. If Montgomery or Thorn noticed the hostility radiating toward them, both were better at ignoring it.

At the bottom row, they cut to the left, curving around the stage. Near the back squatted a concrete building. It had puzzled Jordan that the building that housed changing rooms and equipment for concerts had been built like a bomb shelter without windows. A walking mountain of a vampire stood guard at the only door Jordan could see. He frowned as Montgomery approached. "Please join the others and take a seat. Elder Marcus will address everyone at once."

Montgomery stood as tall as he could. "We need to speak to Elder Marcus before the meeting. It's a matter of life and death."

"Sorry," said Marcus's guard. He—Jordan didn't know his name—looked down at Montgomery. "You'll have to take a seat like everyone else."

Montgomery's eyes narrowed. "I am the blood son of the Elder of Rancho Robles, and I demand entrance."

The guard looked less than impressed by his announcement. "My orders come from the Elder himself." There was the faintest hint of satisfaction in his voice, as if he had wanted to say something like this to Montgomery for a long time. "No one—vampire, Family, or werewolf—is allowed entrance."

"Mac, Mac," Thorn said. He patted his friend's shoulder, angling between him and the guard. "Of course he knows who you are. Everyone here does. And he's probably enjoying taking you down a peg." He turned his attention to the guard. "Okay, Tyrone. You've had your fun throwing around whatever power Marcus gave you. Now let us in."

"Sorry, Thorn." He shook his head, his tone a lot more apologetic than it had been toward Montgomery. "I can't. The boss is in a mood. It's not worth my head."

Thorn squared up to the man. "Tyrone, please. Let us in. It

really is a matter of life and death. I'll intercede with Marcus myself. You won't be punished."

The words shouldn't have worked. But to Jordan's surprise, Tyrone went rigid, staring into Thorn's eyes. He stepped to one side, opening the door without another word.

"Thank you," Thorn said, and walked inside.

Jordan shared a look with Montgomery. Her surprise and worry were reflected in his expression. His mouth twisted into a frown. "How did you—"

"Later," Thorn said. "Who should we look for first? Marcus or Molly?"

"Molly," Mac said. "We'll need her to convince Marcus and Shane."

They looked around the room. She had been in walk-in closets that were more spacious. It could have been due to the folded table tennis table shoved against a stack of chairs and folding tables. Along the side wall was an organized jumble of backgrounds and sound equipment, clearly meant to be protected from the weather and thieves. Three curtained off stalls stood along the side wall, changing areas offering a modicum of privacy. "Are we sure she's here?"

Thorn's question, the obvious one they had all overlooked, jolted Jordan. What if Molly wasn't here? She could be back at the Cataluna with the majority of Marcus's servants. They might be able to delay and get her here in time. She wasn't in this main storage area. Or she might be behind one of the three doors on the side wall. They didn't have time to search both locations. They needed to narrow it down to one place, and she wasn't sure how.

The words of the werewolf in her dream echoed in her mind. *Pay a little more attention to this.*

Jordan lightly touched her nose. She drew her hand away and closed her eyes. "Hey, Jo," Thorn started. "What are you—"

"Hush, Thorn," Montgomery whispered. "Let her concentrate."

She drew in a deep breath and filtered through the commingled scents. There was dirt tracked in from outside, rich and earthy with the fertilizer that kept the grass a more-than-natural green. There were scents of several vampires, Marcus's included. While not able to ignore them, she tried to focus on the human ones.

Unfortunately, there were several female ones. Not all of them were recent, but more than one woman's scent was commingled with Marcus's. Jordan bit back a snicker. Marcus liked to travel with snacks apparently.

Focus, she growled to herself. She drew in another breath, trying to filter through different odors. Rubbing alcohol stung her nose. Doctor Beverly was somewhere nearby. She snorted to clear her nose and inhaled again. This time, underneath the medicinal smell, she picked up the faintest scent of a familiar perfume. She inhaled deeper and sneezed. Her eyes popped open. "She's here."

"You sure, Jordan?"

She walked toward a closed door. "Serenade Breeze is Molly's favorite perfume. Somebody around here is wearing it. This way." Sniffing as she walked, she headed toward the curtained stalls.

They halted when someone stepped into their path. Marcus's senior famulus stood in front of one of the doors like an unbending tree in the wind. He addressed Montgomery. "If you are here to speak with your sire, Mr. Cooper, he has already left to address the Conclave and the Pack."

"I'm not here for him, Reginald," Montgomery answered. "We need to speak to one of the Family, Margaret Griffiths."

"This is highly irregular, sir. If you wish to speak with her, you will need Elder Marcus's permission."

Thorn opened his mouth, but it was Jordan who spoke first. "Please," she said. "We need to talk to Molly before there are more deaths."

He looked at her, a pained, uncertain expression flitting over his face. "This has to do with Da— the killings?"

She met his eyes, heart pounding. "Please."

Reginald slumped. "She's in the farthest stall." He gestured to the one farthest from them.

Montgomery and Thorn walked past him. Jordan paused for one moment. "Thank you," she said before scurrying after the vampires.

Montgomery glanced at her as she caught up. "What was that about?"

"Family business," Jordan said. "I'll explain later. Molly first."

Montgomery nodded. He swept the curtain aside, giving them a clear view of the interior.

Molly was hunched over, perched on the edge of one of the folding chairs. She twisted her bracelet back and forth, fingers brushing against the charm embossed with the Family symbol. She looked up, her eyes going wide and fingers clenching around something black and shiny. "Mr. Cooper, Mr. Henderschott," she said. There was a small tremor to her voice as her hand tightened around a rectangular object. "How may I serve you?"

Montgomery's eyes furrowed. "What's that?"

Molly tensed, hand moving to her skirt to hide what was in her grip. Montgomery lunged toward her, grabbing her wrist. Thorn stepped up to him, face blank. Montgomery reached into her pocket and retrieved what she had tucked inside it. He tapped the screen and then held it to her face to unlock it.

Reginald frowned at Molly. "You haven't been cleared to have a cell phone yet."

"I don't think she'd ever be cleared for this one." Montgomery handed it to Thorn. Jordan's stomach dropped from the steely tone he spoke in. "Read the last text she sent."

Thorn scanned the screen. "V has left the bunker. Will meet W in five minutes on stage." He rolled his eyes and shook his head. "You couldn't come up with more clever code names?"

Molly's chin lifted in something between defiance and resignation.

So that was it. Sadness flooded Jordan. She had believed she just needed five minutes alone with her friend. She'd convince Molly to explain how they'd misunderstood. Except Molly had been willingly going along with the person who had been killing everyone, the person who had shot Thorn while aiming at her. The numbing sorrow wrapping itself around her soul transmuted in a heartbeat to white hot anger. Molly had been aware Jordan was a target and hadn't warned her. There was no denying it, as much as she wanted to.

Thorn's voice snapped her back to the here and now. "This text was sent eight minutes ago." He looked at Montgomery. "We need to get them offstage now."

39

Montgomery led the charge to the amphitheater with Reginald at his side. Jordan and Thorn followed in Montgomery's wake, each holding one of Molly's arms, hustling her toward the stage where Marcus and Shane were about to address the gathering. Despite the anger boiling through her, the part that wanted to believe her friend was innocent babbled a new idea. Maybe this was a chess game and Marcus was using Molly as a double agent to ferret out another traitor among them. She glanced at her friend. Her theory withered on the vine. Molly was pale as marble. Her forearm under Jordan's grip was cold as ice as a tremor ran through it.

"I thought we were trying to be discreet about this, Mac," Thorn said. "Dragging her onstage isn't going to win us any favors."

"Do you think we have time to keep things quiet?" Montgomery shook his head. "I'd rather have him around and angry at me."

Unlike earlier, the bodyguards sealing the entrance to the vampire side of the stage parted before Montgomery without so much as word of protest. It may have something to do with the unusual forcefulness of his stride. Or the fact she and Thorn were dragging Molly along, both equally as grim. More than likely, it was the fact Reginald walked beside Montgomery. Everyone, vampire and Family alike, knew if he was willing to risk his patron's displeasure, it was a dire situation.

Jordan stiffened as they stepped on stage, looking out on the gathered crowd. She always thought of the vampire and werewolf population as large, but she now estimated the gathering patrons, their Family, and the Pack was under one hundred people. It always seemed like so many more, but then she was dealing with them every day. In this city, and the larger populations surrounding it, they were able to blend in. Except, she thought with a mental rolling of her eyes, when they gathered in one spot and weren't being particularly careful about hiding what they were.

The sensation of everyone watching her was the batting of a kitten's paw compared to Marcus's predatory gaze. For the first time, she felt the true weight of his displeasure as he took in their little group. She wanted to slip her currently nonexistent tail between her legs, crouch down, and back away with a placating whimper. And his ire wasn't even focused on her. "Montgomery Cooper," Marcus said. His tone was the velvet fur sheathing the steel claws threatening to burst forth. "What is the meaning of this?"

"My apologies, sir." Montgomery's voice only had the slightest crack in it. He wasn't making any effort to hide the threat to either the vampires or the werewolves. The microphones for Marcus and Shane had to be picking up his words. "We have reason to believe you are both in danger. There is a hunter out there."

Alpha Shane snorted. His eyes narrowed in annoyance, but the smile on his lips revealed his amusement, probably at Montgomery being publicly shamed for this interruption. "That is the entire reason for this meeting."

"No, here," Montgomery snapped. "This is an endgame. A trap."

"You have proof of this?" Marcus asked.

Montgomery gestured toward where Jordan, Molly, and Thorn waited.

Marcus frowned. His eyes met hers for a half-second before settling on Molly. "Bring her here."

Jordan glanced at Thorn. He stiffened his spine, mouthed the word 'idiot,' and walked forward, dragging Molly with him. Jordan, holding Molly's other arm, trotted to keep up.

"You're playing a dangerous game, Montgomery," Alpha Shane growled.

"You can prove this accusation?" Marcus asked.

Montgomery handed over the phone. "She had this on her in the waiting area. She's been sending messages to someone. That person knows everything about this meeting."

Marcus glanced at the screen before handing it over to Alpha Shane. Jordan bit back a smile as Alpha Shane rotated the screen right side up. He slid his finger over the screen as he read. His shoulders tensed. "He's right." His eyes moved to Molly as he stepped past Marcus. "Do you have anything to say for yourself?"

Jordan glanced out at the audience, worried how some of the vampires would take a werewolf ordering the Elder's famulus to speak. A glint of light in one of the rear entrances caught her eye. There were no light fixtures there. Nothing should be reflecting or casting light. Jordan launched herself at Alpha Shane as a crack of a rifle shot echoed. The wolf in her had reacted before she could think. She caught him in the midsection, and they tumbled to the ground. Someone screamed "shooter!" The sound hadn't died away when a second shot rang out. The scent of blood filled the air. She rolled free from Alpha Shane as Molly's legs buckled. Her friend melted to the ground inches from her. A black hole marred Molly's temple.

Screams and howls filled the air around her. The previously

empty stage was filled with a flurry of activity. Montgomery dragged Marcus out of the potential line of fire. Reginald sidled along with them, keeping himself between his patron and the edge of the stage. Pamela had an arm around Alpha Shane's waist, trying to pull the larger werewolf in the other direction. His teeth were bared in a snarl as he began to shift. Angela, already in her werewolf form, led a charge of werewolves and vampires toward the entrance to the bowl. But most of Jordan's focus was on her friend, crumpled on her back as she knelt over her.

Hands reached around her shoulders, drawing her up. She stumbled off the stage. Thorn followed, Molly slung over his shoulder in a fireman's carry. The bodyguards circled around Marcus, leaving them outside of their circle of protection. They hustled to the concrete bunker, making it inside before Tyrone slammed it shut with the echoing thud of a mausoleum's door.

She looked around. Marcus, of course, had made it inside. So had Reginald. Rosanna had also. Jordan didn't think she had been on the stage. Maybe she had been in the crowd backstage. Or maybe she was a fast runner. None of the other werewolves appeared to be in this building.

Montgomery guided her by the shoulders to lean against a wall. Reginald was powering up a two-way radio when Doctor Beverly appeared, carrying a first aid kit. "Put her down." Thorn lowered Molly to the floor. The doctor knelt beside her. She touched her neck at the pulse point, frozen in concentration. She sighed, rocked back onto her heels, and looked up at Jordan and Thorn. She shook her head. "She's gone."

Gone? The word echoed in Jordan's mind. She slid down the wall and pressed her forehead to her knees. Molly couldn't be gone. She couldn't be dead. She couldn't be the one who had been slipping information to the hunter. She couldn't have been responsible for the deaths of so many people.

And, a small, sarcastic voice in her head pointed out, hadn't she done the same thing to Rhys when he kidnapped Montgomery? Why wouldn't Molly attempt revenge for the loss of her boyfriend?

"Jordan!" A hand rested on her shoulder, unobtrusively checking her pulse. She lifted her head and drew in a deep breath. Thorn knelt beside her. "Were you hit?" he asked.

"No. I'm okay." She shook her head, pushing away the shock she wanted to sink into like a numbing blanket. "I wasn't hit."

"This is what comes about from trusting werewolves." Rosanna's voice was sharp. She gestured at Montgomery and Jordan with a knife blade hand as she addressed Marcus. "They almost got you killed."

"This is not the time," Elder Marcus rebuked her. He looked at his senior famulus. "Reginald, report."

Reginald, his two-way radio pressed to his ear, listened before speaking. "They found an abandoned rifle," he reported. "Still warm, just outside of the entrance to the amphitheater. They also said there was some sort of stink to mask whoever was standing there."

"Like when I was shot at," Jordan said.

"They're attempting to track whoever it was, but it's unlikely they can given the amount of traffic on the street."

"So, we have no idea who this hunter is." Marcus turned to eye Molly's body as if disgusted she had the bad manners to die before speaking. "And the only person who could give us any information is dead."

"Not quite, sir," Montgomery said. "We have her phone. We have access to her email. It may take some time, but we can figure out who this hunter is."

Marcus looked at the phone he was still holding. "You can tell all that from this thing?" He handed it to Montgomery.

"We'll need Detective Henricksen's help. It will take a little time—"

"Now, Montgomery. We don't have a little time. We need to stop this hunter before he gets away."

Montgomery looked at his sire, then at Jordan. Wordlessly, he held the phone out to her.

Jordan took the phone. It had been dumb luck she had been able to get into Molly's email. The only things she knew about digital forensics were from the court TV shows she turned on when she couldn't sleep in the afternoon. Pamela could help with her police contacts, but that would take warrants issued by a judge. Telling them she was involved in the attempted murder of a vampire and a werewolf would not go over well, and any story they came up with needed to withstand scrutiny.

She flipped it over to look at the screen, still not sure what to do. The text app was still open. Trying to come up with her next step, Jordan read the message. It was just as Montgomery had said. A name wasn't assigned to the phone number. She was about to switch over to the email app when her eyes widened and her stomach twisted and dropped like a stone. "I know this phone number," she whispered before she could stop herself.

All the vampires stared at her through narrowed eyes. "You know who she was talking to?" Montgomery asked.

Bile filled Jordan's throat. She swallowed hard. The answer had been in front of her all the time. How had she been so stupid? "I can take you right to him."

40

———

Elias threw open the door to his apartment. He grabbed the duffel bag sitting next to the door and shook it open as he stormed through the living room and into the bedroom. He picked up books from his desk and tossed them into his bag. The timer in the back of his mind continued its relentless countdown. He had maybe five minutes before the vampires and werewolves raiding his college office would discover he wasn't there.

He hustled to his desk in the corner, shoving maps and notes waiting to be entered into his laptop into his bag without any concern for tearing the paper. He opened the desk drawers and shoved hanging folders forward, clearing access to the space where he had a handgun, a silver-plated knife, a bundle of stakes, and a box of loose ammunition.

He paused at the wave of guilt flowing over him. Molly had already suffered so much. But he'd had no choice the moment she appeared on stage. A quick death at his hands would be more merciful than the slow death at the vampires' and werewolves' fangs as they tortured her for information, he'd told himself as he framed her in the scope of the rifle.

And, a small sarcastic voice said, it would give him time to escape. Perhaps he'd get lucky, and the vampires and werewolves would be busy blaming each other, allowing him to get out of town unnoticed. Perhaps he should have chosen another target, like Jordan. She may have finally understood their conversation. Or she had put two and two together from how her friend had been acting. Either way, she would have to be eliminated.

Taking out Jordan would have to be another hunter's job. As would be cleaning out the nest of vampires and werewolves. He'd send word through the network and then disappear for a few years. They would have to wait for the vampires and werewolves to drop their guard again, but it would happen.

Of course, that was after his fellow hunters had chewed him out. He had ruined their ability to use the ploy of turning both sides against each other. They would yell that he had been stupid to try. He was a scholar, not a shooter. He was supposed to watch out for and direct them to targets. A decade of work had been destroyed in a single night, and all because he'd wanted to be the one who pulled the trigger. Then in a panic he'd dropped the rifle and left it behind.

He'd made a mistake. He wouldn't make one again.

Elias opened the closet and reached for a backpack. This one had a change of clothing and other necessities packed. There was one last thing he needed before he fled. He unzipped one of the pockets and pulled out a semi-automatic pistol. He popped in a magazine loaded with silver bullets. They'd kill a werewolf and slow a vampire, assuming he had enough warning and ammunition. Or at least that's what the hunter who'd taught him had said. His other instructor at the range had laughed and told him he'd need a magazine of seventeen hundred bullets rather than seventeen to take down charging supernaturals. It looked like he'd find out which of them was right.

He racked the slide and put the gun into his pocket. Then he rummaged in the backpack again, pulling out another magazine.

He slipped the spare into his other pocket. It wouldn't be likely he'd have a chance to reload, but the weight was comforting. After zipping the backpack shut, he hefted it onto his shoulders. Time to get out of here.

He turned and froze. A woman stood in his living room. Her short brown hair looked like a cow had licked it into stiff peaks. Her gray T-shirt was rumpled, but there was no blood on it. Her face was an unreadable blank, but to his relief, she appeared to be alone. "Jordan," Elias said. No point in trying to hide anything now. "How did you find me?"

His hand tightened on the handle of the gun as her arm moved. She held up a business card. "You gave me your cell number," she said. A bitter smile stretched her lips. "It's amazing the personal information you can find on the Internet."

Of course. He gave her that damn card at the first meeting in the dog park. He was surprised she'd kept it after their appointment. If he could get past her, he could still get out of here. Or better still, persuade her to aid his escape. "I want to help you, Jordan. When we talked in the office, it was clear you were hurting so much. I wanted to take you away from the monsters. I still can." He took a step forward. His hand moved to his pocket, fingers wrapping around the gun. "Come with me. Help me get out of here, and I'll help you cure your condition."

Her eyes widened as she inhaled sharply. "You could make me human again?"

He could lie to her. She probably hadn't considered the possibility, if the shock in her voice was any indication. Better to carefully edit the truth than risk losing her trust in him. "I can help you."

"Like you 'cured' Brian and Victor?" Her hands remained loose at her sides as she rocked her weight between her feet. She shook her head. "Emma and David were human."

"They were working with the enemy, Jordan, hoping they would be made into monsters themselves. They wanted power at the expense of their fellow humans." He took a step closer. "There's still a core of humanity to you, Jordan. They'd have thrown you under the bus if it gave them an advantage. The vampire who enslaved you will kill you if it means saving his own skin. You don't have to act like the monsters they are."

Jordan looked at the ground. Her chest rose and fell in a deep breath. Her head twisted a few millimeters toward the door, cocked as if listening to for something or someone. When she looked up, there were tears in her eyes. "I can't say I was friends with everyone you killed. But some of them were human." She shook her head. "I'm not the monster here."

So be it. Time dilated as he drew the gun. She took a step back, raised fingers curling into claws. He leveled the gun with her heart and fired. Jordan grunted. Her legs buckled, and she fell face down like a cut oak.

He kept the gun trained on her head as he edged around her. Jordan lay stone still. *Shoot her!* his brain screamed. *Take the head shot and make sure she's dead!* As he aimed at her temple, footsteps pounded down the hall toward him, confirming his fear. He swung around, pointing the gun at the door.

Something slammed into his knee. He staggered and went down as his leg melted out from under him, his arm swinging wide. Weight dropped onto his shoulders, pushing him face down. Claws sliced into his wrist. He yelped and let go of the gun. Hot breath gusted past his ear. "Move," Jordan snarled. "And I'll kill you."

The footsteps slowed. "Jordan," a male voice called out. Someone paced forward and picked up the gun. "How you doing?"

"Chest hurts like hell," she growled back.

"Get off him."

The weight on his back disappeared. He looked up. A man with a blue mohawk held his gun, barrel pointed at his head. His peeled back lips framed a pair of fangs. Elias recognized him as one of the vampires who had hauled Molly on stage. "Stay where you are."

He lay on the floor, hands held out in front of him. Out of the corner of his eye, he watched a brown-haired man help Jordan remove her T-shirt, revealing a bulletproof vest. The shot had flattened itself into the weave above her heart. "Took you long enough to get up here," she wheezed.

"We were waiting for your engraved invitation," the brown-haired man said.

"Thanks for crashing the party." Jordan nodded toward Elias. "What are we going to do about him?"

"He'll answer for what he's done, of course. I'm sure Elder Marcus and Alpha Shane have a lot they'd like to discuss with him."

So, this was it. He was going to be dragged before the head monsters to be executed. Well, not if he had anything to do about it.

In a fluid motion, he jumped to his feet. Doing those burpees had turned out not to be a waste of time after all. He pulled the stake from where he'd tucked it inside his jacket and charged the blue-haired vampire. Something burned past his left shoulder, leaving a crease of pain in its wake. The crack of the gun exploded in his ears. Something hit him from behind, knocking the stake from his hand. Two sharp points stabbed into his throat.

"Montgomery! Don't!" Jordan yelled as darkness swirled around him. The taste of copper on his lips was the last thing he registered before blackness overwhelmed him.

41

Jordan stood in the corner of Marcus's office, a respectful distance back from everyone. She could finally take a deep breath without a dull ache, although she was sure she still had a beauty of a bruise under her shirt. Angela sat with her father, soaking in all the information. Rosanna stood opposite the young werewolf. Jordan's attention was fixed on Marcus and Shane as Montgomery, with Thorn standing next to him, told them what had happened at Elias's apartment. "And then I bit him," Montgomery finished.

The Elder and the Alpha leaned forward, keying in with a predator's instinct. "You took too much, and then gave back," Marcus said.

Montgomery dropped his gaze from his sire, shamefaced. "In the heat of the moment, yes, I did. I knew you wanted him questioned," he added.

"I know these hunters, Montgomery," Marcus chided. "Any information we extract from him would be suspect. But I have other plans in mind for him." His smile sent a shiver down Jordan's spine.

Alpha Shane crossed his arms over his chest. "Don't tell me

you're making him join the Conclave, hoping he'll have a change of heart and will spill his guts voluntarily."

To Jordan's surprise, Marcus shook his head, unbothered by Alpha Shane's sarcasm. "No. I have a different punishment in mind for him."

"Even though he's of your direct bloodline," Rosanna asked.

Marcus turned his attention to her. "Would you have me trust a hunter—who has already attempted to assassinate both Alpha Shane and me—with the secrets of our society?" His expression hardened. "The fact that he is now of my line does not mean he will escape the consequences of his actions."

Rosanna shot a pointed glance at Montgomery before returning her gaze to her sire. "Clearly," she said in the driest of tones.

Angela growled. "We are not being allowed our revenge for Brian's murder and desecration?"

Shane glared at his daughter. "We are not being denied anything. Elder Marcus and I are in agreement." He smiled. Somehow the flat human teeth displayed in his smile frightened Jordan more than his wolf fangs. "Trust me, Angela. If the elder does what I think he has in mind, it will be an appropriate punishment."

Jordan didn't like the pleasure accenting the word appropriate.

Angela let out a discrete snort that could be mistaken for a heavy exhale. "So when will this punishment take place?"

"Sunrise."

Jordan bit her lip to keep from smiling at how Angela's eyes popped wide. Alpha Shane was enjoying putting his daughter in her place if his smug grin was any indication. Or maybe it was because the hunter had almost shot him and had taken a shot at his daughter as well. Though she wanted revenge for what Elias had put them through, for the deaths and for using her best friend, Jordan's stomach roiled at the thought of watching him die. Part of her rejoiced, though, wishing she could have dealt the death blow herself. The werewolf in her? A dark part of her humanity she didn't want to acknowledge? She couldn't say which. The words she'd told him earlier echoed through her head. "I'm not a monster like you." Were they true?

Alpha Shane spoke and Jordan focused on him. "While we're waiting for dawn, I have some business to discuss with the chaos wolf."

Of course. He was angry she had knocked him over in front of everyone. It would be seen as a sign of weakness by the pack, and one that could not be tolerated. Jordan sighed and turned to face him. Montgomery stepped forward, but Marcus gestured him back. Jordan took a deep breath. Maybe she could head it off at the pass. "Alpha Shane, while I did tackle you onstage, it was not meant as a threat or a challenge to your authority."

"Yet you did attack him," Angela pointed out. "In front of witnesses, vampire and werewolf alike." There was a gleeful undertone to her voice. "You should be punished for your insolence."

Montgomery clenched a fist but stayed next to Thorn.

Alpha Shane shot a hard look at Angela. "I am the Alpha here," he growled. "I will dole out punishment to those who deserve it." He raised his hand before anyone could raise an objection. "And Chaos Wolf Jordan Abbey does *not* deserve it. Although we are not on the best of terms, she acted to save my life from a threat and deserves to be rewarded."

Jordan stood there, eyes wide. Had she heard him right?

Angela made a choked noise, but Alpha Shane ignored it and continued. "I grant Chaos Wolf Jordan Abbey the same rights the members of the Black Oak Pack hold on our territory. You are free to come and go on our grounds without fear of harassment. If anyone does trouble you, after you have registered your displeasure with them, let me know." He gave Angela a hard glance out of the corner of his eye. "I will see to it they are dealt with also."

Jordan swallowed. Everyone, with the exception of Marcus, appeared stunned by the generosity of the reward. But then Marcus had such a good poker face, she was never able to read his reactions. "Thank you, Alpha Shane," she said. "I deeply appreciate what you have given me."

"I hope so, Chaos Wolf Jordan Abbey."

The Alpha werewolf turned to the Elder vampire. "It's almost dawn. Are you planning on telling us how you will deal with this hunter?"

Marcus rose and did the most frightening thing Jordan had ever seen him do. He smiled and turned to face the paneled wall. Reginald slid the panels to the side, revealing a large-screen TV in the recess. "If you turn to your left," he said. "I believe you will all enjoy this."

42

———————

He woke to a burning thirst, the worst he had ever experienced. Elias sat and swung his legs off the cot he was laying on. The bitch werewolf and the bastard of a vampire had knocked him off his feet. He shouldn't be alive. So why was he? What were they up to?

They want your contacts, dummy, a little voice said. Of course. They'd want information on who he had been in contact with, both on the supernatural side and the other hunters he supported. Someone was watching, and word was probably being sent that he was awake. Soon the torture would begin.

Deciding he wanted to meet his fate standing on his feet, he stood up and stretched. There was no pain, not even the faint ache of a healing bruise or the protest of muscles from the aftermath of a fall. He swallowed, hoping the saliva in his mouth would do something to soothe the dry thirstiness in his throat.

He looked around the room to get his bearings and figure out what to do next. The only things in the room were the bare cot that looked like an antique from the Korean War, a wide window without curtains, and a security camera bolted into the corner of the wall. From the position and tilt, he assumed it had it a full view of anything happening the room. The only other item was a door. He walked over to it and tried the handle, even though he told himself it wasn't going to result in freedom. The door rattled the barest fraction of an inch. He sighed. Of course they weren't stupid enough to leave him in an unlocked room.

That left the window. He moved over to it, studying the glass. He looked carefully along the edges where it met the sill. It appeared to be some sort of layered glass, similar to the shatter-resistant type used in high rise buildings. He looked past his reflection in the glass into the darkness outside. He could make out the mountains ringing the valley Rancho Robles was nestled in.

He turned away from the window to stare at the camera perched in the corner. Someone had to be watching him. Why hadn't they come for him when they saw he was awake? It was hard to think through the haze of the thirst. "I know you're watching me," he yelled at the camera. "What are you waiting for?" Anger and frustration welled up in him, fueled by fear and uncertainty. He surprised himself by letting out an angry cobra-like hiss to vent the emotions. His tongue pressed against the back of his fangs . . .

Wait. Fangs?

He opened his mouth wide and crammed his fingers in his mouth. He sliced them open, tasting the coppery salt of blood. The thirst flared stronger as he sucked at the wounds.

He whipped his fingers out of his mouth, horrified as the punctures sealed over and healed before his eyes. He ran his tongue over his fangs and whimpered. "No, no, no." He dropped to his knees and rocked back and forth. It was now clear why the vampires and werewolves didn't come into the room to torture him. They didn't have to be present to inflict pain.

He wasn't sure how long he cowered there, rocking back and forth and whimpering. The growing light in the room snapped him out of his fugue. He ran to the window and looked out. The mountain range's outline was more distinct now, outlined by the light of the rising sun. They wouldn't be coming in to torture him. Not when the sun could do it for them.

The cot! He scrambled away from the window. He could shield himself with the cot. He grabbed the edge and yanked. It didn't move. What appeared to be wooden legs were metal painted in a grain pattern, bolted to the floor. The lining was a loose weave, more a mesh net with gaps an inch wide that offered no protection.

He screamed, his hatred, anger, and fear as pure as the light and heat rolling into the room. Fangs extended, he kept screaming even as his voice cracked and his lungs burned. He screamed as his flesh began to sear and flakes of ash fell from his skin.

Eventually, the screams stopped, but the burning did not.

43

---

*J**ust die already!** Jordan kept her eyes fixed on the screen. She remembered Montgomery's description of what would happen to a vampire left in the full view of the sun. "We get something comparable to second-degree sunburn after half an hour's exposure to sunlight. It would take a couple of hours to kill us." Even then, she had pictured something out of the movies. The vampire might scream once and then burst into flames, mercifully unconscious. She didn't expect the skin to blister and peel and attempt to heal before the cycle repeated. Each time, the flesh deteriorated until muscle showed and then bone was visible.

She swallowed the saliva flooding her mouth in an attempt not to vomit.

All the vampires had flinched and squinted when the sunlight poured through the windows, despite the safety of it being a video relay. Now they had no problem watching the screen. Elder Marcus, Thorn, Rosanna, Alpha Shane, and Angela were all focused on the monitor. Montgomery angled his gaze so he could watch both the transmitted images and her. She swallowed and picked the wood grain panel surrounding it to focus on, hoping the line of sight would be close enough.

Thorn's voice broke the silence. To Jordan's surprise, his arms were crossed over his chest like a bored teenager. "Are we going to watch him turn to ash over the next few hours or can we get on with our business?"

Marcus turned an icy stare to Thorn. Then he glanced at Alpha Shane, who moved his head in the shallowest of nods. Marcus turned to Reginald and gestured. The old man shut off the monitor. Jordan's stomach unclenched, but the tightness in her throat didn't ease.

"Don't tell me that's it," Angela snorted.

Marcus turned to face her. Angela took a step backwards. Jordan did too. Marcus's face was a study in controlled irritation, if she were reading the tenseness of his brow and the flare of his nostrils correctly. Oddly enough, Jordan noted, Alpha Shane didn't move to protect her. "This is part of the traditional punishment for traitorous vampires." He took a step closer to Angela. The young werewolf swayed away from his approach but managed to hold her ground. "After an hour, the windows will be shut. Once he recovers enough to be aware of what is about to happen, a stake will be driven through his heart. His head will be severed. His body will be reduced to ash. So no, pup. That is not it." Marcus looked at Alpha Shane, shaking his head. "And you think Montgomery's famulus is ill mannered."

Alpha Shane rumbled but didn't contradict him. "It's after dawn. I will inform the pack justice has been dealt."

Marcus stood. "Thank you, Alpha Shane, for your part in the events of the past night."

"The pleasure was mine. Now that this menace is no longer hunting us, things can go back to the status quo." Shane glanced at Jordan. "Or as much as they can when a chaos wolf walks among us." He swept out of the room. Angela followed with a glare at Jordan.

Marcus's shoulders relaxed a fraction when the werewolves were on the other side of the closed door. "And that is that." He looked at Montgomery and Thorn. "The two of you are welcome to stay here for the day, of course. Perhaps you'd like to stay in your old room, Montgomery?"

Montgomery squared his shoulders as he shook his head once. "Thank you, but no, sir. I'd prefer to use the guest quarters."

The corner of Marcus's mouth twitched. "Very well. Go get some rest. Reginald will guide you to your quarters."

Montgomery and Thorn bowed their heads, followed by Jordan a half second behind them. They all turned to leave. As Reginald opened the door to let them out, Marcus spoke. "Montgomery?"

All three of them froze. Montgomery looked back, a quizzical expression on his face. Marcus's voice was pure steel. "We will be having a discussion about how your famulus is associated with a hunter."

Montgomery tensed. "Yes, sir." The shake in his voice matched the tremor running down Jordan's spine. Her eyes remained fixed on Montgomery as he turned and walked out the door.

The moment they were in the relative safety of the elevator, Jordan leaned against the wall for support. One hand clenched her stomach. "I don't think I'll be able to eat barbecue ever again."

Montgomery placed a hand on her shoulder with enough weight to reassure her and squeezed. She leaned against him for a moment then pushed so she stood upright. She looked up at him, mouth open and eyebrows arched in a question. He shook his head in the barest motion, eyes shifting to focus on Reginald. Jordan shut her mouth.

The elevator opened in the core of the fifth floor. Reginald led them past the room most vampires and Family had nicknamed the Blood Bank and into a series of halls that Jordan had not been in before. Reginald stopped before one of the numbered rooms. He produced a keycard and opened it.

They stepped inside what turned out to be a suite. Jordan looked around the room. This part of the suite had been configured as a living area and office. As she stepped into the room, she noticed a desk to her right. A couch was positioned at a right angle to the desk, giving it a fine view of the flat screen television sitting on a credenza. Through a wide opening, she spotted another credenza, the end of a king-sized bed, and a set of blackout curtains. The barest hint of light crept around the edges. Jordan shuddered, her mind flashing back to the execution.

"Do you require anything, Mr. Cooper, Mr. Henderschott?" Reginald asked.

Thorn made a beeline to the couch against the wall and flopped onto it, taking up most of the cushions. "Two units from my stock," he said. He glanced at Jordan. "And something breakfasty for Jordan."

Reginald nodded. "I'll have it sent up right away." He backed out of the room, closing the door behind him.

Montgomery looked at Thorn and arched an eyebrow. "You have stock?"

Thorn shrugged. "That's how Marcus paid me for keeping an eye on you. I don't use it often, but it comes in handy now and then."

Montgomery sat down on the bed. "We need to have a talk, Jordan." He paused as she sat down. "Why didn't you tell me you were going to meet with someone?"

Jordan drew a deep breath. "Because it didn't seem important. He was an old teacher. I had no idea he was a hunter. Hell, I had no idea hunters even existed—"

Montgomery raised a hand to halt her. "And that is my fault. I should have warned you about them. But you should have told me you were talking with someone from your old life." He rubbed his temple with the thumb and third finger of one hand, pressing his forehead with his index finger. "When did you meet with him?"

"First time? Just before they announced David's death. Then I went to talk to him the afternoon before they found Victor's body."

Montgomery shook his head. "I should have realized something was off. That's why you were dressed when I told you about the emergency meeting."

"Now that I know what he was, a lot of what he said makes sense. He presented it like he was offering to help me leave an abusive boyfriend, but he was trying to turn me into a spy like . . . Molly." Jordan choked on her friend's name. Despite her anger and hurt at the betrayal, tears welled up in her eyes. Molly, her friend, was gone. And no matter how she turned it over in her head, it was ultimately her fault for not telling her.

"Turn you?" Thorn's eyes went wide. "He knew what you are?"

"He must have been watching her since the incident with Rhys," Montgomery said. He sighed. "The problem now is convincing Marcus you're not part of a grand conspiracy."

Thorn's eyes narrowed. "You don't think he'd threaten Jordan?"

"What do you think? Marcus will protect himself." He turned back to Jordan. His lips compressed into a grim line. "If he thinks punishing you will best serve his interests, he will overrule me and do so."

Jordan looked back and forth between the two vampires. She had to trust Montgomery knew what he was doing. "For this to work, we're going to have to trust each other. Withholding things will only lead us back to this situation."

Montgomery nodded. "I promise not to lock you out emotion-ally"—he looked at Thorn—"if you tell me what you're telling Marcus."

"Fair enough," Thorn agreed.

Montgomery looked at Jordan. "And if you tell me ahead of

time, I won't forbid you from meeting with them. I just need to be ready to run interference in the future."

"Deal," Jordan said.

"I don't know about you guys," Thorn said through a yawn. "But I'm ready to get some sleep."

"As much as I'd like to, I don't think that would be wise," Montgomery said. He looked as weary as she felt. "Marcus will probably send for me the moment the sun sets. We need to go over your meeting with the hunter. Every word he said. Every time you talked with him."

Jordan inhaled. Time to tell them everything. "I first saw Mr. Campbell while I was walking Rex the night after Alpha Shane had me chased off Mount Ponderosa . . ."

44

———

Montgomery, Thorn, and Jordan spent most of the morning going over Jordan's meetings with the hunter. The more they talked about what happened, the more it became clear Jordan hadn't known how she was being manipulated. All she could be accused of was being ignorant of Elias Campbell's true nature. Her actions were defensible since he had not informed her of the existence of hunters. It was a gap in her education he was responsible for. The question was, would he be able to convince Marcus of that fact?

Eventually, exhaustion took over them. They collapsed in a pile on the bed, snatching what sleep they could until shortly before sunset. When they woke, Thorn left to check on his tattoo shop and said he'd rejoin them at Montgomery's apartment before dawn. Not certain how the meeting with his sire would go, he sent Jordan back to his apartment with strict instructions. "If you don't hear from me in two hours, grab the cash and the cell phone I keep in the bedside drawer and drive. Get out of town and drive as far as you can go. Thorn will call you when he can." He hated the look of fear in her eyes, but she needed to be afraid.

It would be for her own good. He hoped it would be enough of a head start. Thorn could guide her somewhere she'd be safe.

He had just stepped out of the shower when the summons came. Montgomery dressed in the same tan slacks and blue dress shirt he had worn the night before, wishing he had a change of clothes. There was probably one in his old rooms still. They would be thirty years out of date, musty, and loaded with memories. He didn't need to face them down tonight. He had enough to deal with.

He walked down the hall leading to Marcus's chambers, stomach roiling in nervous anticipation. Montgomery followed protocol and knocked on the door. As Marcus bade him enter, the butterflies solidified into a knot. He kept his face neutral as he pushed the doors open. "You wished to see me, sir?"

Marcus, sitting ramrod stiff, gestured to the empty chairs in front of his desk. "Take a seat, Montgomery."

He did as Marcus instructed, perching more than sitting, waiting for his sire to begin.

Marcus's eyes never left Montgomery's as he tapped a manila folder on his desk. "I had Elias Campbell's movements traced to determine who else he was in contact with. We confirmed at least one meeting between the hunter and your famulus." Marcus's gaze narrowed. "Am I to understand that she not only knew this hunter, but she met with him and did not inform you?"

The lie was on Montgomery's lips, ready to deny she hadn't told him about the meeting. But the moment his attempt at protecting her by deception was discovered, and he had no doubt Marcus would discover the truth eventually, both he and Jordan would be in worse trouble. "Yes, she did."

Marcus leaned back, looking somewhat relieved. "And what are your plans to punish her?"

Montgomery willed his spine to not stiffen. "None, sir. I do not feel it is appropriate to do so."

Marcus sat taller in his chair. "And why do you believe that?"

"I discussed with her what happened," Montgomery said. "He had been Jordan's teacher just before she was bitten. She had no way of knowing he was a hunter when she met him again recently. She wasn't aware hunters existed at that point. She thought he was offering to help her leave an abusive relationship."

"That is an oversight in her education I fault you for, but it does not absolve her from the fact that she met with someone without informing you." Marcus leaned forward. "She will have to be punished, and publicly, as an example."

"By all means, censure me if you must make a public example of someone. But consider this, sir," Montgomery said. "The moment she recognized the information she held, she informed me. She saved the life of Alpha Shane and prevented what would have been a bloodbath on all sides. She could have easily betrayed Alpha Shane, and had the excuse given his daughter's treatment of her. Instead, she remained loyal and followed your instructions." Now was the time to play the hole card. "Jordan met with the hunter twice, and the initial contact was made by him. Your famulus was in regular contact with him. We have the emails, and who knows how many times she managed to speak with him in person. It's well known among the Family that Jordan and Margaret shared years of friendship. How will it look to everyone when Jordan is punished after saving your life by betraying her friend?"

Marcus sat back, shoulders lowering, eyes hard. "You have a point," he conceded.

"Jordan has promised there will be no such indiscretions in the future," Montgomery continued. "Her involvement can be minimized. At this point, only you, Thorn, Reginald, Rosanna, and myself are aware of it."

"Rosanna could still be a problem."

Montgomery had run the math almost constantly since talking with Jordan. Marcus had to be doing the same now. He and Thorn would do their best to look out for Jordan. Reginald's allegiance belonged to Marcus. For now, both those would dovetail nicely. "I have repeatedly offered her the fangs of the werewolf who killed her famulus, which she publicly claimed would be what was needed to make things right between us," Montgomery said. "I have done so through my famulus and directly myself. When she accepted the fangs directly from me, she stated that she would stop demanding reparations. She also said that she did not forgive me."

"That explains her recent statements during the Conclave." His glare hadn't broken the entire discussion. "She'd lose standing if it became common knowledge you had attempted to make peace and she rejected your offer. It might be enough leverage to keep her quiet. However, are you willing to be seen as the one in the wrong?"

Montgomery shrugged, hoping Marcus would read it as indifference. "It wouldn't be any different from the suspicion and comments I already face."

"Because you have a werewolf famulus?"

"No, because I was a werewolf.

Marcus rumbled like a tiger contemplating a newborn fawn. "Very well. I will tell Rosanna if she attempts to make my famulus's treachery public, her going back on her word will become public as well. Hopefully it will be enough to keep her in check."

"And Jordan?"

"Will not be punished unless you deem it necessary. I leave the decision in your hands. Now, unless there is anything else we need to discuss, you are dismissed."

"No, sir. Thank you, sir." Montgomery rose and bowed.

Marcus waved his hand in a dismissive motion. "Just see to it your famulus doesn't get into any more trouble."

"Yes, sir." Montgomery let himself out of the chambers.

He walked down the hallway, regulating his pace. He nodded

to Helen but didn't say anything. The gossip that he had been called in for a dressing down would spread fast enough.

Once he was out of the elevator, he pulled out his phone. His hand shook as he texted Jordan. "All clear. Meet you at home in fifteen."

And despite himself, he chuckled when Jordan texted back a smiley face.

45

———

Thorn sat at his office desk, reviewing the invoices for payment. He missed the days when he wasn't a responsible businessperson. Sometimes he missed being able to uproot at a moment's notice and flit on to the next town. Lately he had that thought whenever he had to balance the budget or work on the payroll. There were easier ways to blend in that didn't involve so much paperwork. Why had he believed it was a good idea to open a business?

Because he needed a reason to stay in Rancho Robles and keep an eye on things that wouldn't let him leave so easily. And it was a good thing he had. The werewolf-turned-vampire and his little chaos wolf famulus were making things more and more interesting. No, he had to be honest. He had developed a soft spot for Montgomery and Jordan. A huge weight had lifted when Montgomery had texted him that he had talked Marcus out of punishing Jordan. One crisis averted.

Now he had to remain on alert for the next one.

The rapping on his door frame made him look up. Charla stood in the door. "Boss? That detective from the other day is back. Want me to tell her to take a hike?"

Thorn saved the spreadsheet he had been entering data into. He had expected Pamela to call again after the events at Fletcher Park. "No, I'll talk to her, Charla. Bring her back."

This time he stepped out from behind his desk. He went to the water dispenser tucked into the corner and grabbed a paper cup. He produced a bottle of tequila from his desk and poured one shot. He leaned against the front of the desk, drink and bottle next to him. When Pamela appeared, he gestured at the drinks. "Thought we'd start this time on a better note."

Pamela looked at the offered drinks, then at Thorn, lips pursed. "You're not having one?"

Thorn shook his head. "Didn't think you'd appreciate what I'd have to cut it with."

She snorted as she picked up the cup and sniffed at the contents. Her nose wrinkled, but she didn't put the shot glass down. "Thanks." She swallowed it in one gulp. "We had a close call there."

"Yes, we did." Thorn sighed and gestured her to one of the chairs. This was one of the few times he actually felt his age. "You and I should have been the first to realize what was going on. We would have if we hadn't been so busy bickering. Thank Gaia, Jordan said something in time."

Pamela's eyebrows rose. "You must have been worried. You just let a goddess's name cross your lips." A small smile crossed her lips. "And thank Gaia she was able to get us to listen. I don't want to think what would have happened if she hadn't."

"Death. A whole lot of death. That's what would've happened." Thorn dropped into the chair next to her. "This won't be the last time the hunters harass us. They know for sure there are vampires and werewolves here now. They'll be watching for their next opportunity."

"We'll be ready for them. But I'd be more concerned about other packs. Alpha Shane has proven himself complacent, or that's how it will be spun. I'm sure there's others already planning how to take over Black Oak."

"Same for Elder Marcus. And the threat will not be only from the outside. I can think of several vampires who will use this situation to their advantage." Thorn arched an eyebrow. "Can you tell me there won't be any werewolves who will do the same?"

"I don't want to think that Angela would try to overthrow her father instead of waiting, but no."

"Exactly. We'll need to be careful and watch all directions for anything that would destabilize the situation further." Thorn studied her. "Does this mean you're going to stop trying to recruit Jordan to your side?"

"For the moment. It would be detrimental to everyone if she caused more of an uproar by switching sides. When things calm down . . ."

"*If* things calm down. By that time, she'll be firmly entrenched in the Family."

Pamela snorted, a twinkle in her eyes. "We'll see about that."

Thorn also snorted. "Does this mean we're working together for the moment?"

Pamela nodded once. "Don't get used to it."

"Gaia, no! We can't be friends again after all these years. That might break something." For the first time in a long time, Pamela gave him a wide, genuine smile. It made some place deep inside of him ache for a lost time he didn't allow himself to remember often. "Anything else we need to discuss?"

"No, I think we're good."

"Then let me walk you out."

They didn't say anything more as they walked down the hall to the waiting area. He caught some of his employees watching their progress out of the corner of his eye. Thorn opened the door, the picture of perfect manners. Pamela stepped to the threshold and paused. "Thorn," she said, looking over her shoulder at him. "Did you ever think about asking for forgiveness?"

"The thought's crossed my mind now and then," Thorn admitted. "But remember, I tried to ask you once. Do you remember how you reacted?"

Pamela nodded, a frown darkening her face at the memory.

"Do you think they would react any differently, even after all this time?"

Pamela paused and shook her head. Without saying anything else, she walked out of the store.

Thorn closed the door after her. He turned around and looked at the people staring at him. "Okay, show's over. Everyone back to work."

He grinned, watching the sudden flurry of directionless employee energy. It was similar to the flurries of activities he had seen inspired by his current lovers. Jordan and Montgomery were going to make things more and more interesting. And hopefully they would all survive it.

46

—————

Jordan walked out of the small building at the entrance to Mount Ponderosa, naked as the day she was born. Even though she was alone, she couldn't shake the idea someone was observing her as she walked to the tree line. She couldn't see or smell anyone around her. Could another hunter already be in the area?

She sighed. There had been so many losses—David, Emma, Victor, Brian, Molly. Even Elias had been a victim in his own way. They were all connected to her, and through her to Montgomery and Thorn. She wasn't sure what the long-term implications would be for the three of them, but it wouldn't be good.

But she couldn't dwell on those worries right now. Jordan shook her head to clear it. She breathed in the crisp night air to center herself. She had other things to focus on.

Just before she would step among the trees, she stopped. Jordan straightened up and inhaled with more focus. *You told me to pay attention to you.* She envisioned the black wolf she would become. *So, let's do this.* She closed her eyes and reached for the shapeshift, choosing to pay attention to her senses instead of her thoughts. Air currents drifted against her skin, raising goose-bumps. Her mind filtered through the scents—freshly trampled grass, dung from deer that passed by recently. The wind shifted, rustling through the leaves and bringing her the fresh scent of—

Jordan dove to one side before she was fully aware she'd reacted. Her eyes popped open as a white fur blur flashed over where she had stood a second before. Jordan growled, answering the snarl as the white wolf turned to face her with teeth bared. "What the hell, Angela?" she sputtered, too angry to be embarrassed by her nudity. "Alpha Shane said I could hunt here."

Angela changed forms, standing on her hind legs. Jordan kept her eyes fixed on the other werewolf's face as it became more and more human. "You have no right to be here."

Jordan rolled her eyes. "Oh, come on! Even I know you can't override your father and Alpha. He said I have the same right to be here as any other member of the Black Oak Pack."

"Who said anyone else is allowed here? I'm claiming it for me, personally." Angela smiled, her teeth pointy. "So, get out, Chaos Wolf. Or else."

Jordan's fists clenched. She was tempted to claw the smug smile off of Angela's face. Before, the threat would have been enough for her to scamper off. But now she was just tired. Tired of being threatened, tired of her kills being stolen, tired of being bullied, tired of having to watch every step she took. Her body stiffened and she took a firm step toward Angela. "No."

Angela's nostrils flared. "No?" she snorted.

"No," Jordan spat. "You don't like me. Fine. I don't like you. But we're going to be bumping into each other whether we want to or not. So, we either need to figure out a way to get along or we fight it out."

Angela paused for a moment. "In that case, I choose fight it out." She lunged forward, aiming for Jordan's throat.

Jordan had expected her attack. She dodged to one side and, to her surprise, shifted to the bipedal wolf-woman form without thinking. Angela missed her, lightly parting the fur of her shoulder. The other pulled herself up short, turned and lunged toward Jordan again.

This time Jordan didn't shy away. She stepped forward and flattened herself against the ground. Angela, unable to halt her momentum, flew over her. The moment Angela cleared her, Jordan popped up and mule-kicked her. Angela let out an undignified squawk as she stumbled on the landing and sprawled in the grass covering the ground.

Jordan immediately spun around to face Angela. The white werewolf was already on her hind paws. She lunged forward and met Angela's rush. Both werewolves crashed against each other and bounced back.

They shook off the stunning effect and began circling each other. The werewolves snarled and mock-charged each other. Then Angela leaped forward to try to lock onto Jordan's shoulder. Jordan whipped around, slashing out with her paws, and tore Angela's shoulder to the bone.

Angela roared in pain and anger and sprang for Jordan's throat. Jordan stood her ground until the last possible second, then pivoted. Instead of halting, she continued the motion, rotating a full three hundred sixty degrees. Now behind Angela, she bit down on the loose skin on the back of her neck.

Angela let out a screech of indignation and started clawing behind to catch Jordan's belly. Jordan shook Angela, sinking her fangs further in. Angela slowly raised her paws. "I surrender," she snarled in a bitter tone. Jordan froze, not quite believing what she'd heard. Angela barked louder. "I surrender. This mountain is yours."

Jordan held still for another moment, then released her jaws. Breathing heavily, she cocked her head, backing up a few steps. Jordan tensed as Angela turned around, preparing for another rush.

"You heard me. I said the mountain is yours." Bitterness and anger laced Angela's voice. "I tried to claim this territory. You fought for it," she said as if explaining things to a child. "You defeated me. Therefore, it belongs to you now."

"So it is spoken in Luna's light, and is as binding as Sol's rays." Both women turned their heads toward the male voice. Alpha Shane stood there in his human form. Angela cringed and backed away. He fixed his daughter with an irritated stare. "Did you think I wouldn't notice when you slipped away?" He shook his head. "You still have much to learn about being an Alpha wolf."

His attention turned to Jordan. It struck Jordan again how massive he was compared to other humans. She met his stare with a blank expression before deliberately dropping her eyes. Alpha Shane chuckled. "Stubborn and willful as ever," he said. "You should be able to hold this territory against all comers. Shift, pup, so you can ask the questions I know you have."

She tensed, digging her toes into the earth. Jordan pushed up, willing herself to change. It took a few minutes, and a few glares from Shane to shush Angela's derisive snorts. But eventually she stood in front of him, cheeks radiating heat.

"Let me see if I've got this straight," Jordan said. She pointed over her shoulders to the woods. "You're giving this to me?"

"Not giving," Alpha Shane said. "You claimed it by the strength of your jaws." He glared at Angela again. "I hope you're happy, girl. I told you the best course of action was to leave her be."

Angela glared at her father but didn't say anything more.

Jordan still looked confused. "But this is territory for travelers and Chaos Wolves to hunt in. I don't want a territory."

Alpha Shane snorted in amusement. "You, of all people, should know what you want has very little to do with what you get." He gestured Angela over to his side. Once she joined her father, Alpha Shane turned and walked away. "Guard it or abandon it as you like, Jordan Abbey. It's now yours to decide."

She watched as Alpha Shane and Angela disappeared into the woods surrounding the clearing. Once they were out of sight, her shoulders slumped. They kept lowering until she rested on all fours in her wolf form. Jordan took a deep breath, tilted her head back, and let out a deep howl of triumph.

ACKNOWLEDGMENTS

Thank you to my editors, Michelle Dunbar (Michelle Dunbar Editing Services), Lori Diederich (Lori Diederich, Freelance Editor), and Tammy Payne (Book Nook Nuts Proofreading).

Thanks to Fiona Jayde (Fiona Jayde Media) for creating an awesome cover despite my waffling input.

More thanks to the awesome people who have put up with me throughout this process - Isabella, Elanor, Julie, Tabitha, Karen-Leigh, Colleen, Daryle, and Alex. You kept me moving forward, even when it was only inches at a time.

ABOUT THE AUTHOR

Sheryl R. Hayes can be found untangling plot threads or the yarn her cats have been playing with. In addition to writing, she is a cosplayer focusing on knit and crochet costumes. Follow her at her blog http://www.sherylrhayes.com.

ALSO BY SHERYL R. HAYES

Jordan Abbey Series

Chaos Wolf (Book 1)

Chaos Hunt (Book 2)

Short Stories

Reading the Leaves in *AlternaTeas*

Pangram in *Ink: Queer Sci Fi's Eighth Annual Flash Fiction Contest*

www.ingramcontent.com/pod-product-compliance
Lightning Source LLC
Chambersburg PA
CBHW050816190726
48286CB00007B/1882